The Army's Son

MEG BARBER

Copyright page
First published in paperback by
TMK publishing in 2023
Copyright © 2023 Meg Barber
authormegbarber@yahoo.com

Meg Barber has asserted the right to be identified as the author of this work in accordance with the Copyright, Designs and Patents Act 1988

ISBN: 9798394468018

No part of this publication may be reproduced, stored in a retrieval system, or transmitted, in any form or by any means, electronic, mechanical, photocopying, recording or otherwise, without the prior permission of the publisher.

Cover design by GetCovers
Formatting by Sweet 'N Spicy Designs

Also by Meg Barber

The Causton Series (Regency Romance)

The Army's Daughter

Chantel

Elena

Samantha

The Driver (modern heist romance)

Montana Love (modern romance)

Dear Reader

'Leave a review, feed an author', has more than a grain of truth in it. If there is anything you enjoyed about the book, please say so, either on Goodreads (free and open to anyone) or on Amazon if you bought the book there or read it on Kindle Unlimited. Writing is an unpaid labour of love, and the reward is other people enjoying the story. If you wish to be informed when the next book is available, please send your email to authormegbarber@yahoo.com. You will not be bombarded with emails; I have neither the technical know-how to do that, nor the time. That is a promise. When people say that they like my stories, I light up like a neon sign, so if you praise The Driver, glance out of the window; there is a multi-coloured glow out there somewhere.

Happy reading.

'You'll be a bloody general one day.'

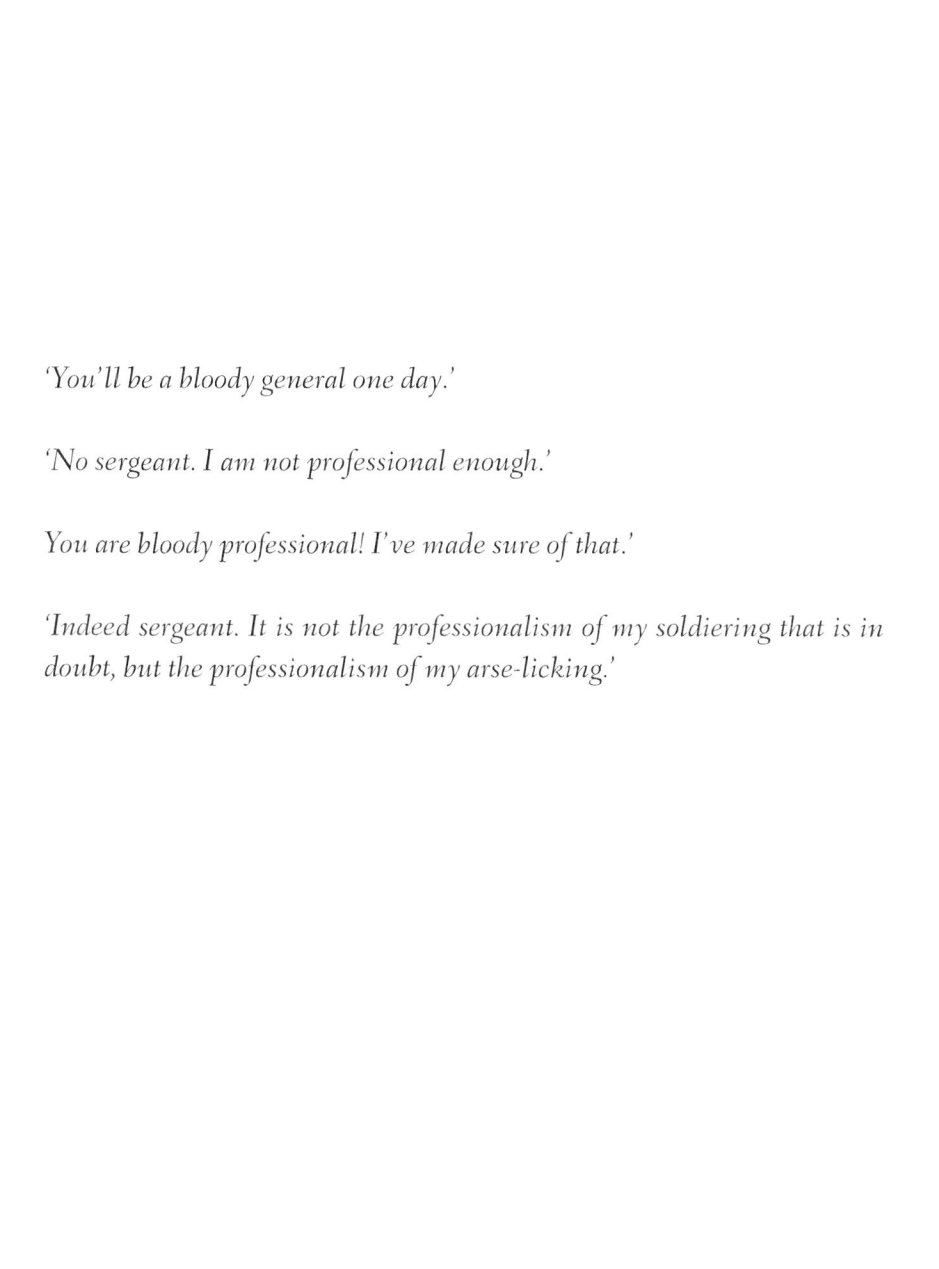

'No sergeant. I am not professional enough.'

You are bloody professional! I've made sure of that.'

'Indeed sergeant. It is not the professionalism of my soldiering that is in doubt, but the professionalism of my arse-licking.'

Chapter One

It was during the hot summer of 1803, when James was nine, that the first worry niggled at him. He was dashing in through the front door, aiming to shoot straight through the house to the kitchen pump in the yard in the hopes he would not be noticed. He was filthy and, worse, had torn another shirt. He had been trying to scrub himself clean in the pond set to one side of the front of the house, but in high summer the pond scum had begun to stain him, and his clothes, green, so he had decided it was the pump or nothing despite the risk of being caught. As he flew over the stone flags in the hall, racing past the various weapons hung decoratively on the walls, he had caught a glimpse of his mother up on the stairs. She had been bending over, her face white and screwed in pain. He was running too fast and too intent on cleaning himself up so the whipping his father was likely to give him would be as light as possible to do more than frown.

He raced through the kitchen and out into the yard and belted round to the pump. He yanked the handle furiously and shoved his upper body under the icy water, shirt and all. He scrubbed at his arms and neck then leant back and let each leg have a shot of water, before scrubbing at his knees. His consideration was that wet but clean with a tear was far better than dry and smothered in mud and with a tear. And with the day as hot as it was, he might even end up dry and clean with a tear. And before dinner time!

It was only as he ran his dripping body around the main barn and back out into the fields beyond that he remembered his mother and the look on her face. His Ma had a personality ten times her size, so it was easy to forget how small she was. He was already as tall as she was, but then, he was reckoned to be big for his age, which pleased him. His Pa and eldest brother were both big men. Pa was big all over, big boned and tremendously tall and, while Sam was the same height, he was long and thin. Like a piece of string his other brother, Lucian, used to sneer. Lucian had a good line in sneers and thinking of him curdled James' guts a little. They curdled more when he remembered his Ma. He stalled his run. Should he go back? He regarded his wet breeches and boots and decided, perhaps not. The house was full of women who could care for her. Perhaps she had yanked her ankle on the stair, or pricked herself with a pin; she was always sewing. Having reassured himself, he ran on, letting the bright sun dry his back and his hair even as his boots squelched.

He was busy with his friends for the next few days damning a tributary of the local river and flooding the vicar's blackcurrent bushes. Then he was occupied hunting for beetles in the fields and woods and marvelling silently over some of the iridescent colours while his friends argued over whether body size or antler size was the measure of greatness. For the while he forgot about his mother and her scrunched face of pain. And then he fell out of the oak. And the thing about oak is that it has a rough bark. And the thing about this fall was that he was tossed backwards as he lost his balance and his back rubbed down the main trunk all the way to the ground. Along with a cut that filled his eye with blood and numerous scratches he was giddy and nauseous. Even Ned the blacksmith's boy, who was as tough as his father's metal, was concerned. As a group, they all decided that he should head home. And then they all scattered. Which told James that he looked in a bad way and they were all afraid that they would be in trouble and be blamed for the injuries to the local squire's son. Swallowing and thinning his lips, James began the long hike home.

To his horror he was met by Lucian. His brother never missed an opportunity to belittle him or clip him around the ear. A privilege James wasn't sure an elder brother was entitled to, but one he had not found a way of countering. Except for putting the occasional spider in Luc's boots. Rather than pick on him, Luc's usual way of interacting, he frowned hard and told James to go straight to the still room while he found their Ma. James could have wept with relief. The one person he wanted right that moment was his mother. And admitting that to Luc was simply not an option. He limped to the still room and let himself into the cool herb-scented air. His mother arrived with her usual hustle; Ma never moved slowly if she could rush. She too thinned her lips and began to ease the linen away from his lacerated back.

'*Alors!*' she exclaimed as she edged the fabric out of the dried blood, '*et comment est-ce arrive?*' She asked him in French, which made him smile slightly. Ma always reverted to French if her mind was doing two or three things at once.

'*Pardon maman,*' he murmured between gritted teeth, 'the tree spat me out.' And she laughed, as he hoped she would.

She washed his cuts and wound a bandage of ripped linen around his head to staunch the wound over his eye, then bundled up his shirt for the fire. James wanted a mirror. He suspected he looked remarkably dramatic with his bound head and was anticipating playing the wounded soldier at dinner that night, when he turned to ask if he looked sufficiently warrior-like. He found she was bent away, her back towards him and folded forward, her arm bent. He guessed she was gripping a fist to her abdomen. The same pose he had seen before. The nausea, which hadn't gone away, intensified. He looked away sharply, not sure what to think, but uneasy again. Once could be ignored. Twice might mean something. But what? His mother turned with a wide smile on her face, kissed his cheek, and told him to go to the kitchen for a slice of bread and jam and to curl up in the big rocking chair and doze for a while. 'For,' she said, 'you need a little rest, my son.'

James followed her instruction, but the worm of worry had made its bed in his guts and would, from now on, be a permanent resident.

The summer ended and James returned to Eton, sharing the carriage with Lucian as he always had to. Luc ignored him for most of the journey, turning away to stare out of the window before leaning into the far corner and dozing. James wished they were closer so he could discuss his concern that nagged at the back of his mind and was cutting up his peace, but Luc had simply given a sharp jab to his guts when he had settled into the coach and muttered,

'Be quiet grub, I intend to sleep.'

Luc was bright, no doubt about that, but lazy. Where his sister Chantel was already obsessed with understanding everything to the most particular degree, Luc just sneered and did the minimum. He had enough pride not to want to look an idiot, but couldn't be bothered to get out his books and study on his own, or make a push in a classroom where he was one amongst many.

James turned to gaze unseeingly out of the opposite window to Luc. He supposed he loved his brother, but Luc made it difficult. There was something within Luc that was disjointed. He didn't seem to be able to be content, let alone happy. James didn't think he had seen Luc smile in an age. His unhappiness and bitterness seemed soul deep and James could not understand why. His eldest brother, Samuel, was far older, being the son of their Pa's first wife, but had the sweetest nature imaginable. Nothing was too much trouble for him, including younger brothers. He wore a permanent half smile and had the lines in his face already to show that. He had often told of how excited he had been when Luc had been on the way and how wonderful it was to have brothers and a sister. Luc even admitted that Sam had been his first playmate and how he had hung out of the upper windows to anticipate Sam's return home when he had been at Oxford. To James, Luc came out of the stories as a happy and loving brother, so why he was such a cross-patch now was a puzzle.

He turned to gaze at Luc, but his tongue once again stayed behind his teeth rather than risk being ridiculed by Luc yet again. He decided he would confide his fears to Sam when they returned at Christmas.

Christmas came and went and was a happy time for James, but Sam seemed to have moved completely out of the manor and was living at the Dower house, so James rarely saw him and when he did it was always in full company. He pondered why Sam might wish to live with Miss B, who was old and had arrived years ago to be a tutor to Sam, but decided in his own mind it was reasonable, as Sam was a man now and fully sharing the running of the estate with his Pa. No doubt, he wanted to be more independent and not live with the ramshakleness of him, and Luc and Chantel, who was eleven and incurably noisy, constantly breaking the peace.

He and Luc returned to Eton in a similar unfriendly and miserable way as always, so James imagined being back with his friends and anticipated happily his return to school. He wasn't keen on lessons that made no sense to him, but when they studied battles, be they Roman or Marlborough's, he was completely absorbed. His father said that he had no idea why his youngest son wished to be a soldier when all of his forebears had been Wiltshire farming squires at Causton Manor. The comment caused James to wonder about his father's intelligence. The current Caustons may indeed be farmers, but the weapons on the walls of the hall told another story. In decorative display that denied their lethal purpose were swords, halberds, pikes, crossbows, axes and maces spread all across the walls. He had been born amongst those tools, not ploughs and hoes. And he had painstakingly taken one of the suits of armour apart when he was seven to see how a man might wear it. The pair of silver suits had always stood at the foot of the main stairs, and along with all the weapons, were constantly visible. All he could suppose was that his father was so familiar with it all that he no longer saw it! Though he had taught James how to use the crossbow properly to prevent him making more holes in the young silver birches around the pond when they weren't targets. So his father was a trice more militaristic than he liked to admit, was James' deduction.

He was fine about going back to Eaton. Luc complained about it, about the food, the beatings, the cold in the winter, but James took it all in his stride. If he had to be at a school, Eton was as good as anywhere. Nothing lasted forever. As a place to be until he could join a regiment it served its purpose. He had arrived as a naive seven-year-old. At home, Sam had been like a god to him, tall and kind and defending him when Luc became too harsh. He had expected the biggest boys to be like Sam. On the side of the young ones when they needed a bit of a helping hand. His assumption had been thrown out like so much dirty water on his second day. Three nine-year-olds had taken exception to his size and decided to 'put him in his place'. A ring of older boys, looking like adults to James' eyes, had stood off to one side and taken bets amongst themselves on the likely outcome. James had taken a beating. As he had lain on his bed recovering, he had regrouped.

The second time he was ambushed he had lit up like a wildfire. He had kicked and punched and bit and thrown blows like a wild animal. He had forced the same three boys to withdraw along with two others who had taken exception to his 'no rules' fighting straight after. He had stood blowing like a bellows with blood pouring out of his nose and fists clenched making sure any and everyone knew he was still ready to take on all-comers. One of the younger masters had run over and taken him by the ear. Instead of whipping him, he had offered to teach him how to box.

'Can't just use your right, old man, you will end up with one arm like a melon and the other like an apple.'

James had listened. And learnt. Now, he lived with satellites, younger boys who hung near him in order to avoid the bullying. Daft thing was, he almost never had to fight these days. And that had taught him about the importance of reputation.

School plodded along in its usual way. The minutes dragged, but the weeks flew past. James was failing to pay attention in a Greek lesson when he was called out of class. He was quite glad at the time as who cared if some idiot flew near the sun and got his wings melted, or wrote a play about some woman dying of grief. Load of nonsense to his way of thinking. And when they wrote about a war, there wasn't enough strategy discussed. So he headed off to the headmaster's office with no particular concern. Until he found Luc there as well. They were told nothing. Just that the Causton coach was outside the door and they were to travel home. They found Bates the stable master waiting by the coach, feet apart, hands behind his back, face grim. He had come to tell them that Sam had died, that they were to go home for the funeral, and that their trunks were already on the coach.

This time James and Luc didn't speak for a different reason. Shock had immobilised them. The news was inconceivable. Luc was bone white and rigid with eyes that remained inside the coach but saw nothing. James huddled in a corner and pretended to look out of the glass to hide the fact that he was silently crying. The journey went on forever.

James was home for a week and couldn't get back to school fast enough. Lucian tried to refuse to go, but their father, grim in a way they had never seen before, was insistent. Once again they shared a carriage and a journey and nothing else. James was still in shock. He wanted to be back inside a routine he understood so he no longer had to deal with the idea of a world without Sam. What Lucian felt, he had no idea. If anything, Luc had been closer to Sam, being that much older, but he clearly didn't want to talk about him. It was the first time James had lost an adult he loved and the hole Sam had left in life was inconceivable. So he forced his emotions inside and willed the coach to go faster.

His mother had been frail and pale, but that was not surprising. Sam had been devoted to her, telling the tale of how he chose her to be his second mother to anyone who would listen. Certainly, James had been told the tale of how she had been stranded on a Plymouth dock in a tempest. She had been dressed in green and his father had always teased her by calling her his mermaid. She had been escaping the revolution, which seemed eminently sensible to James. Strange lot the French. That his beloved mother wanted to come and live in Wiltshire with his Pa and Sam made perfect sense to him. The shock about Sam had shaken his niggling worry about his mother out of his mind.

Time slipped by and James was eleven. Losing Sam had made him grow up in a way he couldn't articulate. All he knew was, that when he ran about the estate during those two summers, getting up to mischief and falling out of trees, after an hour or so he found the need to go home and see that everyone was still there, where they ought to be. The lines on his father's face were now deep grooves and Luc seemed ever more deeply embedded within himself and unreachable, but that second summer it was his mother who had changed the most. She seemed tiny. Yes, he had grown at an alarming rate and never seemed to know where his arms and legs ended so was constantly breaking things and falling over, but she felt as fragile as a baby bird when he hugged her. And she slept a lot. And she was hiding the fact. When James crept back into the house when everyone thought he was out in the woods or swimming at the bend in the river and stealthily hunted around for her, he would always find her curled up in a ball, fast asleep. He found her in the linen room once, then in an unused bedroom and another time up on an empty maid's bed.

He hunted for her as silently as warrior seeking his enemy; learning how to place his feet carefully on boards that creaked, edge along walls so the servants below wouldn't hear footfalls, climbing along the roofs of the outhouses. And on hot sleepy afternoons and dull damp rainy ones he sneaked off to the barns with two of the swords from the wall and practised hefting them. And never forgot the lesson he had learnt on his first days at Eton. He hid them deep in the straw and he hefted and feinted with his left hand as much as his right. His world was out of joint, and he had a feeling that he might need the skills he was trying so hard to teach himself.

Whenever he thought about asking his father about his mother, the sadness in his father's eyes stopped him. He certainly wasn't about to discuss it with Luc, or Chantel, she was just a girl, and although they were all close to various members of the staff it seemed disloyal to mention it to any one of them before his own family. His mother brushed off his concerns. She would put a finger to her lips and whisper, 'Hush my little one,' (which was a joke, he was twice her size), 'I am not as young as I once was. It is not so unusual to need a little nap in the afternoon, now is it? But don't tell your papa, it will make him feel old too!' And she would send him on his way with a smile and a kiss. And it was all a deceit and he knew it. So he kept his worries to himself and planned his future. A future where he would need to be able to use a sword.

Two weeks before he was due to return for the autumn to Eton the nebulous worry that had been fretting at James for so long turned into reality. Only at first, it seemed he had got everything so very, very, wrong. He came out of the barn where he secretly worked on his sword practise to see Luc walking towards the house. James didn't know why, but something about the way he was walking stopped James in his tracks. Luc looked about one hundred years old. Now Lucian was always a misery-guts these days, but this looked different. James moved forward slowly. By the time he had reached where Lucian had been he realized Bates, their senior man, was standing by the barn door Lucian had come out of and that he looked white as chalk. James began to run, his chest too tight for breathing.

'Stop lad,' Bates said as he drew near and looked to be heading for the entrance to the barn.

'What is it?' James asked. His voice, mostly deep but sometimes uneven, sounded high-pitched in his own ears.

'It's your Pa, he had taken a turn.' Bates' voice sounded unusually gruff.

'What do you mean, a turn. Why aren't you with him?' James felt as though the world had stopped quite still.

'He's dead lad. Quite dead.'

James felt the world tilt. 'No. Not my Pa, he is as strong as an ox!'

'Master Lucian saw it. Sir William came into the barn and fell down in front of him. We think his heart must have stopped he fell that heavy. He didn't put out a hand to halt his fall, he just went down.'

Bates put out a hand as if to draw James into a hug, but James span on his heel and ran off. He didn't stop running until he was deep in the wood, lacerated with brambles, his boots wet from boggy ground and his shirt stuck to him with perspiration and ripped. He tucked into the bole of an old oak and curled into a ball. He didn't cry. He couldn't.

He had been told that his mother was laid up with a bad chest cold, so when she again wasn't at dinner he was not surprised. He, Lucian and Chantel sat looking at their plates as their food cooled and said nothing. James was still in his muddy boots and torn shirt, but there wasn't anyone to mention it and he didn't have the energy after dragging himself home to wash or change. He spent the night staring up at the ceiling. His mind seemed to have entered a stage of frozen inertia. He didn't think about his Pa. He couldn't. He desperately wanted his mother, but she was too sick to see him.

In the morning he was told that she too was dead. He supposed she had died from the shock of his father dying so suddenly. It was Lucian who told him. James went deeper into himself and hated everyone. Lucian especially. He had no idea why, but it all seemed Lucian's fault.

When it dawned on him that Luc was now the head of the family he felt struck by yet another blow. The idea that his brother now held his and his sister's lives in his hands was beyond conceiving. When Luc told Chantel that she had to go to live elsewhere with a distant female relative the row saw fit to lift the old red tiles off the manor roof. James kept very quiet and still in the hopes that he might be forgotten. With all the staff in tears and Luc and Tilly bawling at each other day and night he didn't know where to go or what to feel. He hurt, and he had no idea what to do with the pain.

Chantel was beside herself at the idea of being sent away from her home. Worse, she was convinced that at fourteen she knew how to run the whole estate. James thought that she was probably right. When Lucian admitted that he was not only sending her away, but that he was leaving the estate to live elsewhere, she was incandescent. 'Who will run everything?' she demanded. 'Why wasn't he going to stay and manage his inheritance?' She insisted over and over that she could teach him how. James crept away to the barn where he could practise with his swords. If life was to fall apart, he knew exactly where he was headed. As a third son he didn't mind farm work, but he had never had any inclination to learn how to manage the estate and had no intention of learning now. Life at the Manor was unbearable. When Luc told him brusquely that he was to return to school and Chantel was being sent away the following morning he was glad. Some deep part of him knew that life had altered irrevocably. All his happiness has gone and he couldn't believe it would ever return. He was ready to step into life as long as it was elsewhere.

James watched Chantel's carriage leave with misgivings. The fact that she was being sent off to a total stranger bothered him, but on the other hand, if anyone could look after themselves it was Tilly. He trotted off to the stables to see Daniel. He found him mucking out, so he picked up a pitch-fork and helped.

'Did you see her leave?' he asked Daniel.

'And heard her,' Daniel was grinning widely. 'What a racket! I was up in the old oak. I wanted to see if she really was going to go.'

'Are you worried about her?' James couldn't help asking. He wasn't sure if he should be or not, and Daniel was sixteen, a man, to his eleven. Daniel and Tilly had always been fast friends.

Daniel stopped shovelling and leaned on the haft. 'A little. Is it true she had been sent to some relative in Bath?'

'In a way. Only none of us had ever heard of her before. She lives at 14 Muster Street.' James gave the information deliberately.

Daniel said nothing. He just looked straight into James' eyes. He bent to continue working and James stayed alongside. He had never been told to join in with the work of the estate and Lucian never had, but he liked the feel of his back flexing and his arms working to lift, and he even enjoyed the way the sweat broke out and soaked his shirt. The estate was home and his father and Sam had always leapt off their horses to join in any of the work anywhere they thought they could be of help and James had simply done the same. He worked when he wanted to, ran off about his own business when he didn't, and it seemed to suit everyone. He was the squire's son, after all.

When they had finished Daniel stood wiping his brow and said, 'Thank you.'

No,' James said with emphasis, 'thank you.'

They both knew that Daniel would do what James couldn't; go and see that Tilly was well. James loped off; he had to pack for Eton, he was leaving in the morning.

Lucian did not send Bates with James. He said he needed him on the estate. James didn't argue, in fact, he made no comment at all. Not even to recognise the extraordinary fact that Lucian was now Lord Causton and the squire. His trunk was loaded and he entered the carriage for the first time on his own. Lucian was leaving for Oxford in the autumn and considered that he was finished with school. He was going up early, but so had Sam, and it wasn't that unusual. James thought that Luc might get his comeuppance; Luc wasn't clever the way Sam had been. No one commented on the old haversack that he also took with him that he had found up in one of the attics. If they had, all they would have found were some underclothes and a couple of darned shirts. And one shilling.

The carriage drew up at the front of Eton and the coachman wandered off for a smoke of his pipe while the under-coachman hefted the trunk up to James' dormitory. James stood for a while by the empty coach, the door still swinging open, and looked around casually. Some boys were tearing around on one of the fields over to his right. He swung the haversack over his shoulder and headed in that general direction. Once he reached some trees, he simply turned to his left and vanished into the undergrowth.

Late one hot and heavy afternoon the previous May, one of the younger masters had walked with a group of boys out of the grounds and along the dusty lane towards Windsor. The hulk of the massive castle had floated above the treetops gleaming silver as the sun warmed its old stones. At the bank of the Thames they had hired a half dozen boats and rowed their small flotilla out across the water. When they had reached the jutting land the locals called Hamm, they had beached and hauled the boats above the waterline. They had settled to roaming the green tunnels under the trees where the undergrowth reached in places higher than their heads. The air had felt thick and tasted of pollen and the scent of blackberries yet to come. When they blundered into a camp the master had firmly taken charge.

The camp had consisted of a dozen or so men sitting huddled around a stick fire above which hung a pot of something stewing. Rabbit and nettles, James had suspected. The food had smelt wonderful. In answer to the brusque master, the men, forelocks well tugged, had explained that they were waiting for a recruiting sergeant and that they were all off to join the King's army. The master had nodded then shepherded the boys back to the boats, where they had rowed towards home with enthusiasm, stomachs growling for their supper. It had been a blissful afternoon, ending only as the stars had emerged popping out one by one above the rooftops. This was where James was headed. West, towards Hamm. Towards where recruiting sergeants could be found.

He found the sergeant mid-way through the following morning after a comfortable night stolen in an inn hay loft. He signed his name, handed over his shilling, and joined the army. The sergeant asked his age, he said sixteen, and no one seemed to find that a problem. He would join a Wiltshire regiment as an infantryman, the 62nd Regiment of Foot. When he met the other recruits as they marched out of town he received some odd looks, but he was as tall as any of them and bigger built than most. He could hear the accents of his own county all around him, but there was also a group of Dorsetshire men at the back. He tuned-in to the rhythms of their speech and smiled. It was like music, listening to them. He was as strong as any, enjoyed the march and being outdoors and had finally arrived exactly where he wanted to be.

Chapter Two

The threat of war in the Iberian Peninsula had been rumbling for some time. It had often been the main topic of conversation, as it was now. Like a fish darting in the shallows, it had sometimes been the only topic of conversation, then it would flick away, and not be mentioned, only to return to the main stream yet again. The whole idea thrilled him. If there was to be a war he was perfectly happy to join in. It seemed they were marching to Kent for training. The Duke of York had removed corporal punishment some years previously for many offences and Sir John Moore had set up the Shorncliffe System for training the light infantry. Lt Colonel Mackenzie had introduced the idea that the infantry, instead of marching straight into cannon fire might, a revolutionary idea, think for themselves. He also made the officers train with the men; that had caused reams of comment by the newspapers who were horrified by the idea of the classes mixing in such a way and were unconvinced that the comradeship this engendered was at any of value. James had studied it all and made up his own mind. This new army was definitely for him.

He arrived, slung his knapsack on the bunk in his quarters, then followed the sergeant outside for his first day of training. The sergeant frowned at him.

'How old are you, lad,' he demanded.

James had got away with it so far, so he said calmly, 'Sixteen, sir.'

The sergeant frowned, but let it slide. Few boys of eleven were as large as James, and a year here or there on the rule of being sixteen was often let slide. Just not by five years James knew. But so far luck had gone his way.

They were marched over the field and paused to look at a gun carriage while their sergeant spoke to another. James laid his hand on the cannon and took in the wooden carriage, mentally eyeing up the geometry and working out how the wood was supporting such a massive piece of metal and wondering if his classroom geometry would be of any use. Then he spotted something. He raised his head and gazed around. They were standing at the top of an open field looking down slope. He saw what he wanted and charged off, running as fast as he could.

'Here!' the sergeant shouted. He swung his head looking for the new recruit and saw him bent talking to a man far down the field. The lad was pointing back up at them. Then the man, who he could now see was a carpenter, had picked up a bag and was hurrying back with the lad. They arrived with the carpenter puffing and blowing. He dropped to his knees and peered at the gun carriage. As the sergeant reached to haul on James' ear and pull him back into line the carpenter called,

'Sergeant, have a couple of your lads help me out here!'

When he looked down he could see the carriage wood was sheared and minutes away from breaking. He quickly ordered the new lads into line and they supported the cannon while the carpenter hammered a 'quick fix' into position. He rose, sweating.

'Well done, sergeant for sending for me. When these buggers collapse it is the devil's own job to haul the cannon about and put matters to rights. Had a few lads injured when that happens.'

He packed up his tools and headed back to his previous job. The sergeant frowned at James, whipped them all back into line and herded his new batch of novices away. James got into line well away from the sergeant and kept his mouth shut.

The sergeant, James learned, was called Harris and James was to be under his command for the following month. As he didn't seem to be in trouble for breaking rank, James was relieved and content. He quickly found he was fit enough and strong enough for the training and began to relax as everyone around seemed happy enough to accept him. Then disaster occurred. He was hauled out of line by Sergeant Harris and marched off to the tent where some senior officers were gathered around a table leaning over maps. To James' horror, in amongst them, was Lucian.

'I want him back!' Lucian was shouting.

James felt sick. There clearly was a disagreement going on. Two of the officers moved towards Lucian and began to edge him away. Sergeant Harris and James followed. Once they were out of earshot, the discussion continued, but with Lucian still red in the face but quieter.

'He is a school boy,' Lucian was saying, shoving a finger in the chest of one of the officers.

James settled all of his weight on the sole of his left boot, feeling it settle against the earth and took in a breath. He was getting ready to unleash a right hook powered from his right foot as he stepped forward and aimed his right arm. He was about to put his whole body into the punch. He would beat Luc to death then swing for it, so help him. What stopped him was Sergeant Harris gently gripping his right upper arm. James flicked him a look and Harris gave a tiny shake of his head. James paused, frowning deeply.

'Furthermore,' Lucian was continuing, 'if anything happens to me he is Lord Causton. You can't have a bloody Lord of the realm as a common soldier!' James tensed again and Harris gripped tighter.

It was Harris who spoke up, 'Excuse me sirs,' he began, looking at Lucian, 'but how about you buy him in as an Ensign. He is young, agreed, but will soon grow.'

'A what?' Lucian demanded.

James was frowning now at Sergeant Harris, but kept quiet. One of the officers, from his insignia James knew him to be a Lieutenant, spoke to the other, a Major.

'Not a bad idea, sir. What do you think?'

'Don't see why not. All the Ensign's are babes in arms, this one might fit right in.' At that, the major strode off, indicating clearly he had better things to do.

The lieutenant turned to Lucian.

'Ensign is the lowest rank of officer. The boy will be training with boys not much older than he is. He will just have to stay in training for longer.' He turned to James, 'What do you think, boy, willing to serve your time in that way at first? Still want to be in the army?'

'Yes sir, and yes,' James shot back.

There was a bit more arguing on Lucian's part, but as it was clear that if he didn't agree James would simply run away again and find another regiment to join, he eventually gave in.

Lucian was walked away by the lieutenant to complete the paperwork. Before he left he said quietly to Sergeant Harris, 'Keep the lad alive until he makes lieutenant, there is a good man.'

Sergeant Harris agreed and saluted smartly. When they left he turned to James.

'Quite sure, are you lad? Once the army has you it won't let you go, no matter what age you are.' He paused, 'What age are you, anyway, lad?'

'Fifteen, sir,' he said firmly. Lucian had called him a school boy, but hadn't in his hearing mentioned an actual age.

'Well, the way you acted over that gun carriage was impressive.' He leaned forward, 'But you ever do it again and I will personally whip you until your back is raw and you are sobbing for your mother. If anyone had been practising range-firing down that slope, you could have been shot to ribbons.'

James suddenly saw the open field in his mind's eye and blanched. 'Yes, sir,' he agreed. 'Never again, sir, I promise.'

'There is a reason I am a sergeant and you are not, lad,' Harris commented.

'Yes sir,' grinned James. He was a soldier, or as good as. He didn't care if he was an officer or not, but if it kept Luc off his back, all was well and good for him.

Sergeant Harris kept James busy, but not as he had expected. He was amazed at the amount of paperwork the army generated.

'Right, lad,' Harris told him. 'Accounts. Boots, muskets, salt, doesn't matter what it is, it all has to be accounted for.' James raised his eyebrows. 'And you are going to learn from the bottom up about stores. An army doesn't just march on its stomach, it needs a bloody lot of other stuff as well. Look sharp.'

Harris had thought that his insistence on stores and paperwork might disillusion the lad, so they could send him home to his mother. But nothing seemed to deter him. He soaked up knowledge like a sponge. His writing was bloody awful though so Harris found an infantryman who was a drunk, when he had the chance, and had joined the army to escape a couple of too-persistent creditors, who had received a decent education. He set the man to teaching James penmanship. 'As an officer, you will be writing orders. It is bloody important that people like me can read them!' he spat at James one morning as he tried to interpret James' scrawl and splotches. Once more, to Harris' surprise, James took his orders seriously, perfecting his writing for hours with any scrap of chalk or ink he could find, on any scrap of flat surface or paper he could find. And he improved. Harris sighed, there was no getting rid of the lad, so he decided to teach him how to fire a musket.

James' response to this idea was met with a thoughtful frown. 'Who is the best at firing a musket in the regiment, sergeant?' he asked. Harris had been expecting boyish excitement not this thoughtful appraisal. When he didn't immediately reply James asked, 'Is there anyone more skilled than you?'

The Army's Son

'I taught the lads that teach the skill, so all my lads are good.'

'But who do you consider the best?' James persisted.

'Well, I am still one of the fastest. These lads,' he gestured at the humming camp around them, 'can fire four times a minute.'

'Then I would like to learn from you,' James told him with a wide grin. 'Bad habits are hard to unlearn,' he commented.

Harris raised his eyebrows. 'Indeed,' he muttered. Normally he would delegate a corporal for the task, but this lad was an officer, allegedly.

One of the lieutenants had walked over to watch. Harris took James through the workings of the long gun of the modern army.

'Commonly called the Brown Bess, this, lad, is the Land Pattern Musket. Ever shot one before?'

James shook his head. He was skilled with his crossbow and so had never bothered with guns. They went wrong too often and made too much noise to his mind.

'It is faster now we have paper shot,' Harris commented. 'We used to have a powder horn and had to measure the powder each time, but now it comes in a paper tube, so we have improved our rate of fire considerably.' James was watching keenly. 'Pay attention,' Harris told him sternly, 'you have two grades of powder, course in the paper shot and fine for the pan. Use course in the pan and you are more than likely going to blind yourself permanently.' James nodded. 'The difference is in the saltpetre. There is more in the fine, so it goes off with less spark. Don't forget boy,' he finished fiercely.

Harris ran him through the procedure, showing how to take out the shot from a pouch held on a strap that ran diagonally across his shoulder, hold the paper tube and bite off the end. It left black marks on his lips. He then tipped the paper tube into the end of the musket, took his ramrod from where it hung below the barrel and used it to shove the tube down hard. Then he took a lead ball from his pouch and shoved that down on top of the powder and paper.

'Acts as wadding,' Harris said. 'When I was a lad we had to wrap the ball in a piece of wadding before we shoved it down. It is all much quicker now.' As he spoke the replaced his ramrod. 'Never forget to put your ram back, lad,' he said. 'In the heat of battle when your fingers are all thumbs you don't want to be scrabbling on the ground for it because you have lost the bloody thing.'

Then he flicked open the pan and lifted a powder horn from around his neck. He pushed the stopper off the horn and tapped some powder onto the pan. James peered closely to see how much. 'This is your frizzen, lad, you need to close it properly.' The metal clicked together with a small snap. 'And this lad is your cock.' He pulled back the hammer that would crash forward and ignite the powder in the frizzen by making the flint spark. Normally there would be bawdy comments about, 'My cock is bigger than that' or 'My cock sparks more than that', but James simply looked interested. Harris lifted the gun to his shoulder, set it firm, aimed towards the targets and pulled the trigger. There was a flash and then a spurt of gold where the lead had landed as fragments of the yellow straw target went flying.

Harris handed the gun to James. He took it calmly, no sign of childish excitement. The first thing he did was point it into the ground and pull the trigger. Harris noticed the lieutenant raise an eyebrow. James then ran his hands over everything. He stroked the metal and wood of the gun as if learning its contours, lifted the frizzen up and down to feel how it worked, popped the end on and off the fine powder horn, felt around in the pouch for the paper wrapped shot, removed and replaced the ramrod. He stood for a few moments with his head on one side and seemed to think. Then, he set the gun with its stock on the ground and went through the whole procedure smoothly and slowly before sending a lead into the straw. He then proceeded to do the same thing twice more, each time slightly faster. The lieutenant stopped him there.

'Ensign Causton,' he said briskly. 'Head over to the gun crew by that cannon,' he gestured with a hand. After returning the musket kit to Harris, James trotted off.

'How old is the lad?' the officer asked.

'Says he is nearly sixteen, sir,' Harris told him. The lieutenant's expression suggested he believed that as much as Harris did.

'Little bugger is a born soldier. And likely to make General before me. I thought we could scare him back to his mother, but it is clear we are stuck with him. If he is that good with a Bess, let's try him out on a cannon.' He strode off after James.

Harris took out his pipe and sucked on it. He considered the officer's words. In his opinion, not to be breathed aloud, James was already a better officer than many. The lad was unfailingly cheerful, took on any task with interest and good humour, soaked up knowledge like a sponge. On top of which he was decisive and had opinions he had clearly thought through. Just needed to polish up his bloody writing so I can read it, he thought with a wry smile.

James, for his part, had no regrets. Whatever the army threw at him was better than sitting at a desk at Eton breathing in chalk dust and listening to stuff he had no interest in. He never strayed far from Harris. He knew if he was caught on his own, there were plenty who, if they could keep their identities secret, wouldn't mind 'turning him over'. And not all of them were in the ranks. He was viewed, on the whole, as a curiosity. The only good thing was that no one, not even the other Ensigns, had divined his true age. He was twelve and a half now. Bit longer and he could stop fretting about being caught out.

He had friends among all the ranks. The women who did the laundry, or repaired tunics, were the most acute about his youth. They teased him, but gently, and he enjoyed their off-hand and often foul-mouthed mothering. The aching loneliness and loss he buried deep and refused to acknowledge. He often wondered how his sister Tilly was getting on. He could write a letter to the address he had given Daniel, he supposed, but every day he put it off as there was something more interesting to do and the days slipped into weeks, then into months, until he was no longer sure he could remember the direction accurately. Lucian he despised and tried to forget. Apart from them, there was no one left.

A few weeks later he and Harris were part of a detachment sent to Ireland. He was feeling much more secure. He had actually seen the notice in the London Gazette of his commission, the entry declaiming him as the brother of Lord Causton. It still shook him to see Luc mentioned as the one holding the title. It should have been his Pa. And his Pa had always stuck to being Sir William. Apparently when his Pa had been knighted he had gone mad with irritation. It had meant stiff new clothes and a visit to court. He had hated it. His Ma had sailed through it all completely unconcerned. His father had returned and immediately given his court clothes to the vicar telling him to find a home for them. James didn't remember any of this, but he had been regaled with the tale often enough.

As the youngest Ensign it was his job to carry the guidon, or standard. It was the first army task James had disliked. They had marched through Dublin to cheering crowds who were all clearly enjoying the flutes and drums and as one of the standard bearers, James had felt the attention of the crowd as a physical blow. He always hated being the centre of attention; he knew he would have been far happier tucked next to Harris in the ranks. It hadn't helped that some of the other Ensigns had been openly jealous of the role, one or two being younger sons of dukes and earls. As the brother of a lowly lord, he had come in for some unpleasant bantering. Those boys had been brought up to be gazed at and admired. Sir William had seen himself as a simple farmer, content on his acres and keeping as far away from towns and cities, especially London, as possible and James had absorbed his instinctive humility. Harris just told him it was good practice for him. James had kept his face as blank as possible as much as possible, but suddenly when a bad egg hit the scarlet jacket that he was so proud of, it was a shock.

'Why did someone do that, sergeant?' James asked Harris when it was all over.

'Many see us as a foreign army. The Irish, after all, have their own army.'

'But we don't mean them any harm, do we?' James pressed.

'No lad, but we are recruiting and there are a lot of people who don't want all of their young men scooped up and taken off to fight foreign wars. They know that there are many who will have no future but that of being a farm labourer in the same spot they were born in and who will never even get the chance to visit their own capital. So the army with our pipes and drums and the guidon you were carrying will look far too attractive. And besides, this is a poor country for all that it is called the bread basket of England, and poverty is enough to make any man, or woman, angry.'

James mulled it over, but later, when they had marched far from Dublin he was surprised he had been hit by only one egg. The cottages most of the Irish labourers lived in compared poorly with the neat stone cottages his father had provided for his tenants. Made of sod earth with soil floors and turf as the only protection to keep out the weather, he wondered how they navigated the famine months of January to March when his father and Sam had ensured every cottage had sufficient food to last the winter. The people he saw standing by the road looked thin by comparison to his own Wiltshire folk and were mostly bare footed. He developed a dim opinion of the landlords they were beholden to. If a man couldn't look after his folk better than that he had no right being a landlord, in his view. But he kept his mouth firmly shut and was glad he had. It seemed some of the other Ensigns had families who were drawing rent from this destitute population. James hoped that the folk he had left behind in Causton were still being looked after. He had a feeling it was a forlorn hope. Lucian had never intended to be a landlord and James had never had so much as a letter from him, let alone a visit. He quite deliberately put Causton and his remaining family firmly out of his mind.

. . .

James' sojourn in Ireland, it seemed, was coming to an end and they were all to disembark for India. So the regiment required a little entertainment before leaving home shores and as their newest officer recruit, the younger lieutenants decided James required 'blooding'. He had no idea what that meant, but it seemed to be some kind of initiation ceremony and as he had been rather expecting something of the sort he had given Sergeant Harris the slip and gone along with the crowd.

He was now sitting frozen into immobility amidst the noise of bellowing voices, shivering lights, sickly odours of cheap perfumes mixed with stale perspiration and the wild intense colour of red uniforms and scarlet satin corsets. And flesh everywhere. Breasts hanging low and billowing out, almost covered nipples pressing against satin, plump and puckered thighs revealed by the toss of skirt hem framed with equally white petticoat flounces. His head was spinning with the gin and he thought he was going to be sick. A woman was yelling at him above the noise, calling him deary, and then she was pulling on his wrist, trying to make him stand and he knew he was going to spill his guts on her dress. There was no lull in the noise, only an intense pain at the side of his head. He glanced up blearily to find Sergeant Harris had him firmly by the ear. James relaxed and lifted his backside and was pulled by the yanking hand, bent almost double with only the floor in view. Harris was elbowing his way to the door, kicking when necessary taking no account of rank, and inch by inch he found the outer door and shoved it open.

'Wanna be sick,' James muttered.

This was greeted with an emphatic, 'Good.' Harris changed his grip to the back of James' neck and held him head down over a patch of grasses at the corner of the building. James heaved for a while, then stood. Harris silently offered a canteen of water and James swilled his mouth out and then drank deep. Without a word, they began striding back to barracks, James keeping up but drifting a little now and then.

He slumped in a chair in Harris's room as the sergeant heated water for some tea. There was the sharp smell of rosemary for a moment and James was catapulted back home. When the water had boiled he sat cupping his hands around the herbal brew and breathed in the steam. Harris was cleaning his pipe and as he scratched at the white bowl, he was watching James.

'How old are you really, lad?' he asked. He had been careful to remain ignorant so far.

'Not quite thirteen,' he admitted.

This was greeted with a snorted 'hummph'. The boy would have to go back home, Harris thought. He had known the lad wasn't anything like the sixteen he claimed, but he hadn't thought that he was as young as he was. It wasn't really his age that mattered; boys aged into men, no one had yet found a way to stop that happening, but this boy wasn't mudlark from the rookeries and stews of the London hovels, nor a runway sweep's apprentice, nor from any of the other crevices that the boys in the army had crawled out of. His brother, a young shiver, had appeared and claimed to be a Lord Causton. And so it seemed. The father had been knighted for services to the army, leather and grain, and been raised from a mere sir to the ermine. Harris scratched the back of his neck. This lad still needed his ma and pa. The boys who normally rolled up at his age were already battle-hardened by poverty and aggressive neglect; for them the army was the first home they had known.

'You need to go home, lad,' he said. 'You have had an adventure, now trot off back for a few years. If you still want the life, it will be here waiting for you, not to worry about that. Wars ain't goin' to end any time soon.'

James lifted his head and looked at Harris in horror. And then it hit him. Like a sledgehammer to the guts. A horrific wail came out of his mouth. He tried to stop it but it had him in its grip. He screamed his pain and loss, then jack-knifed his head into his knees, hitting bone to bone with an audible crunch.

Harris watched for a while, then lay one hand on the lad's back. To his surprise, and embarrassment James swivelled sideways and sobbed into his chest. Harris patted him awkwardly and let the lad be. Better out than in, was his motto. The storm went on for a long time, until finally James found some measure of control. He lifted his head muttering apologies. He sat for a while gathering himself and Harris thought that now the lad would turn to his own crib. James turned to meet his eyes and said quietly and calmly,

'I have no home to go to. None at all. It is the army or nothing for me.'

'Come boy, what do you mean,' Harris pressed, not convinced. Everyone had family. Well, he didn't, but he considered himself unusual. To his surprise, James gave him a wry smile. He swallowed and said,

'Recently I have lost my eldest brother, my father and my mother. My sister has been sent to an aunt who isn't an aunt and I have no real idea where that might be, and my only family, my elder brother, has vanished. I have written three letters, two with a return address yet have heard nothing from him. The two came back as 'undeliverable'.'

Harris sat and gazed at him. 'What about other aunts and uncles, second cousins and the like?'

'My mother was French. She escaped the revolution in 90 and her family were guillotined. Pa was an only child. So, no. That is why my sister has been sent off to a woman no one has heard of. But I don't worry about her. If she were here she would be a general in five minutes. I have never seen anyone best her.'

Harris was surprised into an unexpected bark of laughter.

James drew himself up and swallowed. 'I apologise Sergeant Harris. I assure you such histrionics will not recur.'

Harris looked at him hard. The lad didn't sound or act like a child of his years. And he remembered the gun carriage. James had probably saved one man at least an injury. He sighed.

'You may be an officer, but you don't move out of my sight for the foreseeable future. And we need to work harder on your numbering.'

One day the lad would be presenting a butcher's bill, he would need a sharp understanding of what the death toll after a battle meant to his fighting strength. But that would come in time. And it was always too soon for any man.

'Get to bed,' he said. 'I want you on duty at ten sharp.'

He was gratified to see James rise and nod, and quietly take himself off. He sucked on his pipe thoughtfully and gazed out at the stars. The lad would have to grow up quick, that was for sure.

James stood against the frigate rail and let the wind blow salt spray into his face and speckle the shine on his buttons. They were on a frigate bound first for Plymouth and then for the port in southern Spain known by some as Rooke's Rock and by most as Gibraltar. James had read up on the history of the rock avidly. He longed, secretly, to be like Admiral Rooke and to win something historic, but on the other hand, he was more than content to be lost in amongst the mass of the army. It was proving a home to him, however brutal and unthinking it could be at times. On others, the comradeship and company reassured him that he was where he should be, doing what he should be doing.

Harris was standing with him some days later when, fully provisioned, they watched England slip away into the morning mist.

'Well, we won't see home again for some time,' Harris said quietly.

James turned and looked at him. 'Not quite true for me, Sergeant Harris,' James said just as quietly, 'I am with my home.'

They stood watching the waves and clouds as the sails bucked and bellied above them. 'Do you have any family?' James asked.

'A sister somewhere. Not sure where anymore.' Harris sucked on his pipe. He gave James a smile and went about his duties. James twisted his head and watched him walk with steps as sure as the sailors to set men to duties that were pointless but would keep them from gambling and fighting their days away, he supposed.

Harris continued to keep his eye on James as the journey progressed as did Lieutenant Greeves, the man who had taken James off to learn how to command a gun crew.

'How is he doing?' Greeves asked Harris one day.

Harris tapped the stem of his pipe on his bottom teeth and thought for a moment. 'He is like the ship's cat. I never know where he is but he is always being useful. Found him learning how to whip a Turk's cap yesterday.'

Greeves shot him a look. 'Isn't that a knot that ends a rope decoratively?'

'Indeed, sir.'

Greeves gave a snort of amusement. 'Did you hear what he got up to the last time I had him practising his gun crew?' Harris turned an enquiring gaze on Greeves so he continued. 'He had the lads weighing the powder they used for the shots. Then he reduced it by a proportion and had them see if the ball went as far. By the time I intervened he needed some help with the mathematics; had got himself into a bit of a muddle and the crew were pitching in unhelpfully, but he had worked out that the ball would go as far with eight percent less powder than they were accustomed to using. He was trying to scale his results up to show what the effect would be in saving resources in battle.'

'Ah. Useful, I suppose, but a bit of a problem.' Harris was grinning.

'Indeed.' The two men smiled at each other. 'As we know, it is usually the cannon balls that are the limiting factor, not the powder, but I liked the way he was thinking.'

As they stood there they became aware of the men on deck. It wasn't anything in particular, just a ripple along the senses of experienced men that something was not quite right. Turning, Harris saw James stripped to his drawers following a seaman up the rigging, climbing almost as fast and grinning like the boy he still was. Greeves took a step clearly intending to order James down and Harris risked a flogging by catching his arm.

'Don't distract him, sir,' he hissed.

They both watched as James climbed higher and higher. At the crow's nest both lads climbed inside, panting and grinning. Out of nowhere came a yell, 'Navy and Army evens!' and there was a great roar of approval. Looking up made Harris feel more than a little sick.

'Little bugger,' he muttered.

'That's why we don't take them that young!' Greeves spat out, and stormed off to bring the men back into some kind of discipline.

'Brave, though,' Harris muttered to himself. 'Little sod is going to take years off my life.'

He was going to have James scrubbing decks for the foreseeable future. Trouble was, the lad would set to with a grin and a will and Harris would be left feeling he had rewarded him not punished him. He shook his head, 'Little bugger,' he said again, this time louder.

James explored Gibraltar with a will and was sad to leave. Many a pretty girl had shot a glance his way and he had come into much teasing from the other Ensigns, but he just blushed and felt queasy. He still had the odd nightmare about the whore house and would wake sweating and shaking. Strolling the streets, he had loved the colours and scents of the vegetable markets, the lushly embroidered clothes of the women, the sound of so many tongues in the narrow streets. Let alone the multi-coloured population who varied from tanned, to every shade of brown to solid black. It had all been exotic and exciting.

India, on first appearance, seemed a more lush Gibraltar and even more colourful. It smelt different though and as they eased into port he took deep breaths, never wanting to forget his first sight of this new land. Causton Manor seemed a long, long, way away.

He was billeted in a wooden cabin called a bungalow with one of the other Ensign's, but when that lad was moved to other duties for some reason James was left on his own. He had a room to sleep in, a sitting room and a bony old woman to cook and clean for him who inhabited rooms at the back. It was basic and the cockroaches were the size of English mice, but James loved the veranda out the front that he could sit on in the evenings and the simplicity of it all. Not all the men had such unattractive housekeepers and on those evenings he might hear shouting where the occupants found cause to complain about their care or rattling and gasping as others made the most of their female house companion. His own housekeeper seemed unable to keep flesh on her bones and looked as though she had grown up with Methuselah. They lived together quietly and when James went down with an inevitable fever a couple of weeks after he arrived she nursed him as if she were a mother cat and he her sick kitten. When he heard a small girl in the market yelling at her mother he began to call the old woman 'Mata', which he hoped meant what he thought it did. As her response was a grin showing every one of her brown and broken teeth, he guessed he had done something right.

The first time they went into battle he was sick with nerves the night before. The routine of marching into position began to calm him and he knew Harris would never be far away. Until the first shot he thought he would disgrace himself by wetting his trousers, but with that first volley everything slowed down to half speed and he found his breathing was steady as his mind calculated angles, risks and opportunities. He emerged from the battle unscathed, filthy and temporarily deaf. But now he was a soldier in truth.

When he had been in India a year he marched back into their billets on a warm and insect drowsed evening exhausted after yet another skirmish. He was not too pleased to find Mata with a young girl, who kept her sari pulled over her face. He had picked up a little Hindi and from what he could understand Mata had to go somewhere and the girl was to look after him. He couldn't help but show his displeasure. He was used to Mata, enjoyed her cooking and hearing her potter around the place when he was there. They lived in harmony and he didn't want his peace disturbed by a foolish girl who would not know his likes and dislikes. Standing in front of a fusillade was one thing, but not having that peace he was accustomed to when he returned was quite another. James was irritated.

He saw Mata off with a kiss on her brow and a frown as she walked away. Then he strode after her and stopping her, he walked once around her, thanked her for looking after him and bowed. She gave a gleeful bow in return, clearly glad to be parting on good terms. Sighing he went to wash and then sit on his veranda to process the day's fighting. As he walked to the water barrel at the rear a flash of colour let him know that the girl had witnessed the parting. His frown returned. Later he would go and join his colleagues, but he liked to calm his mind first and he wasn't sure he could do that with a stranger around.

He ignored the girl for over a week. She seemed to sense how out of sorts with her he was and kept well out of his way. Her cooking wasn't as tasty as Mata's, his shirts didn't feel as clean and instead of being deeply content in his quiet home he felt out of joint. Then he asked her to tell him her name in his limited Hindi. 'Priti', she said quietly and gave him a mischievous grin, which suggested she knew some English at least. In fact, as it turned out, she knew quite a bit and James began to warm to the idea of improving his Hindi. Mata's lack of English had proved a substantial barrier to his progress.

After some time, James and Priti began to settle together and even talk a little in the evenings. Eventually she asked,

'Why did you walk once around Mata when she left?'

'Out of respect. The god Ganesh walks around his mother because she is the world. I wanted to show Mata how much I thought of her.'

Priti watched his face thoughtfully and then left him alone. He could hear her washing in her room, sloshing water about and humming as she dried. The thought of her naked bothered him a great deal and he tipped back his head and felt like howling at the moon. Why, oh why, had Mata had to leave him?

That night he was awoken as the moon rode high. He thought it must be either animals or birds calling in the tree canopy that had disturbed him, but then, as his eyes adjusted to the dark, he realised that Priti was standing with the open window behind her. His soldier's instincts suggested that she had chosen that spot so that she would be outlined against the lighter night sky and he was therefore less likely to attack her as an intruder. He swallowed and it sounded as loud in his ears as a musket shot. As he watched silently she slowly unwrapped her sari and slipped out of her blouse. Naked she slipped in beside him. It was James' sixteenth birthday and he had never received a nicer gift.

Chapter Three

Hal Whitlock was leaving the army. Only leaving was not the correct word. The correct word was deserting, which was probably why the skin on his back was jumping around and his spine felt like it would prefer to curl up inside his guts. With every step he took towards the port he was expecting a hand on his shoulder. The result then would be simple. A man didn't leave the army. And he didn't continue to serve either.

He had known what he was doing when he signed on and he was confident in what he was doing now. It had all started when his Ruth died. He had always privately scoffed at the idea of hearts breaking, but when she had died he had felt his very soul fracture. He hadn't realised how much she had meant to him until she was gone. She probably had known. She had been better at that stuff than him.

His two boys had grieved too; Christopher, blonde and blue-eyed and Stephen, tawny of both hair and eye. They had both had the height and girth of his own father, unlike him. He was, to be polite, stocky, with huge feet that had always amused his Ruth. He had been taken down by measles when he was a young'un and his ma had always said it had opened him up to all the rest; the swollen throat of the mumps where he had sweated and swallowing had been agony, the scarlet fever, when he had seen devils and angels dancing in his room his fever had been so high and so he had never reached the size his feet had suggested he should have. But his lads had. They had been lucky and although they too had been through a selection of childhood illnesses, they had shrugged them off and come through. And as a result, the little buggers had grown to twice his size.

Both boys had helped fill the pot from an early age snaring rabbits and pigeons and the odd duck or fish, but it was when they had come home with a deer that the problems had begun. They swore that they hadn't intended to kill it, but it had been panicked by something else and Chris had arced his knife at it instinctively as the thing had sprung into the hollow where they had been hiding. They had both been soaked in blood and every stitch of clothing had needed to be secretly burnt. None of them had enjoyed the meat either. The knowledge of what the magistrate would do to them if the death of such a protected animal was discovered spoilt all of their appetites. Poaching deer, like deserting, was an instant death sentence.

Time had passed and then Ruth had been taken ill and slipped out of their grasp. They had only just begun to recover when the gossip began to circulate. There were rumours going around about both Chris and Steve bringing home a deer one night. Why they had emerged so long after the event, it must have been more than a year, Hal didn't know. The boys hadn't waited to find out. They had taken the shilling when the next recruiting sergeant had come around. Chris had leant forward, his elbows on his knees, his shock of blonde hair drifting into his eyes, as he had tried to explain to his father why they were both going to leave him. He had shocked them both when he had accompanied them and signed on too. The army was more than happy to take on three experienced blacksmiths, and then they had ended up in India, and to both boy's disgust he made sergeant while they remained firmly in the ranks. And now he was going home.

. . .

The evening was sinking to a humid purple haze. James was sitting in his breeches and boots with his jacket open over his shirt drinking a cup of something delicious Priti had made him. He was gazing tiredly over the tree tops trying not to think about the previous three days. The fighting had been brutal and they had lost a lot of men. Now, the compound was quiet and he was glad of it. He needed time to unwind and rest. Then, out of nowhere and with no warning, two men were running towards him with swords raised. James darted inside for his musket and sword but by the time he returned to the veranda the two men were right on top of him with another close behind. He fought like a mad man, with no idea what was really happening except the bastards were here and trying to kill him. He had laid out the closest two when he realised he had lost sight of the third. The compound was full of the sounds of women's screams and men's shouts.

Then he heard Priti scream. He spun around and hurdled the table and chairs flying like a wild thing towards the rear of the bungalow. The third man. He would have been checking who was at the rear of the house. James reached the back to see Priti being hauled through the open window by her long hair. He rushed forward, but something crashed into his head and he went down, struggling up, an explosion deafened him and his left shoulder flew back, pulling the rest of his body with him.

He came round to find he was full of pain but it all disappeared when, lifting his heavy head, he saw Priti huddled under the window. Hauling his body across he went to pull her into his arms but the sight of her neck stopped him. Her throat had been sliced from one side to the next. A different kind of pain caused a silent wail to scream up from his guts. He laid his head on her breast and forced his right hand up to her stomach to rest it on the faint swelling that they had not acknowledged except for an exchange of looks. Dark swirled, and he gave up caring about staying in the world.

. . .

Hal knew that the barracks had been attacked. He spat into the dust. Complacency. It killed more men than the bloody cholera that did the rounds in this bloody country like a clock ticking. Here it was. Now it wasn't. And then back it was. Stephen had died of it and he and Chris had been devastated. 'Why not him?' he had asked. What kind of perverse god would take his beautiful boy and leave his worn-out father? And after three days of solid vicious fighting his Christopher had gone down. Well, it was more than a father could stand, and he didn't care what the bloody hell happened to him, he was leaving.

He strode to the dock to see if he could talk his way onto any vessel that was heading for anywhere that wasn't India. There was what looked like a likely craft busily being provisioned as he shifted himself between wooden crates and huge piles of canvas wrapped cloth. Someone had told him over a million bales of cloth were exported from India to Britain every year. He could believe it looking at the warehouses and heaps of cargo ready for transporting. He managed to force a porter to pause as he ran back down the gang plank in the search for another load to carry aboard.

'Hey, mate! Where are you headed?'

'London docks, soldier, what is it to you?'

'How do I get a berth?'

'You a deserter?'

'No, I have permission to head home.' Like hell he had.

'Captain is up there,' the sailor pointed.

'Right oh.'

Hal hesitated. He was indeed a deserter, so might it be better to wait until closer to cast off so the captain couldn't send for the army? He didn't really care if he was shot, but there was no point in asking for a bullet. He would rather go home first and be put beside his Ruth. He decided to walk around the wharf a little more. He ducked and dived under ropes and dodged around amongst rushing seamen. And then he saw the injured. They were lying on stretchers on the stones of the wharf in rows. A sergeant with a book was demanding names of the men as they lay in the unrelenting heat of the sun. Bloody fools.

Why weren't the lads in the shade? And then he began to understand. They didn't want to ship them home. There were too many of them. If they died on the wharf, problem solved. Sick to his guts Hal walked closer.

One lad caught his eye. He had lieutenant's insignia but was young, but then lieutenant was a rank that held all sorts. It was his size Hal noticed. He was big, just like his lads had been. Hal walked closer. This lad had a bandage around his head and another around his left shoulder. He seemed to have a couple of knife wounds too. Hal knelt by his head. A pair of dazed blue eyes opened and looked into his. Hal took out his water bottle and dribbled a little into the lad's mouth.

'Sergeant!' Hal shouted. 'This here's my lieutenant. I am supposed to be escorting him home.'

Recognising another sergeant, the man walked over. He peered at his book. 'Lieutenant James Causton. He yours?'

'He is indeed,' Hal insisted.

'Very well, he is booked on the Princess Marie-Claire. I will send a couple of lads over to help you carry him aboard.'

The man hustled away, clearly glad that at least this was one less stretcher he had to deal with.

This Lieutenant Causton did not appear to have any possessions. Hal wasn't surprised. The barracks including the compound had been set on fire. This lad was lucky to be breathing still. Something rose inside Hal. He had lost his two lads, but he would be buggered if he would let the army kill this one. Without help, he surely would be finished and, from the callous way the army was treating these poor sods, few of them were going to survive even the next few hours.

It seemed officers were to be given berths on the Marie-Claire. Hal supervised his charge being taken aboard and then went to find a hammock to sling in the same cabin. Space was clearly going to be tight.

Hal nursed the young lieutenant as if he were his own. He dribbled drinking water into his parched mouth, dribbled soup in when he seemed a little more conscious and dribbled brandy in when the lad seemed to sink too much. He barely slept and changed the bandages twice a day. Most of the time the lad seemed to be in a deep, deep sleep. When the fever began, Hal was not surprised.

It took three weeks, but finally one morning the lad woke and said, 'Who are you?'

'Sergeant Harold Whitlock.'

'Thank you,' the lad murmured and went straight back to sleep. Hal grinned to himself. The lad was doing well. The fever was down and he seemed to have his wits about him. Hal celebrated by drinking some of the brandy.

Within days his tame lieutenant was becoming restless and beginning to haul himself out of his bunk and walk up and down.

'How do you feel?' Hal asked, knowing the answer.

The lad just looked at him. He stretched and twisted and walked a few more steps before collapsing back onto the bunk.

'Is there any food around?' he asked.

Hal grinned and headed to visit the cooks.

Once he started eating, there was no stopping him. Within a couple more days he was walking up and down the deck and then he began carrying filled buckets up and down.

Hal's, 'Steady sir, take it gently now,' received a long cool look.

Eventually they sat and discussed their situation.

'What is the ship's name?' James asked.

'Princess Marie-Claire. She was one of the *vaisseaux fregates* in the *Marine Royale*, what the French call their navy. She was captured off Trafalgar and as sailors don't like their ships being renamed, they painted out an 'e' off the end of Princess, and Bob's your uncle, she is an English ship of the line.'

James gave him a long look. 'Fancy your French pronunciation, do you sergeant?'

'Was it bad, sir?'

James gave a low chuckle. 'Not really. My mother was French. I grew up bi-lingual.' He took in a breath and gazed into the middle distance. 'Her name was Marie-Claire. I thought I was hallucinating when I saw her name on the bow, that is all.' He paused and turned to

Hal again. 'So, how do I come to have a devoted valet who I have never seen before?'

'Deserting, sir. You should shoot me.'

'You haven't deserted far if you are spending your time nursing me.'

'Well, truth is, I haven't got around to actually leaving the army yet. I wanted to get back home, some bastard was going to let you die on the dock side, so I thought I could kill two birds with one stone. Get us both back home in one piece. So, I suppose I don't quite deserve shooting just yet.'

'Well, my powder is almost certainly damp, so you are safe from me.' He held out his hand. 'James Causton.'

Hall shook it, 'Hal, just Hal, if you don't mind.'

James didn't answer, only gave a slight nod. Not a man for chatting, Hal thought and liked him all the more for it.

Hal was smoking his pipe and gazing over the rail. It was a fine day of breezes and sunshine and the sails were gently bellying. It was on days like this he quite liked boating, he thought, though if any of the sailors heard him call their beloved stolen frigate a boat they would probably gut him and drop him over the side. He turned to see James pull his shirt over his head, ball it, and throw it to a watching sailor. 'Hang on,' thought Hal, 'I washed that damn shirt!' James was now dressed in nothing but his drawers. As Hal watched he untied the drawstring around the waist and retied it more firmly. He was now talking to a sailor whose dark hair was tied back in a queue. James stood head and shoulders above the man, so was bending down to speak to him. The two shook hands then James stood upright again and, shielding his eyes, peered up at the rigging above them. 'Oh no,' thought Hal and took a step forward.

All work on the ship had ceased. Even the bloody Captain was leaning forward to watch events. 'What if a pirate appears? Or a storm?' Hal looked around wildly. Being on a boat was bad enough but the bloody things could sink easy as winking. They weren't made of nice strong metal like he was used to working with, they were made of bloody wood! Even insects could chew through that!

The two men lined up and there was a sharp whistle. James began to climb steadily to a point about fifteen feet above the deck. He stopped there, gazing below and Hal's breathing began again; perhaps this was it. But no, there was another shrill whistle and James resumed climbing as the sailor leapt up to chase after him. Gazing up made Hal feel queasy, but he couldn't tear his eyes off the men. 'I'll bloody kill him,' he muttered aloud.

They made it to the crow's nest together, but James' long reach meant he clearly touched the wood before the sailor. The soldiers watching below gave a huge cheer and as the two men up above shook hands, down below money changed hands.

Later that night Hal gave James a tongue lashing. When he stopped to draw breath James said,

'Fancy the 95 th Regiment of Foot, the Green Jackets?'

Taken by surprise Hal paused his tirade. 'What?' he asked, pulling his head back on his neck in surprise.

'Have you seen the Baker Rifle they are using. It is marvellous. And I reckon I could do a good job with it.'

Hal felt rocked. 'So?' he asked.

'Just wondering if you would like to remain my valet? I have been thinking, when a skirmisher lays down to sight, his back is wide open. How would you like to be behind me and keep an eye out. Nothing destroys an enemy faster than losing all the officers. I fancy going just for them, crawling close and, well, taking pot shots.' His grin was infectious and split his face from ear to ear.

'Sounds like a recipe for an early grave,' Hal grumbled. 'I am turning in.'

A week later he was off again. 'A cart load of monkeys would be less trouble,' Hal grumbled to himself. They had been becalmed for three days. The weather was stifling and the men ill-tempered and here and there facing up to each other, like small flickers of a fire that shot into life then settled, leaving everyone feeling that an inferno might flare up at any moment. This time the Captain was taking a more active part. He was standing out on the deck with his pocket watch, a huge gold monster, open in his flat hand. James, meanwhile, was gazing up at the yard arm.

Then James began to climb. As before he flew up the rigging as if born to the trade. At the yard arm he walked out, holding on where he could at first, and then steadying himself he edged out to the end holding both arms out for balance. On deck the men were silent and watching. There wasn't a man aboard who wasn't on deck waiting for the young fool to plunge to his death. At the end, James stood for a moment, then bent his knees and threw his arms up above his head. It was only then Hal realised what he planned. Like an arrow he dived straight for the sea, entering with an audible splash.

Hal bent over the rail anxiously waiting to see if he emerged. When he did, he was far along the ship towards the stern. Instead of heading back on board, he set out with a strong over-arm stroke Hal hadn't ever seen before, not that he knew anyone who could actually swim. Paddle around and keep afloat, but not this smooth cutting through the water. The men rushed along the sides to follow his progress and it was obvious most were betting their wages on the outcome.

James eventually arrived back where he had entered and began to race up a rope that had been thrown down for him. He arrived on deck and fell to his knees, head forward and gasping. Grinning up at the Captain he asked,

'How did I do?'

'Beat me by one half minute,' the Captain sighed, and held out his hand.

'What does he mean?' Hal asked a seaman.

'Cap'n did it as a lad. Your boy was aiming to beat his time and he managed it.' The man ran off to collect his winnings. Disloyally he had bet on the soldier not his own man.

That night Hal agreed to try to enter the 95th if they would have him.

'I ain't leavin' you on your own. Bloody dangerous, you are,' he grumbled.

James just laughed and slapped him on the back as he shook his hand. As he lay in his hammock that night Hal thought, 'Well, life won't be dull, that is for sure.' And the more he thought the more he began to think that James was probably a bloody good officer. This ship had been on a knife edge if not of mutiny then of a troublesome disturbance. James' display had caught every man's attention and they were still talking about it amongst themselves, happily. That was the word. Happily. His dive and swim had altered the whole mood of the company. Hal couldn't work out if it had been deliberate, instinctive, or an accident. So he went to sleep.

A month later they were working their way up the Thames when James began the conversation. They were both men who had done a great deal and seen a great deal more; personal conversation was not their style. 'Thank you for bringing me back from the dead,' he began. 'I will never be able to repay you and I want you to know how genuinely grateful I am.' He wasn't looking at Hal, but was gazing at the misty, or possibly smoky, city in the distance.

Hal moved beside him and set his gaze on a parallel line. They stood quiet for a while as the sailors rushed around doing what sailors did. Eventually Hal said quietly, 'I am not sure the gratitude shouldn't be the other way around.'

James didn't ask for an explanation, he just turned and gave Hal a frowning look, before looking away again. Hal cleared his throat.

'I had two boys, Stephen and Christopher. Big lads like you. Cholera got one, the last battle t'other. When the rebels headed for the barracks I decided I didn't care if I carried on breathing or not, I just walked away. Without them, what point was there in living?'

James turned once more and looked at Hal. Now it was his turn to be quiet, before he said, just as quietly, 'There was a sergeant. Harris. He went too. He trained me. Made me who I am.' The deep emotional connection between the two men didn't need to be explained. Harris had been more of a father than his own had been. No one's fault. His

Pa had just died too soon to finish the job that Harris then picked up. Priti and the babe, well, that was his business and he would grieve inside his own heart in his own time.

Tales of the siege Ciudad Roderigo were circulating as James and Hal made their way through London towards the Headquarters of the British Army at Horse Guards Parade. James was desperately impatient. He wanted to be where the action was once more, whether in the Americas or the Peninsula. Personally, he was hoping for the war in Europe as it was closer and he could get there all the sooner, but realistically he knew he was considered a 'Sepoy soldier' having battled only in India and was the more likely therefore to be dispatched over the Atlantic. He had finally been made up to Lieutenant on his sixteenth birthday while still in India. Despite his five years of service, he was a long way down the rolls of what the Horse Guards might consider a 'useful' soldier. Inexperienced Lieutenants were two a penny.

Hal strode along beside him, amused by this different James who was normally so imperturbably calm one wondered if he had a pulse. This morning he was almost jumping out of his skin with impatience. Hal, on the other hand, was in no hurry. Dying always came too soon in his book. And a siege was bloody miserable. And Spain in the winter was especially bloody miserable. And he didn't like the cold. He was a blacksmith for heaven's sake, intense heat was where he felt most comfortable! But he tagged along. He would wait until he saw where the boy was being sent and then he would make up his mind.

James had his interview and came out defeated. He had requested the 95th Foot, the Green Jackets who went ahead as a skirmish line and explored for weaknesses or picked off individual troops, hopefully senior officers, with the near miraculous Baker rifle. James was desperate to get his hands on one.

'What happened?' Hal asked.

'He laughed at me. Told me no one my size could ever make a skirmisher. There would never be a big enough rock to hide behind.'

Hal covered his smile with his hand and then hunted for his pipe. The same thought had occurred to him. 'What do they want you to do?'

'Instead of light infantry they want me as a heavy infantry detachment commander. They ran me through the gun crew procedure as if I was sitting a school boy's exam.'

'Did you remember it all? Like how the ventsman has to ensure he doesn't blow off the loader's hands?'

'Good grief, man! Of course I did.'

James looked decidedly irritated, but Hal guessed it wasn't him he was annoyed with. Gun crew procedures needed eight or nine men to work in absolute precision. James turned to Hal with a slight frown,

'I learned how to manage a gun crew before I was thirteen. It isn't something you forget.' Hal was coming to realise that if the army taught James anything, it stayed taught. He shoved his finger in his ear and scratched. He wasn't sure if he should apologise or not.

Hal watched as James, he thought, sulked. So he was somewhat surprised when James looked up and told him cheerfully,

'I have a plan. Come on, we need one of those markets for second-hand clothes. There must be many in London. In fact, you go and ask around, it might be better coming from you.'

'I being the one with the common touch,' said Hal with asperity. So, not sulking, planning.

'Absolutely sergeant,' James responded with a straight face.

'We need to get over to Tower Hill,' Hal said. 'There is a Rag Fair on Rosemary Lane.'

They walked. It was good to have solid ground beneath their feet and they were used to walking. Once they arrived they found that Rosemary Lane might have smelt sweet once upon a time but now the overwhelming smell was of stale humans. However, they were they were used to that. Sometimes, it had even been themselves that had stank; soldiering wasn't always a clean occupation. They emerged from the crowds with a calico wrapped parcel of a huge brown cloak. Hal was none the wiser, but decided he was up for the adventure, whatever it was.

The lodgings Horse Guards had sent them to were clean and basic. Once there, they shaved, washed down and James smartened himself up as much as possible with his second-hand jacket and breeches the army had found for him. His own uniform had been soaked in Priti's blood and once he was well enough he had made Hal throw it all overboard. Army efficiency, an oxymoron, whatever that was, James insisted, had somehow sent a stock of old uniforms home on the boat with the wounded men. The jacket was for no regiment James had ever served in, but it did have a lieutenant's insignia though the breeches were so huge round the waist he needed both a belt and pins to keep them up, but they both decided he would do.

'Wish me luck,' James requested.

'What for?' Hal grumbled.

'I am off to Whites.' James was grinning like he was up to mischief.

'That is a club for rich gentlemen!' Hal expostulated. 'How are you going to get in?'

'Now, now. My brother is a lord, remember.'

Hal refrained from further comment but looked decidedly doubtful.

With an evening free Hal tucked himself into a corner of an inn called the Grey Goose with the intention of downing an ale or two. He would sit there perfectly content to suck his dry pipe and make his drink last, enjoying not being on a boat. He was keeping his ale consumption low as he had seriously had enough of being tipped to and fro, and the idea of becoming tipsy enough for the floor to undulate had no appeal whatsoever. And that was where he was when James came in and found him.

'Drink up, we are heading north,' he told Hal. 'We have two tickets on the night stage. From there we will need to hire horses.'

Hal gave him a resigned look, downed his ale, and followed. He was too busy wondering if the rocking of the stage might be akin to the movement a ship made to ask too many questions.

They walked into the cobbled yard of another inn through a fine mizzle in the centre of Bakewell the following lunchtime. Their trip had been cold, uncomfortable and as Hal had feared, unsteady due to the bad roads north of London. After leaving the coach they had agreed with the ostler to hire two horses and that he would have them ready early the following morning.

'Now food,' James commanded.

'No argument from me,' Hal rejoined, 'but when do I find out where we are going?' As no answer was forthcoming, he shook his head and gave up.

After a decent meal of roast beef and potatoes with a synonymous Bakewell tart afterwards, they retired to their room. They had two narrow beds up in the eves, but at least it was fairly private.

'Don't know why Bakewell is so proud of its pudding,' Hal complained. 'It is sitting fair heavy in me!'

'Your fault for having seconds,' was the unsympathetic response. At which point, James tugged out a map from his knapsack.

'We are going where? To do that to him! I have thought it before and I am thinking it again, I should have left you on that bloody wharf to die,' was Hal's response. James ignored him.

As it was January, first light came late, so it was not until half-past-eight that they could head out into the bitter cold. At first there were snow flurries, which worried James as his disguise was not intended for a white background, even if the whiteness was partial. As they climbed upwards on their horses, to their relief the snow ceased and an intermittent sun brightened the bracken and gorse covered hills they were climbing. Gradually, the inn yard they had left fell away and, blowing on their fingers for warmth, they found the copse of trees they had been aiming for set high on the uninhabited hills above the little town.

Major General John Winterton smothered the kick of his gun with his shoulder and with great satisfaction watched the pheasant flutter from the air. His gun dog needed no instruction, but excitedly raced off to claim his master's prize. The day had evolved into a clear cold brilliance that made England a country to long for while overseas. Bracken gilded the rolling green hills around him and in the near distance ran a pale rock face of a local crag. Yellow gorse flickered in the intermittent wind reminding him of the old saying that kissing was always out of season when gorse was. Gorse, of course, showed egg-yolk-yellow flowers all year round. He was about to call to his shooting companions some witty retort about his superior aim, when he was vaguely aware of a rustling behind him and the bitter chill of a small round circle against his cheek. He stayed perfectly still and waited, aware that his heart beat had ratcheted up alarmingly.

'Good afternoon sir, Lieutenant James Causton at your service,' came a voice.

Turning slightly and therefore pressing the gun barrel yet further into his cheek, Major General Winterton tried to see the man standing beside him. What he saw was of little comfort. The man was perfectly calm and controlled. Not someone Winterton was inclined to take on at just that moment.

'Is this an assassination,' he asked. Both his companions and his dog were far enough away to probably not be aware yet of what was happening.

'Absolutely not, sir.' The voice sounded offended. 'I am currently on the lists at Horse Guards awaiting detachment. I have been told I am quote, 'too bloody big to ever think of being attached to the 95th Foot'. I believe they are wrong, sir, and I hope, now, you do too.'

The gun barrel was now gently removed. Winterton turned to face his assailant properly and found a dishevelled and indeed large, young lieutenant standing to attention, gun correctly at his side, draped in a huge muddy-brown cloak.

'Is that gun loaded?' he asked.

'Absolutely not, sir. Pointing a loaded gun at a senior officer sir, not something I could ever do.' And suddenly the young man's face was split with a huge grin.

'How long have you been here?' Winterton asked.

'We arrived at about nine-thirty. I have been down here in the bracken tracking you ever since you arrived.'

'But the light is fading, it is nearly four o'clock!'

'Indeed sir. I am rather cold.' Again, the grin crept back.

'Who is we?'

'My sergeant is up on the ridge with a spy glass. It was easier for him to see where you were than I could down here.'

'How did you communicate?' Winterton was horribly aware that he had had no idea he had been tracked.

'Hand signals, sir. Tricky, but we seemed to be making it work.'

'And what do you hope to achieve?'

'Your support so that I may join the 95th. They need good shots and men who can cover ground secretly and I can do both. This is the shape of future warfare, sir, I really believe that. In India I saw how the native armies could defeat us by using local cover and letting each man think for himself. The devastation they could wreak upon our forces was horrific. I should like to turn that horror on the French.'

'You realise that many senior officers believe such warfare to be ungentlemanly; indeed, beyond contempt and totally dishonourable.'

'They are out-of-date, sir. There is likely to remain the need for ranks of soldiers in pretty uniforms marching into battle to the fife and drum for a long time yet, but this kind of flexible warfare is the future, dishonourable or not. At the end of the day, it is about winning while losing as few men as possible.'

Winterton was startled into a laugh. 'Thought about it have you?'

'Of course sir. I am an army officer.'

'Causton, you say?'

'Yes sir.'

'Well bugger off, and report to Horse Guards Monday fortnight with a green uniform with all insignias and ask for Major Hustings. He will give you your orders.'

And as James turned to move away Winterton couldn't help asking, 'How did you know I wouldn't faint?'

'Not you sir. Too experienced and too good a soldier.'

With that James turned and headed back to Hal in the increasing gloom of the winter afternoon. As he moved through the bracken he heard Winterton mutter, 'Cheeky young sod.' James' face split into a huge grin. He and Hal were off to the 95th. He was going to have a Baker Rifle to play with. 'And heaven help the French,' he thought to himself. It wasn't just officers with their pretty uniforms he wanted to pick off, but the sergeants. Sergeants ran the army, every army. Take them out of the equation and troops would soon fall apart. It was a hypothesis he was aching to test.

Chapter Four

The weather in the Peninsula was even colder than in the northern sweeps of England. James and Hal spent Christmas day with their faces turned into a sleeting wind on board a rackety ship ploughing its way to Oporto. Once there, they had been instructed to find Wellington and the army as rapidly as possible. James felt alive. This was what he had lived and trained for since he was in leading strings. Hal watched the excitement on his face with resignation. It was going to be a bloody war, he reckoned, and keeping his man alive was going to take some doing.

Wellington's camp was bleak. Accommodation was inadequate for the troops and Hal almost immediately went down with a fever that turned his guts to water and laid him out for days. James grinned and nursed him and chided him for giving in to such a minor illness. Hal closed his eyes and wondered if he ought to give up now and let the army bury him where he lay? He found his feet again just in time to begin the march to the fortress Ciudad Roderigo, Wellington's target. They began marching in rain, which turned to sleet and snow. Hal began to cheer up. The air was clean and moving was keeping him warm enough. James, he noticed, was almost bouncing. The bounce didn't last for long. They had to wade through a river chest deep with blocks of ice crashing into their bodies and then, while soaking wet, dig trenches. The wind howled around their heads and cut into their bodies. Once the French general, Marmont caught news of their attempt, he would march his forces here as fast as possible and, until the trenches were dug, they would be unlikely to hold against the French. There was going to be a battle and, Hal predicted again, it was likely to be bloody.

His commanding officer was rounding up his officers. James trotted across, smothered in mud and still dressed in wet clothing, but keen to discover his next orders.

'We will breach the northern defences. For that we will require volunteers for two Forlorn Hopes.'

Standing to one side and apparently busy, Hal listened with a sinking heart. Sure enough, James stepped forward. 'I'll take one detachment,' he said clearly. It was a good job Hal's language remained in his head as it contained every curse word he knew. A Forlorn Hope was just as described. The men would all be volunteers and they would rush forward and attempt to scale the walls against almost impossible enemy fire in order to make the way clear for the larger force following behind. It was rare for any of the volunteers to survive or, if they did, finish in one piece. But survival often led to promotion and it was one of the only ways a man like James could progress in the army without money to purchase a higher rank. James didn't want a higher rank, Hal knew, he just thought he was invincible. Hal felt sick. The fool lad had spoken up; there was no way of getting him out of this now. He had lost the two sons of his blood and now, almost certainly, he would lose the son who had lodged in his heart.

They didn't speak much in the following days. What was there to say, Hal wondered? Wellington had ordered a cannonade, and the booming seemed to shake the very hills and mountains. The night before the assault was to begin, the nineteenth of January, James ate well and teased Hal like the boy he still was under the carapace of an experienced soldier.

Hal was roused from a fitful sleep a little after midnight. James was attempting to get out of bed, but his greatcoat, used as a blanket, had tangled in his legs.

'Need a piss, lad?' Hal asked. He reached and lit a candle. James seemed unsteady on his feet. Frowning, Hal too slid out of his bedding. Then James tumbled forward, before hauling his body into a hump and beginning to crawl.

The next two hours were spent in digging a hole for James to vomit and void in while attempting to keep him conscious. Despite his worry, Hal was jubilant. As dawn broke he hied off to find their senior officer. At the news, he gave a small nod to another officer who followed Hal back to where James lay, wrapped in his greatcoat, semi-conscious and curled around a stinking hole in the ground.

'Ah. Lieutenant Causton is indisposed, I see.' The he glanced at Hal. 'Get him well. If all goes to plan we can send him in when we take Badajoz.'

Over my dead body, thought Hal.

Ciudad Roderigo was taken without his help and James was well and back on duty within three days. The two of them were now sent out to scout for any French that might be in the area. With a small force of eighteen men, James led them out to scour the surroundings for any French advance guards or Portuguese bandits. And if they managed to bring back some game for the evening pot, all well and good.

James was enjoying being useful and he had some good men with him. The weather remained bitterly cold, but at least they were no longer wet to the skin. They were scouting west about ten miles from the camp to check what was over a ridge. From the top they should have been able to see for some miles distant. General Marmont was out there somewhere, and he must know that Wellington would head towards Badajoz next and anyone who thought about it would know that he would send scouts out to keep an eye on Wellington's army. There were at least two French armies in Spain and the idea of them meeting up gave James an itch between the shoulder blades.

They came out of nowhere. One minute they were reaching the

edge of the ridge and the next they were engulfed by horsemen and sabres. James wasn't sure who was the most surprised, his troops or the French. Infantry against calvary was usually a forgone conclusion; infantry died. But James had strung his group out along the whole length of this part of the ridge and the horsemen were all together. He launched himself forward and, rolling under the first horse, shoved his knife up into the beast's belly. Rolling again, as the poor creature floundered in pain, he swept his rifle forward using it as a club and took the man out of his saddle. James finished him as he hit the ground. Spinning around, he knifed the horse that was now close beside him in the neck, shoving the blade in hard and twisting. Again, the wounded creature reared up in shock and pain and, as his front hooves landed, James sliced the rider's leg behind the knee. Both man and horse were screaming now, but James heard nothing. As always, when in battle, sound faded away and time slowed down. It was as if he had forever to reach up and grab the man and, hauling him from his mount, slice his throat under his chin strap. There was another cavalryman swinging his sabre above James' head, but his target was suddenly hit in the chest and flew backwards from his horse. James' men were moving in, firing, stabbing, closing a loop around the milling horses. It all became a blur of movement and countermovement, parry, thrust and step back. And then it was over. The remaining French swung around and headed back up slope to the ridge peak and then vanished over the other side.

    James raced to the top of the ridge and throwing himself flat, loaded and sighted his beloved Baker rifle. He took two riders down before they were out of range. Losing men so unexpectedly had caused the others to lay low across their horse's necks and race even faster. James had his men cover the French dead in brush in the hopes that it might keep scavengers away until their comrades could return and bury them. He looked the other way as his men looted the bodies; little would be found, he knew. But even a morsal of food was valuable in this bleak and frozen country. Their own fallen and wounded they would take back. Stopping to dig graves might get them all killed; the French knew where they were and knew how many they were.

The Army's Son

. . .

He had reported. He had given his butcher's bill. Of his eighteen, four were dead and two wounded. And he was exhausted. And filthy. And heartsore. The four had been good soldiers, the best. He had known them all well and liked them. They had been rough tongued and insolent, and had done everything he asked them to at a trot and willingly. He picked his way through the camp stepping automatically over tent ropes and pegs, ducking under washing and smelling the numerous pots that hung over fires cooking suppers. His feet felt heavy, as if his boots had taken on a life of their own and independently turned to lead, and his head still rang with the sound of shots and the scent of cartridges. He spat, unthinkingly, his spittle landing streaked black with gunpowder. Somewhere further on, through the alleyways of tightly-packed fawn tents lay the river.

At the river bank he paused. The water would be cold. Fed by the mountain snow melt, even in high summer it would strike chill on the skin. But at least the actual lumps of ice had ceased to appear in the water. Before Ciudad Roderigo the cavalry had been forced to walk their mounts in a line four across into the water to act as a physical barrier to the ice so that the men could cross. Until then, men had been knocked under and injured as they attempted to wade, but the cavalry had not been amused to be used in that way.

The bank immediately in front of him was bare, the local growth of shrubs, brambles and saplings having been cleared to allow a camped army access to fresh water. Somewhere downstream, behind a copse of almond trees, the horses were tethered so that they could be brought water easily and not foul the drinking water with their waste. Upstream, the cooks had set their own camp. In front of him was an open area for all to use, but for the moment it was quiet. Right that moment he ached for the cold, clean water. 'Washing away my sins?' he asked himself ironically. Out in the water, perhaps twenty yards away, the trunk of a tree swirled past. Fast. Quite a current then. Perhaps that was why he had found the bank deserted this late in the afternoon; dark would drop soon. And it was supper time. He watched the trunk disappear as he unbuttoned his tunic. Shrugging it off he grabbed the back of his shirt and hauled it over his head and then sitting down, pulled off his boots. Standing once more he pushed his trousers down. They were so smothered in mud that they could have been any colour, so much so, the dark green with the black stipe was barely visible. In only his drawers, he stepped forward into the edge of the water.

He didn't hesitate, but kept walking forward until the river bed fell away and the current took him. Taking a breath, he ducked under and pulling against the water with his arms and kicking with his legs, forced himself forward and down to the very bottom at the deepest part of the river. Then, he let himself be bobbed up back to the surface. He emerged whipping his head around to shake the water from his hair and off his face. He never thought about his childhood. He didn't let himself. He had no family now, no home, and no wish to revisit the grief of how he had lost his beloved brother and his adored parents in such quick order. He had always deliberately turned his mind when memories had surprised him. The water now reminded him vividly of swimming in the river in Wiltshire on the Causton estate with a hoard of other boys. Instead of shoving the memory away, he floated in the current and remembered childhood shrieks and boasts, the heat of every summer and the cool of the deep water that lay in the bend of the river. Of diving in, of pushing other boys, of being pushed. Of being unthinkingly happy. He could let go, he thought. He could just let the river take him. Eventually the cold and the current would take him under; he just had to allow it.

Instead, he turned towards the now far distant bank, oriented his body in a line facing the way he intended to go and began to swim with all the power of his body. He had been exhausted, but now he was exhilarated with the challenge. Him against the fury of the river gods. Even as he began to tire, he felt laughter within, bubbling up. The water was so cold. The strength of the river great. He pulled harder and bit by bit he began to make headway.

He stood when the water was thigh deep. He would sleep soon; no nightmares tonight. On the bank in the gloaming, stood a woman. Maeve Butcher. She was broad and bold, with wildly curling dark hair and full lips outlining a wide laughing mouth.

'Well, Lieutenant, now ain't you a sight for sore eyes,' she called out to him.

'Clear out, Maeve so I can remove myself from this river and maintain some modesty.'

'Now why would I want to do that? A lovely body like yours would gladden the heart of any red-blooded woman.' In the fading light he could see her eyes and he was aware that standing out in the water as he was, she could probably see him clearly. Her head moved slowly and he was keenly aware that he was being appraised, she just stood there, hands on hips her mouth grinning her approval.

'Maeve, clear out or the innocent and unsuspecting Corporal Butcher is going to find himself on the discipline list.'

'Now then sir, you wouldn't do that.' And she laughed with cheerful confidence. A boy appeared tumbling down the bank with arms and legs flailing with his haste. Behind him, was the solid outline of Hal. With a nod, she took her lad by the hand and with swishing hips she vanished into the greenery.

Hal's voice boomed out. 'Been told you need a clean shirt.' James waded out with a sigh. By the time he reached the shore, Hal was handing him an unmuddied shirt and trousers. 'What is the sense in scrubbing yourself clean and then putting that lot back on?' He asked rhetorically. 'Poor planning and preparation, if you don't mind me saying so.'

'I do. And you can follow Maeve and bugger off.'

'Now then lad, I've supper waiting at the hovel the army have dished out to us.'

'Criticising my Colonel, are you now Sergeant?'

'Now would I ever do that, sir?'

James laughed and shook his head. His teeth were chattering and a hot supper sounded wonderful. Tomorrow there would be more men to kill. And more men to watch die. Tomorrow.

Later, Hal sat and sucked on his pipe thoughtfully. The swim had done the lad good; he was sound in his sleep now. He gave Maeve a thought. James was no innocent; he knew that, but he was careful. Army women, to him, were completely out of bounds. An old soldier who had been in India at the same time as James had recounted the tale of a lovely Indian girl, and of how some wizened old hearts had found a pulse when observing two who so clearly cared for each other.

The old warrior had said, 'Never made a wrong step, that lad. But they were both so young, and they just had to look at each other for you to know what was up. No one minded. On the contrary, it warmed our hearts some. But the insurgents slit the lass's throat when he was there. Bad business, it was. Still, he couldn't have taken her home now, could he?'

Hal wasn't so sure. His James could be a stubborn bastard when he was in the mood for it. But a woman now. He would think on that one a bit.

Chapter Five

James was swaying on his feet. He had been digging trenches around the fort of Badajoz all night by moonlight and all day in the rain. Every shovel of earth had been wet and heavy. His arms ached and his back screamed. At that moment, he had no idea if they could take the citadel or not and he didn't have the energy to care. He needed to collapse for a while before he reported back for duty.

He entered his lodgings to find a woman sitting by the fire sewing. He paused in the doorway, too drained to ask what the hell she was doing there. He ignored her and walked to the side of the bed and unhitched his sword, laid his rifle on the shelf, then lifting his chin begun to loosen the buttons at his neck. The woman had risen and was adding a steaming kettle to what he realised was a round metal tub of water. She shook out a clean shirt and laid it over a chair-back so that it might air by the fire before pulling a screen forward to shield the tub.

'Who are you?' James asked, aware his voice was unwelcoming.

'My name is Elfie. I am a widow and Hal said I could stay here and care for you.'

'I don't need anyone else. I have Hal.' He knew he sounded petulant, but he was too tired to care. And he had only the one room that acted as both bedroom and living room.

'Very well. But might I suggest you rest for now.'

Her tone was calm and to James she appeared impervious to his bad temper. This made him even more irritated. But she was right, he was in no state to have a discussion about her unexpected appearance in what he considered his private space.

He stripped to his drawers and strode to the screen and went behind to bathe. He sank the bits of him he could into the warm water and instantly felt a little better. As he lay there he began to doze off. He didn't move until the water cooled considerably. As he rose from the water a hand appeared over the screen with a towel. He took it and scrubbed himself dry. He tugged on his shirt and some clean drawers that had also appeared and then went lifted the screen out of the way and folding it, leant it against the wall. The woman had set a place for him with a plate of cold beef, a loaf, and a large jug of ale. He downed the ale, every drop, then walked to his bed and dropped into it. He was asleep before his head had sunk into the pillow.

In the early hours he awoke with a jerk. His mind had been fighting an old battle and as he came to he wasn't sure where he was. Then he realised a foot was resting against his. He twisted slightly to discover the woman had rolled down the worn slope of the mattress towards him. She was in his bloody bed. He sank back into oblivion in a state of irritated resentment.

'What the hell is she doing in my room!' was how Hal was greeted in the morning.

'I put her there.'

'Why?' The word was spat out. James' bad temper seemed to have grown.

'I think she will be good for you. You don't use brothels, so why not have a paramour.'

'You don't use brothel's either. Why don't you have her?'

'Because I have my pipe and am a good deal older than you. I don't have the same needs.'

'My needs are none of your bloody business. Find her a pallet before tonight, or she is out on the street. She can sleep by the fire, not in my bloody bed!'

Hal watched a furious James stride away and sucked on his pipe with a smile. His very anger told him he had done the right thing. And there were no pallets available. And if there were he would burn them.

That night James returned to his billet to find Elfie had again anticipated his needs. There was a good fire, warm water and clothes airing by the flames. And a meal bubbling in a pot that smelt blissful. James knew he was being surly, but didn't seem to be able to help it, and wasn't sure he wanted to lose his anger in any case. He washed, shaved and ate, then headed out to spend some time with the other junior officers. When he returned the candles were all extinguished so that only the fire gave off light and in its soft glow he could see the woman, rolled in a blanket, asleep on the floor in front of it. The floor was made up of rough bricks laid, no doubt, straight on the earth and tipped uneven with a century of wear. He kicked her gently with his boot. When she awoke he told her gruffly,

'Get into the bed.'

She was clearly bewildered as she awoke, blinking around her in confusion. 'No sir,' she said softly and curled up again. James lifted her up and deposited her on to the bed. Tugging back the covers he hauled her back into his arms and shoved her unceremoniously under the sheets. When she tried to sit up, he pushed her down. An hour later, after more brandy than was good for him, he rolled in beside her. This time she had her back to him, so he curled around her and went to sleep. It was a bloody cold and wet night, and they had the outpost of Picurina to take in the morning before they could make an attempt of the huge fortress of Badajoz.

Days later he noise of the guns hammering from the successfully taken Picurina was deafening everyone and it was to go on for eleven days. Badajoz was a fierce old fortress. It would take more than a breath of air to take her and so the cannons bellowed and nipped at her walls repeatedly. On the morning of April 5 the sun arrived to everyone's surprise. The guns having created a breach, they all knew that the attack was to be imminent. As James strapped on his weapons, he saw Elfie in clear light for the first time. She appeared older than him by a decade or so, but her skin was clear and what he had believed was a head of grey curls turned out to be actually a light but dull blonde. She had piercing pale blue eyes that held intelligence and a more than reasonable figure. As he buttoned up and pulled on his boots he asked,

'Why are you here?'

'I asked your sergeant if you might take me. My third husband was killed at Ciudad Rodrigo and a wedding ring hasn't stopped any of my men from dying on me. I liked the look of you. You are younger than you look, or people take you for, I believe, and you are known not to use the camp women.'

'How did you know I didn't like men?'

At that she gave a slight smile, 'Woman's intuition,' she stated flatly.

'So, you will be my whore?' He kept his tone harsh.

She breathed in deeply and lifted her chin even higher. 'Yes. But only yours.'

He gave a grunt and walked out. There was a battle to fight, he had no more time to think about the woman. Even so, the thought that she might be there, ready and waiting when he returned, warmed him more than he wished to admit.

The day was interminable. Wellington's orders for his division had seen James and six of his lads despatched to see if they could pick off any of the men inside the fortress. As the day wore on and there was no attack, everyone's nerves became strained. James told his corporal to calm down and that it was a bloody sight worse for the men who had volunteered for the Forlorn Hopes. He had again volunteered, but been refused. He had been firmly informed that it was his long-range accurate shooting that was required.

'Think what it must be like to have volunteered for that duty and then have it deferred? You, my man, are bloody lucky to be up here with me taking pot shots.'

James' outburst had settled the men and they again set to finding somewhere to lie and seek a head or even an arm that came within the sights of their Baker rifles. James knew that the worse matters became the calmer he was. It was as if the Earth turned more slowly for him.

It wasn't until ten at night on the sixth that the attack began. James and his men had slept out, constantly trying to pick off officers, anyone, that came into view. They moved down to support the attack and were subsumed into the bloodbath.

By the time James limped back to his room he had lost his jacket his shako and his sword and had a deep sabre slash across the back of his left shoulder. His shirt was more red than white, but he was alive, which was more than most were. It had been a battle like no other. The butcher's bill was horrendous and he had no idea yet if Hal had survived. To his surprise, Elfie was waiting for him. She stripped him so efficiently he was reminded that she had already survived three husbands and had no doubt stripped and cared for all of them at times.

'You didn't lose your rife, then,' she commented softly as she bathed and tied up his wound. He was sitting naked on a chair by the fire, too exhausted to sit fully upright.

'Never,' he muttered, before she helped him to the bed and tucked him in as if her were a child.

When he awoke it was full dark. Elfie was tucked into him and the warmth of her body was a delight. As if sensing his conscious state she reached up and stroked the hair away from his brow. He pulled her towards him and rolled on top then pushed inside. Then he lay, deep within her, blinking in the dark and not sure that he could move. She pushed on his right shoulder and rolled him gently onto his back again, before repositioning herself on top of him and riding him gently to completion.

James slept for two days, barely even eating and drinking. Elfie pottered around the room, doing the chores of washing his linen, polishing his boots, she was good at that and it surprised him, scouring for food and cooking it, and generally staying close in case he developed a fever. Hal looked in once or twice, but left when he saw how sound asleep James was. On the third day he brought news.

After they had discussed the battle Hal said,

'Have you heard about Harry Smith?'

Smith was a Lieutenant General of the Light Division, and wealthy, handsome and intelligent. He was one of James' heroes.

'No, what of him?'

'It seems that after we took Badajoz the men did a good job of sacking the place. Talk about rape and pillage. Smith came across a young Spanish girl of only fourteen and she asked him to protect her. He is only going to marry the child today!'

'Good for him,' was James' comment.

'Bit young,' Hal muttered, not having received the shocked response he was hoping for.

'I am nineteen,' James replied quietly, 'I am not sure age can be measured by the calendar.' He felt rather than saw Elfie's sharp look.

After Hal left he fretted until Elfie helped him sit up and into a chair. She didn't fuss, she just ensured he was propped upright with his feet up and comfortable, then ignored him. She hardly spoke and as he dozed on and off, he had to admit it was good to have another living being around. He wouldn't have been able to abide chatter. As the day moved on he began to feel slightly less feverish and light-headed. Elfie was now sitting sewing by the window. His shoulder hurt like hell, but it was no longer burning and he took that as a good sign. More than once he wondered if they really had engaged in sex, or if it had been a dream. He was honest enough to admit it had been a relief, like having a boil lanced. The tension of the previous days, waiting for battle, preparing the trenches, the often filthy weather preventing them seeing attacks before they happened, and then the utter slaughter of the battle itself had left him as tight as a drum skin. And she had ridden him to release. It had opened up his wound, but it had been worth it. Yet it bothered him. He knew he was not yet sufficiently hardened to being able to take a woman without some emotion involved, yet that was what he had done. He knew his soul was wounded. But then he closed his eyes again. That wound was a small one.

Hal's next visit brought the news that when Wellington had walked amongst the dead, he had wept. Furthermore, he had apparently been heard to say that they should never attempt a siege of that like again. 'The butcher's bill is huge. We have lost five thousand good lads,' Hal recounted. James felt the small amount of energy he had gathered during the day drain away. Yet they now controlled the entry to Spain. Two French armies had been nearby, yet they had not arrived in time. To wait might have meant an even greater slaughter. Behind his closed lids he remembered that Lieutenant of long ago joking that he, James, would be a general one day.

'No,' he thought. 'To be the one to make that decision,' he breathed in, 'no. I don't want that.'

That night when Elfie redressed his wound he asked her how it was.

'Better than I hoped. It was deep and I thought might be infected, but it seems clear.'

'Is your sewing neat,' he asked over his shoulder.

'Neater than any surgeon's,' she claimed firmly.

And he grinned. He had become used to her and had begun to like her. She was calm and efficient. A lot of people, men and women, irritated his nerves. They talked too much, or fidgeted, and he found he quickly lost patience and wanted to be off on his own or with just Hal, but Elfie had a soothing presence.

'Why me?' he asked. She didn't pretend not to know what he was asking.

'You are a fine man, tall and well proportioned. You are known to be private. And your men respect you.' She paused, 'But I didn't know quite how young you were.'

'I don't feel young,' he told her, watching to see her reaction.

'No. War does that to a man,' she said softly. It seemed it wasn't to be an impediment.

That night he pulled her to him and she came willingly. He breathed in the scent of her and slid his large hands over her softness. She felt like comfort. And affection was already growing; she was a good woman. He had lost more men than he could at the moment face at Badajoz but, it seemed, he had gained a mistress.

The battles rolled on and James didn't become any younger. He survived Salamanca and Vitoria and became a major. The fury of Badajoz had played a part. So many men had died there he had floated up the lists. Few men had not only his experience but his skill with the Baker and a looted bag of coin had helped. His life was progressing exactly as he had anticipated at eleven when he had run away. He was a soldier, he was good at his trade, and the sun rose each morning and set each night. And then Napoleon was defeated. James was in London waiting with Hal to be shipped across the Atlantic to the colonies to fight in the war there, when the impossible happened. History kicked every British soldier in the teeth; the living and the dead.

Waterloo, it was the battle they had not expected. Napoleon had not taken his retirement to heart. On the contrary, he seemed determined to expedite a comeback. Blucher and Wellington won the day and James had been in the thick of it. And now Napoleon was once more subdued, James was to be shipped home with hundreds of other wounded men. Hal, who seemed to live a charmed life, had survived without a scratch. But he had been the one who had hauled James over his shoulder and fought through the mud of the battlefield to get him to a transport cart. Unconscious, James had been trundled into Brussels and then lain on a floor in a private house. He came to, to find Hal sucking on his pipe and peering into his eye.

'What happened he asked?'

'We won, and you have a lump of metal large enough to fashion a coal scuttle in your thigh.'

'Ah,' said James and passed out again.

It seemed the surgeons had not even tried with him, but had assumed he would die within hours. Instead, he had survived and Hal had managed to get him to London.

They took cheap lodgings overlooking a cobbled yard, mostly inhabited by similarly exhausted soldiers, few of them officers. James had some money, but not a great deal and as the future was beyond uncertain, they had jointly decided to keep expenses to a minimum. Each night Hal sat in the yard and smoked his pipe or pretended to. James wasn't sure that there was often tobacco in the bowl. Hal would chat to the whores who strolled by at dusk seeking business. Lying in his bed, feverish and riding waves of pain, he could hear their conversations through the open window.

'Evening Nell, how are you this evening?'

'Oi'm well, Hal me dearie, are you up for my charms tonight?'

'No thank you love, there are plenty of other lads who need you. You will do fine for business I am sure.'

'But none as 'andsom as you, Hal.'

'Go on with you love, and you be careful, you mind me?'

And with a cry of cheerful farewell the girl would move off to find customers aplenty amongst the worn-out men who hung around the yard, some still shaking with the shock of what they had witnessed. As comforts went, the girls were probably better than most as long as they didn't carry the pox, always a risk with their profession. James envied the other men that comfort. He longed to bury himself inside the warmth of a woman; feel her arms and legs wound around him, however false the pretence of intimacy. Perhaps then he might feel some sense of peace. His wound was healing, however, but parts of him were still stubbornly refusing to function. At least he could make his own way to the earth closet these days, though the effort almost brought him to a faint.

That night, when Hal came in James mulled the question that had been filling his mouth for hours. He waited until Hal had settled beside his bed and was quiet before he chewed it into sound.

'How is she?' he asked. 'Did you see her?'

Hal took in a breath. 'I did lad. I saw her and spoke to her sister. She won't be across to see you.'

James swallowed audibly. 'She means it, then?'

Hal sat quiet for a long time and James began to hope. He longed for Elfie. She had been his companion for a long time. He missed her quiet competence, the comfort of her silences, her company. Listening to her when she brought home gossip, always crisply told and often with quiet amusement at the failings of others. Elfie was never unkind and loved the foibles of others, like the wife who had discovered her husband with another woman and had silently planned her revenge, before unleashing it by hitting him with the half-rotted back leg of a donkey until he was unconscious. Elfie had loved that. And she had been the one to hold the wife as she sobbed out her hurt at the betrayal, before then bathing and binding the husband's head. Everyone turned to Elfie; he most of all.

When they had been furloughed home, before Waterloo, Elfie had left him. She had told him that he needed to find a wife of his own class and start a family. James had been devastated. At first he had let her go in state of anger at what he saw as her desertion. Then, when he had cooled down, he had begun to wonder if he might woo her back. He had offered marriage and she had turned him down. He had offered to continue to live with her as they had been and again she had refused him. Reluctantly, he had backed away, unwilling to become that bore, the persistent ex-lover. But he still cared, and was confused with how she could have just walked away when there had been no signs that she was unhappy with their life together. It nagged at him that she might, indeed, have been unhappy and he had missed it. The thought sat deep within and fretted his dreams. That she wouldn't cross a few streets to see how he did after such a wound as he had, hurt terribly. Had she been able to cast him off so easily? It seemed so.

Hal didn't speak and the moon rose high and higher as they kept each other company in the darkening room. James was surprised when Hal cleared his throat.

'They want to keep it from you, but it doesn't sit right with me. She is sick, lad, grievously sick. That is why she left you. The sister told me this afternoon. You are trapped in this bed, and she in hers most of the time. She looks frail.'

It took a while for the sense of the words to fully make sense. Elfie ill? And she had kept it from him. And he knew why. She had known that the battle was brewing. She had wanted to save him worry when he needed to have all of his concentration on what he did so well. Killing other men. The thoughts hammered at him, pulsing alongside the waves of pain that constantly ripped through him from the, hopefully, healing wound.

'Brandy, Hal,' he said. And as Hal held the glass to his lips, they both ignored the tears that rolled across James' cheeks and over Hal's hand.

Autumn drew on and James was now hobbling around the courtyard with a stick and was gaining in strength day by day. He was in constant pain and it seemed that this might be the rest of his life. He was chewing over whether he was prepared to accept that. Maybe not. He was not going to become an opium eater, like so many other lads who had come back broken; he would eat a bullet first. He and Hal did not discuss it but he suspected Hal had read his mind.

'Go and see if your sister still lives,' he continually insisted to Hal.

'Not yet, lad. Soon,' Hal would prevaricate. He insisted that as both James and Elfie were far from well he would put off seeking out his sister, his closest relative, until they were both better.

James had made his way over to Elfie's sister's house just once. The sister had refused him entrance until he had swayed on her step, clearly about to pass out. He had been shoved into a chair until a modicum of strength had returned to him. The sister's anger, coming off her in waves had infuriated him. Why the hell shouldn't he visit his friend, he had demanded. Loudly. And then the moaning had begun. It had wailed down the passageway from behind a closed door. The sister had teared up, trembling.

'Is that my Elfie?' he had asked, horrified.

'She is in so much pain,' the sister had whispered. 'She couldn't bear to see you. She talks about you, when she is conscious, but most of the time she floats either in pain or with the opium.'

'Opium?' He couldn't imagine his proper Elfie taking opium. It was against her grain!

'It helps,' was the only answer he received.

'What does the doctor say?'

'To increase the opium as the pain increases. She should let go, but she just hangs on!'

'Tell her I love her,' he said, and pressed what money he could spare on the woman. And he did. Not the intense passion of lust and romance, but the love of respect and care.

'She knows,' the sister whispered, 'that is why she won't see you.' And then she asked, looking him over, 'Will you live?'

'I don't know.'

And then Hal had arrived, puffing, guessing where he had got to. Hal had helped him home and no more visits had been attempted. The illness was in her guts, and they both knew how undignified that was and James began to accept that the woman who had been such a comfort to him for so long, was dying slowly and painfully and would never allow him to see her again. For days afterwards he lay on his bed, now careless of the attempts he had been making to become well again. The hope of being able to see Elfie had driven him on for weeks, but now his spirit felt broken. And then the letter arrived.

It was nothing special in itself, except for the directions. The original address was to Lord William Causton at Causton Manor, Causton, Wiltshire. As James' father had been dead for many years now, James' initial thought was to wonder how long this letter had been roaming around? Someone at Causton, perhaps the vicar or the magistrate, had sent it on to Lord Lucian Causton at Oxford university. From there it had travelled to a bank in Bristol, and then to a bank in Bath. Finally, it had arrived in Whitehall, where a clerk had, either cleverly or in a desperate attempt to find a home for the wretched thing, sent it on to him. He supposed the name Causton was not that common, so someone somewhere had hoped that he might know where the letter was bound.

'What is it all about?' Hal asked.

'It is from a Lady Mary Swann, writing on behalf of her father, the Earl of Swann. It seems my father and hers were at school together and my father once promised to do a service for this Earl. And now she wishes to claim that service.'

'What are you going to do about it?'

James tossed the letter aside, 'Nothing. Never heard of the woman. Or the Earl, come to that.'

Something about the letter nagged at James. Like an irritation to the nerves. Or a bout of the flux! He found himself getting out of bed and roaming the courtyard with his stick once again, round and round, until he could do a couple of circuits without nausea or dizziness stopping him. Then he roamed out to the local inns. He never took more than a few pennies with him. The local children while at first attempting every pick-pocket trick in the book had finally given up and now called cheerful greetings to him. He had finally become part of the local scenery. So Hal had his whores to chat to of an evening and he had his ragamuffins in the day, he thought with a wry smile. Horse Guards or Whitehall or whatever had finally put him on half-pay and from somewhere came a monetary bonus. According to the letter that brought the information it was for some act he had committed in battle. He personally couldn't remember such an act, but he took the money. After more than a decade of putting his life in the hands of his country, he was sure he had done something else to deserve the award if not that particular act. And the idea of trying to give it back and the red tape that would most definitely ensure if he made the attempt, was enough to bring him out in a cold sweat. So, more cheerful now he was solvent, he went to strengthening his leg with a will. But the letter still nagged.

Winter was firmly in charge of metrological events when he first attempted to mount onto the back of a horse. Not Satan, his huge black, but a mild chestnut of numerous years with a mouth like an iron bucket. Having ridden almost every day of his life, he was left in deep shock at how much muscle a man could lose in a handful of months. The Guards corporal who had walked the horse over from the stables watched him with a wicked grin on his face.

'Corporal, I should have you whipped just to get that look off your face,' he snarled.

'Yes sir, absolutely sir,' the corporal replied, still grinning.

'Well give me a bloody hand then!'

Once he was on board the corporal was all efficiency. He helped James to stay in the saddle as they walked the chestnut around and James reacquainted off-duty muscle with its responsibilities. As the corporal helped James to slide off the horse's back in a shamefully ungainly fashion, James told him, 'Thank you, lad. I couldn't have done that without you.'

'No sir, I don't deserve thanks. You are a brave man and I honour that. Few men would have the guts to try. The pain is bad, sir, isn't it.' They both knew it wasn't a question.

'Aye lad, but it was worse in June. How is Satan?'

'Ah now, there is a real horse. Missing you, I believe, sir. He is a bad-tempered brute. But,' he added, 'a wonderful ride.'

'You mistake, lad. Satan is bad tempered whether he has me there or not.' They both grinned. 'Who rides him?' James asked.

'A Colonel Mannenheim. Excellent horseman, sir. Excellent. Even he says, though, that he is a handful.'

'Well, whisper my name in his ear, perhaps the old boy might improve his manners.'

'The Colonel or the horse, sir?' the corporal asked.

James breathed in deeply, 'How you have lived to make the age you are defeats me,' he told the wide grin. Shaking his head he said, 'Tomorrow, lad, same time.'

'Yes sir.'

Snapping a salute, the perfectly dressed, if not perfectly respectful, young guardsman swung easily up into the saddle and managed to wheel the chestnut and trot away as smoothly as a pot of cream. James shook his head again as he watched him merge into the burly London traffic of coal carts, cabs, carriages and inebriated pedestrians that jammed the city streets. Feeling exhausted but in far better spirits, he began his slow walk back to their lodgings.

When he returned, the letter was still there, propped on the mantle. James re-read it and sat to pen a reply. He explained briefly that he was not aware of the location of his elder brother who had the honour of being the current Lord Causton and here he snorted aloud, but he would be delighted to attend her as soon as he was able, perhaps in the new year. He read over his words and decided to delete the word, delighted, but in the end left it as he couldn't scratch it off the paper without making a hole and so removing it would mean re-writing the whole thing and that he could not face. So he sent it off.

'What the bloody, damnation hell do you think you are doing?' Hal demanded. 'I haven't nursed you back to bloody health for you to go on a wild goose chase all over the bloody country!'

James couldn't help it. Hal's fury caused him to laugh out loud, something he hadn't done for an age. This only increased Hal's fury.

'You are spluttering, old man,' James informed him.

Hal was so incensed he could barely speak, 'Old man! Old man! You insolent puppy!'

James roared so much tears of laughter rolled down his face. They ended up in a local inn imbibing the excellent, for London, local ale. It was agreed. They would see out Christmas in London and when James could once more ride Satan, Hal would take a coach to see if he could find his sister in Dorset and then make his slow progress up the country to meet with James at Lady Mary's.

'Where does this woman live?' he asked James again.

'Lincolnshire,' James informed him.

'Back of bloody beyond,' Hal muttered, crossing his arms and sucking noisily on his pipe.

Woozy with ale James grinned. Perhaps life was going to be alright. Then his smile faltered. There was one part of his anatomy that still wasn't working that he hadn't mentioned to Hal. Well, a man had his pride, didn't he?

Chapter Six

James was not enjoying his introduction to Lincolnshire. The sleet was now horizontal. The pain in his left thigh was so intense that he was slumped over his horse's neck letting the beast take him where it willed. Their roles had been reversed. He was no longer in charge; the horse was. And the horse was as miserable as he. The journey had taken three days already and he was not going to reach his destination tonight. Not in this weather. He lifted his head and searched for shelter, but in this God-forsaken land there was little to none. Lincolnshire. Flat. Uninspiring. Full of huge ditches that could swallow a man and a horse and leave not so much as an ear tip showing. Full of a wind that blew straight from the North Sea and the frozen northern lands, shredding the very soul of a solitary traveller. 'Buggering place,' he muttered. He'd be buggered if he would die here.

At last there was a hedge. Hawthorn probably and knowing his luck. Full of thorns, but, he had to admit, good at filtering the wind even in the dead of winter. He nudged his knee and Satan, too exhausted to be anything but obedient, trudged along some of its length to where a couple of stunted trees that grew in the thicket allowed a smidgen of shelter. He slid sideways and in ungainly fashion out of the saddle and leant for a while as the pain heated him from the inside and swirled in his head, blanking out all thought. He swallowed as the waves retreated and rummaged in his saddlebag for food for the horse. Then loosened the girth and tied the reigns to an unhandy branch. Reaching for it sent such a tsunami of pain along his nerves he almost passed out.

Hauling his oilskin out was his next challenge. Tucking it under his arm he kicked at the leaves in the lee of the hedge and then lay it down. Rolling himself in its folds flat along the shallow trench he had created he crashed down into sleep, beyond caring if he should wake again, his last thought only that he should have left the horse loose. If he died in the night Satan too would be in serious trouble. On the other hand, bugger it.

He woke in darkness, a layer of snow covering him. Kicking himself free of the oilskin he tried to look around. He had bivouacked in some unholy places, but this took the biscuit. It was as if even in the grey light of pre-dawn the horizon was as far away as if he were at sea. He tugged the horse loose and shoving the rolled oilskin back into the saddle bag, attempted to mount. It took four goes. What bloody army officer took four goes to get on his horse? He'd have been laughed out of the regiment. Even dead drunk he should have been able to do better than that.

The two of them, lost souls in a bleakly frozen land, moved slowly back to the road. In his view it was more of a cart track and was giving him no confidence that he was heading in the right direction, but he plodded slowly forward. The weather had settled, leaving the snow-smeared land to reflect what little light was coming from the dawn.

Far in the distance he thought he saw a candle flicker into life. Focusing on it, he kneed the horse and hoped upon hope they might at last find some warmth and shelter. Buggering land.

Gradually the candle was joined by others and the vague outline of windows beckoned him forward. Neither he nor the horse had much of a hurry left in their bones, but they did their best until the house was there, firmly in view. Satan, suddenly recognising that food, water and shelter were nudging into a promised reality, shifted into an awkward canter, nearly unseating him. What the hell, it seemed they had found somewhere, though whether that somewhere was where they had intended to be remained to be seen.

Jack had been up before first light, jumping out of his skin with excitement at seeing the snow-covered land outside his window. Mary wondered if she could even remember being six and being excited by a snowy day; if so, it was a day way back in the distant past as far as she was concerned. But Jack's enthusiasm was catching and so here she was, at day break, outside her door, her hair tumbling over her shoulders, tossing snowballs with freezing hands to her son who whooped and yelled with the sheer joy of being young and outside in the cold with the safety of a warm house to run to when it all became too much. But that time was surely not yet.

Mary had stooped to fill her cupped hands and as she looked up to find where her aim should be to decidedly delight her son with a strike, movement caught at her. Standing straight she peered into the dark grey dawn to see a man and horse heading towards her at a steady speed. Both horse and man were flat black shapes against the landscape and sky and both looked unnaturally large. Breath caught in her throat and against her will there was fear in her voice as she called Jack to her. The man and horse cantered onwards, closing the gap, his cape flying out behind him emphasising the image of movement and threat. 'Jack!' she called again, even more urgently. Jack, as was the way of all six-year-old boys, merely turned to see where she was looking and stood stock still with curiosity. 'Oh, rats!' she muttered, in exasperation. But her nerves were jangling. Yes, she was expecting a visitor, but one in a coach and the visitor she was expecting had not exactly promised to come. She had not looked for this huge black apparition, so felt suspicious and she didn't believe she knew anyone who might fill the outline heading inexorably towards them.

The pair arrived and she looked up to the shadowed face of a large man on a large horse.

'I don't suppose for one moment this is Swann Manor is it?' he asked.

'Actually, it is,' she told him. Jack, she could see, was running towards her now keen to see who the arrival was.

'Ah. Well lass, would your mind running to tell your mistress Major Causton is here, there is a good girl.'

Mary wasn't sure how to respond. Part of her wanted to bob a curtsey and stretch her Lincolnshire accent to make out she was the nursery maid or governess he assumed her to be and part of her wanted to respond in her most haughty manner as being offended at being called both 'lass' and 'good girl'. Instead, she nodded and pointed towards the front door. It was her that had asked him here, after all.

Robert arrived, hurtling out of the door and tugging on a coat to take the horse and the man leaned over the horse's neck and slowly slid down, standing for a moment with his head pressed into the saddle as if in prayer, or thanks that he had finally arrived, she concluded. Then he turned and made his way up the two steps to the open front door. She noticed he was limping quite badly, favouring his left leg.

James stood for a moment in the hall as the girl and a young lad heaved the door to. To his right another, older, lad was throwing great hunks of wood onto the fire. And that was all he remembered afterwards. The sensation of warmth, the walls being panelled, and a flagstone floor.

Tom, over by the fire watched as the huge man's head tipped forward and instinct kicked in. He shoved himself to his feet and threw himself forward, only aware of how the man's arms were hanging down from his shoulders, his hands dangling towards the floor. As he toppled forward Tom threw himself underneath the man. He landed flat on the flags with the man's head on his back between his shoulder blades. Mary gazed down at him.

'That was quite heroic, Tom,' she told him. 'Are any of your ribs broken?' Tom was spread-eagled face down on the flags with the man unconscious across his back.

'I think I am alright, ma'am,' he gasped from now empty lungs.

It took four of them to lug the brute of a man up the stairs to the front bedroom. Tom got on with lighting a fire while Mary and Mags stripped him down to his drawers and woman-handled him into a thick nightgown and wool socks. Finally they had him in the bed with a warm brick and enough covers over him to keep him warm in Siberia, wherever that was.

'Think he will wake up?' Mags asked.

'No idea,' Mary told her truthfully. 'But I suspect it is just exposure. Warm him up and no doubt he will be good as new.'

They both shrugged and left him for a while. The horse was probably in no better shape and Mary wanted to ensure Robert had fed the great beast and smothered that too in blankets.

James came to slowly. He was buried in the mattress, which billowed around him, which told him he was in fact on top of a number of good feather ones. His feet were far too warm being smothered in heavy socks and being beside a hot brick, and he seemed to have some kind of fur cover over the top of him. Might be wolf, he mused. Didn't ships bring wolf pelts into Hull? That was in Lincolnshire. He lay with his eyes closed as someone did something repetitive. Saw wood? Sharpen a sword? He wasn't sure. He opened one eye to find two green-gold eyes gazing back at him, unblinking. A cat. The only cats he had ever known had been scrawny ratters and if you caught them with the sun behind them you could clearly see the fleas dancing off their coats. He forced a hand free of the sheets to shove it off him, but as his fingers reached the animal they encountered a softness he had not expected. Gently he allowed his fingertips to explore the wondrous experience of a clean cat's coat. The purring only intensified. Smiling, he allowed himself to sink down again into the depths.

When he next awoke the cat had gone, but a face was gazing down at him. A woman. She had a strong bone structure with a huge black eyebrow that ran from one side of her face to the other, unbroken and only dipping where it crossed over her nose. She also had an eye tooth jutting out into the air beyond her lips. That must put the boys off, he mused. Oddly perhaps, he liked the face. Its strength. It was the face of a warrior. The kind of female face that might win battles. He smiled to himself and passed out again.

When he eventually came to properly another woman was leaning over him, offering water to his parched mouth. This one had a round face. Older, sweeter, and with the kind of smile a man wanted to return.

'Thank you,' he managed, as he took in as much water as he could manage. 'How long have I been out?'

'Three days. Do you want to piss?'

He nodded and between them he managed to stand up enough to aim for the chamber pot she held. She helped him perfectly calmly, as if helping men to piss in pots was quite a normal part of her usual day. He sighed, managed to finally toe off the hated socks, and crashed back down to sit on the bed. The woman simply took hold of his legs and swung them up onto the bed, pushing his chest gently so he once more lay down again.

'I am Mags, rhymes with rags and short for Margaret, I will go and fetch you some soup.'

'Why not Meg?' he heard himself ask.

'No idea, but Mags it is. I will be back in a moment.'

James lay and gazed at the cracks in the ceiling and watched the light from the fire make dancing shadows, turning the old plaster into an almost three-dimensional map of rivers and hills. He supposed he had made Swann Manor at last. And he wasn't dead. Well that was two plus points. Now all he had to do was help Lady Mary, whoever she was, and he could finally pass away a grand success. He decided it was a good thing he had written to Hal from a tavern two days ago to ask him to meet him with the coach as soon as he could. There was no way in hell he could make it back to London on horseback. He wondered if Satan was alive too. Perhaps he was, they seemed skilled in bringing things back from the dead if he was any example. When she returned Mags helped him to sit up and slurp some broth and suck some soft bread. Hell, he was in a bad way. Just after she had left the room and he had begun to sink back into oblivion there was a scrabbling at his left shoulder. Obediently he hefted the blankets upward and the cat slid downwards, finally curling into a ball at his waist. James ignored it, while enjoying its company, and again slept.

The following morning Tom helped him to dress and all the while boasted about how he had thrown himself below the toppling man to break his fall. James made grateful sounding grunts and wondered at the stupidity of the boy. He might have suffered bruises if not broken ribs, but the lad seemed pleased at his prowess. He shook the boy off when it came to making his way down the stairs. He was not a bloody invalid. Well, not completely.

The hall below appeared deserted, so once he had reached the safety of the flags he aimed towards the door that seemed to have the most light around it. It did indeed prove to be the kitchen and was suffocatingly warm and filled with the scent of baking bread and roasting meat. He clomped in and was met by a round woman wearing a scowl and a huge white apron. She had her hands on her hips and seemed about to repel boarders. James forestalled her,

'Do you have a boot boy?'

'We have a boot girl,' was the response. Then came a yell, 'Sally!'

Sally was not tall but was wide in a solid sort of way with a smile that lit her face from ear to ear. James had once had a lad like Sally on his regiment and had loved him. Nothing had ever been too much trouble and he greeted each and every day as if the sun was shining and all was right with the world, even when they had all been knee deep in mud and two days without food. He met Sally's smile with one of his own,

'Do you think you could find me something to clean my boots with?' he asked. True to form, Sally shot off in her own clumsy way and returned with brushes and clothes and a pot of beeswax.

She watched with interest as he levered each boot off in turn and applied liberal amounts of wax and scrubbed the leather until it gleamed and all of the white water-marks had been cleaned away. Sally said something to him that might have been, 'Good job.' James grinned and returned her materials while thanking her gently for her good opinion of his efforts. The cook with the apron grunted something that he took for approval. Clearly Sally was held in affection and he had passed muster. He made his way over to the rocking chair that sat beside the range. It was stuffed full of cushions so he threw most of them off and sank gratefully into the comfort of the ones he had retained. He stretched out his legs and crossed them at the ankle and let the heat warm his thigh at the side. Opening one eye he viewed the cook. She gave him a snort and returned to whatever she was doing at the table. Her chair, he guessed. It took all of five minutes before the cat was up on his lap, purring away. As it kneaded its claws into his thigh he flicked its ear with a finger to deter it. Clearly he wasn't the only one to object to pin holes in his skin as it immediately turned round to make itself into a ball and settled to sleep again. James let himself smile a little and dozed off.

That evening he managed to sit at the dining table with Lady Mary and Mags to eat some solid food. He was regaining strength and knew he would soon have to face discussing why he had crossed the country in the dead of winter to respond to her summons, but for now he was too tired. Let some food reach his guts and with a bit more sleep he might be able to face the challenge. For their parts, Mary and Mags questioned him lightly about his journey and at no point did he have to admit to sleeping in a ditch in a snow storm. He was quite sure the warrior queen, which was how he thought of Mary, would have given him a tongue lashing about his stupidity.

The three of them retired to a small parlour beside the dining room, which was clearly where the women spent their evenings. James took one of the chairs beside the fire, stretched out his legs, crossed his ankles and closed his eyes. Eating had worn him out. He sensed more than saw Mary and Mags pull up a third chair and settle so they all sat in a ring around the fire. He smiled slightly. He had expected to be turfed out of whosoever seat he had purloined, but you didn't get to be an Army Major without taking risks, and he was beyond exhausted still. And the women had, as he had rather expected, simply taken the problem and resolved it. Good lasses, both, he thought.

The following day he made his way to the kitchen once again. Was handed his ration of sour brown bread with lashings of salty butter and raspberry jam along with a mug of warm milk stolen from the cow that morning for his breakfast. Once he had eaten he settled down to nap again. Today he was finding he was more aware of what went on in the kitchen. The cook he worked out was Mrs Gibson and there was a lass called Sarah alongside little Sally. It was Sally who had handed him his breakfast and he had thanked her gravely. Her smile could have lit up the world, he thought. From behind his closed eyes he heard the interplay of the three women and they chopped and scrubbed and did what women, and men, in kitchens did the world over.

He cracked one eye open to watch them all for a while, when Mrs Gibson was busy. Sally was scrubbing pans industriously, standing in a pool of water on the stone flags. Taking in a breath he scooped the cat up and dumped it on the floor. Then, heaving himself to his feet, headed to the outer door. No one said a word, but they all watched as he hauled the door open and headed out into the bitter wind outside. Lincolnshire was full of bloody wind, in his opinion. It needed a few mountains to slow it down. He would have a word with his maker, if he ever met the chap.

He found Tom in one of the stalls in the stable chopping wood in his shirt-sleeves. Together they found what James wanted and fashioned what he had in mind. It took about an hour and when he again crossed the yard back to the kitchen there were bright spots of light in front of his eyes. He banged back into the kitchen and forced the door shut. It had no doubt swollen with the wet of winter, but that meant fewer draughts, so it was probably a good thing it was such a bugger to open and close.

He carried his handiwork over to where Sally was once again washing pots and laid it down at her feet. She gazed at it a moment and clapped her hands, smattering him with dirty water. An improvement over blood, he thought. The wooden stand would lift her up a little so she could reach the big stone sink all the better and the wood would be warmer than the freezing flagstones on the soles of her feet. He received a nod from Mrs Gibson and returned to his (or rather her) chair by the fire. This time his sleep was not at all feigned. Bloody hell but he was in a bad way. The sooner Hal arrived with the carriage the better and then he could work out a solution for the woman and be on his way.

Mary was doing accounts when Mrs Gibson interrupted her to tell her that the Major was sound asleep in her chair and grey as dust.

'Been outside and wore himself out,' she informed her. 'Came back fit to collapse. The man should be in bed.'

'I quite agree. And just how do you suggest I get him there? And make him stay there? It nearly killed four of us to get him into bed when he was not conscious. How we might manage it when he is, I couldn't say.' And that ended that conversation. Meanwhile, James, oblivious, snored softly and made a bed for the cat with his lap.

Hal arrived that afternoon. James heard the commotion and made his way into the hall in time to see Hal being ushered in, brushing snow from his shoulders. Hal eyed him up and down and commented,

'Been poorly have you lad?' before the two men fell into a hug.

'Poorly!' thought Mary. The man was more corpse than was comfortable! But she kept her opinions to herself. Clearly the men were fond of each other if that hug was anything to go by. At least when the Major left he wouldn't be alone this time, which was a measure of relief.

Hal hadn't only brought himself. Up, alone in his room, he revealed that he had brought a letter. It had taken a long while to reach him and had been penned by a curate, but it told him that Elfie had finally died.

'From the sister?' James asked.

Hal took a deep breath. 'Aye. They have buried her in Whitechapel. She says a surprising number of mourners turned up, her own friends and lads and their wives from the army. It seems word got out.'

'But not me.' James' voice was flat.

'She says that she made it clear to everyone that that had been

Elfie's choice. That Elfie only wanted you to have good memories of her. She cared for you lad, she wanted to spare you.'

James lifted his face to the ceiling. 'But she didn't spare herself.'

They stood silent for a long moment. 'I think she was afraid,' Hal said.

'Of me?' James couldn't hide the hurt from his voice.

'No, herself. I wonder if she didn't trust herself not to ask you to put her out of her pain if you saw her. She knew you loved her. How could you have denied her? That day you tried to visit, she was screaming with the pain.'

'What a bloody awful way to die,' James murmured. 'Don't you ever let me go that way.'

'Nor me lad. I am happy to agree to it now!'

'I wouldn't have done it,' James said.

'No lad, of course not,' Hal agreed.

But neither of them was sure that was true. Either of them might have helped Elfie on her way had she begged them. They had both cared for her in their own way and had seen and done far worse over the years. Neither wished to investigate too closely how hardened they had really become. It was easier to mouth the words they knew they ought to say and leave deep examination of the truth untouched. Both of their lives had been tough and brutal for as long as they could remember. Now the war was over, perhaps it was time to investigate if souls could become renewed; if they could learn to approach life with hope rather than constantly be on their guard for danger. Only time would tell.

That night Hal regaled them over dinner with tales of his journey; toll keepers whose character and comments had amused him and taverns where various incidents had occurred. James sat and picked at his food, still clearly frail, and smiled quietly. Mary watched him covertly and tried to make him out. So far mostly all he had done was sleep. Except for making that stand for Sally. Yet Mrs Gibson, Sarah, Sally, Tom, Robert and Mags, which made up the entire household, all seemed his cheerful slaves, willing to watch for a need before he ever

The Army's Son

voiced it. How this had happened she wasn't sure as his face was often uninformative and his favourite way of standing was straight upright with his feet apart and his hands clasped behind his back as if he were on parade and he rarely seemed to open his mouth. Yet they all seemed to adore him. To her consternation the big, silent, and half-dead man seemed to fill the house with his presence. The very air in the corridors seemed to vibrate with him, the walls seemed aware of him and, worst of all, she prickled at the thought of him. Her skin seemed to be alive with the knowledge that he was in her home. It was all making her irritable.

Later they made a ring of four chairs around the fire and sat quietly watching the flames. Mary heard the Major take a deep breath.

'You wish for some help, I understand,' he began in his low voice.

Despite her boldness in writing to his family and in even making her plans, as far as they went, she blushed what she knew was an unbecoming scarlet. Putting her thoughts into speech had been hard enough when it had only been Mags listening, but now the same words needed to be out into the world at large.

'I would like a husband,' she admitted. 'I understand that London is the place to go for one, but I have no real idea of how to go on, or contacts to help me.'

'Lady Mary,' he began, but Mary stopped him with a raised hand.

'Major, I have stripped you naked and helped bathe you let alone spooned soup into you, and I am baring my soul to you, I think we have got beyond Lady Mary and Major Causton, don't you?'

He gave a cough of a laugh, 'Indeed. Mary and James it shall be.'

He watched her eyes, so fierce, like an eagle's, and her manner, which she wrapped around her like a cloak, of power and determination. He could have done with more troops with her attitude when he had been wielding command.

'So, a husband. You wish to attend the marriage mart in the spring.'

'Indeed. Are you able to help?' Now he was here she was wondering. How exactly could an army Major help her?

'The Duke of Southwald has claimed for some years he owes me some service. I believe it is time I requested he honour his promise. His wife is a powerful force in London society. With her behind you I believe you will find many doors open to you. What kind of man are you looking for? I imagine you have a list of requirements.'

His gentle smile held no sign of censure and Mary drew courage. Marriage was a business. This was no different from buying a property or some new stock, like a ram or a bull, after all. His pragmatic attitude helped her courage to settle.

'Jack is now six and I have so far tutored him myself. He will have to go to school soon and mix with his peers and make contacts that should last him a lifetime. As indeed your father's school friendship with my father has led me to requesting your help. The letters I found from your father gave me the impetus to write to you. As I explained, I have appealed to the House of Lords to request that Jack inherits his grandfather's title of Earl of Swann, and the response has been favourable. The Lords seem reluctant to allow the title to die out and in his favour, Jack will be a major landowner in the country. They seem to believe it makes sense for him to have a seat in power one day.'

'So Jack's future seems assured, why a husband?'

James' eyes never left hers.

Mary took a breath. 'To act as a role model for Jack, primarily. I can teach him to shoot and run the estate, but not to fish or go on as a man in society. If he never leaves my side he will be handicapped. I have to let him go for him to grow into a man who can stand on his own feet and make his own decisions. I cannot keep him tied to me all his life. He would grow to hate me.'

All James did was nod once, then gaze into the fire. Mary noticed suddenly that Hal had left the room but before she could wonder where he had gone, James turned back to look at her.

'Your Lincolnshire accent is not overwhelming, but it is too noticeable for London society, and do you dance?'

Mary's blush, having faded, returned. 'Not well,' she told him.

'I would advise you to take speech lessons to lesson your accent. It shouldn't take long, all you need to do is make your vowels shorter. But dancing is a must. That might be harder. My view is that you should prepare for your entrance to society as if you were applying for a post like say a lawyer, or sea captain, something where you would be expected to exhibit sufficient skills for the job.'

'You are saying that I am not good enough as I am?' Her stomach had sunk and she felt a wave of coldness sweep her. She was chilled with failure already!

'I am saying that girls of sixteen will be on the marriage market beside you and they will have trained for their debut from birth. If you go in against them without due preparation, then they will shred you to pieces. In my opinion, there is nothing more unkind than an ambitious girl. They will throw so many knives into your back you will be unable to stand upright.'

Suddenly Mary laughed. He was absolutely right! And he was also right that she could prepare; and she would.

'Thank you,' she said. And then, 'And how do you know all this?'

'Ah. I was a child of eleven when I became an officer. I too was totally unprepared, but I was so young I had time to pick up the skills I needed. I reduced my country accent first, then learnt to read and write fluently, because I couldn't, and last of all I had to learn to dance, to bow, to make conversation about innocuous matters such as the weather with nicely brought up young ladies. And when I made mistakes, they did indeed shred me. But the advantage of the army over London society was that I was frequently moved, so my mistakes did not follow me. You, however, have only the one platform on which to perform.'

'It is going to be a performance, isn't it?' she asked. All he did was nod.

Mary looked up to see that Hal had returned. He was standing before her undoing a leather roll of what seemed to be tools.

'Let's see to that tooth, lass,' he told her.

'My tooth! No, it stays as it is.' Her tone was emphatic.

'Nay lass, out it comes and right now. Here, open up. I will rub the gum with clove oil to numb it as much as I can. After that, it is for you to bite on the spoon.' Sure enough, he had a wooden spoon with a round handle in his hand.

'No,' Mary said, 'the tooth stays.' To her terror, she felt Mags' hands bear down from behind on her shoulders. It was Mags who spoke up,

'Her father told her that little girls had died in the past when their teeth were pulled. He put a dreadful fear into her.'

'Right then,' said Hal, 'fear is best faced head on. Here we go.'

Mary's eyes flew around the room like wild birds. Then they met James'. His face was grave, but his dark blue eyes watched her with intensity. Mary gazed back and knew he was willing her forward. He gave her the slightest nod, and she opened her mouth.

Hal was quick and he was strong. He gripped the pincers around the tooth and began to pull. Mary bit down on the spoon and felt the tug on the root. Then the root began to cave under the pressure and discomfort ripped through her head and her nose began to run. She tried to gasp in air, but pain suddenly roared through her and now tears poured unchecked and against her will down her cheeks. Mags had all of her weight on her shoulders and Mary felt her spine buckle as Mags held her one way and Hal pulled in the other. With a ripping sound the tooth came free and with it a mess of saliva and blood poured down her chin. Spitting the spoon out Mary gave a gasp of agony, then clamped her lips shut. For the first time since she was a child, they closed together without the eye tooth pushing out into the air. Mags was wiping her face and making quiet soothing sounds. Mary glared at her with fury, hating her at that moment. Hating Hal, and hating James especially. Already her jaw had begun to swell. Hal held a spoon of brown liquid out towards her. Bright spots danced before her eyes as she regarded it.

'Drink it,' he said, 'it is an opium mix. It will allow you to sleep tonight.'

Mary weighed up her options. The pain had made her faint and dizziness was coming at her in waves. And she was afraid to sleep in case her father had been right and she never woke up. On the other hand, if she slept with the opium, all control would leave her and at the moment that was exactly what she wanted. To float away and wake, hopefully, when it was all over. And if she didn't wake, the opium would make her leaving the world a painless process. With thoughts swirling, she opened her mouth and took in the syrup. Right that moment, with pain flooding her, she was utterly indifferent to whether she lived or died.

The room grew hot, her eyelids heavy, and sensation fell away. Mary didn't fight, she just let every worry she had ever experienced float away leaving her boneless and content. She was still in pain, but it was a benevolent sensation, no longer something to fear or internally scream about. When her head fell to one side Mags laid it firmly onto the side of the chair. Then she took some tweezers out of her apron. Her hands flew over Mary's face, plucking hair out of her thick brows and creating two elegant wings over her eyes. Hal blinked and gave a cough of amazement.

'What are you doing, lass?' he asked Mags.

'Might as well finish the transformation. I have been wanting to do this for years.'

'Might she sack you?' Hal asked.

'Humph,' was Mags' reply. 'Last time I looked I hadn't been paid since she was sixteen.'

Hal gave a cough of a laugh. He prodded Mary but sure enough, she was out cold. He gave a great sigh. 'I should have got her upstairs first, now I will have to carry her up.'

'No, I will bring down some blankets and leave her by the fire for the night. She will wake up as mad as a nest of hornets and having everyone around in the morning may, well, it may, make her still her tongue.' Mags looked over to see what James made of it all. He was sprawled out as always in the chair, crossed feet towards the fire, with his eyes closed. But he was smiling. Mags gave her own smile. Young Mary had met her match with these two.

The following morning Mags was heading towards the linen cupboard. The hallway was gloomy, but she was well used to it and didn't need light to find her way. Outside the wind was gusting sleet that didn't seem to want to lie, but appeared to prefer to fly around annoying everyone. She laid the sheets and other linens carefully flat, then closed the door and turned to head back to the warmth of the fires elsewhere in the house. As she drew level with the window embrasure a huge hand flew out and grasped her left wrist, while at the same time a firm kick to her left ankle took her feet out from under her. With a gasp she toppled backwards into Hal's lap and his two large arms surrounded her, clasping her firmly to him.

'And what do you think you are doing?' she demanded. 'I never even saw you there!'

'I didn't mean you to. You were focused on where you are going and I kept still. Movement attracts; stillness doesn't.'

'Caught many women this way?' she demanded, struggling slightly.

'Now lass, what do you think?'

His huge work-roughened hand reached up and stroked her cheek, smoothing her hair back from her face as he did so. With gently pressure he pulled her head down onto his shoulder and shifted slightly to settle her more comfortably. Mags gave a sigh and let herself be embraced.

'Those two will have to work themselves out. But it is time we did our own working out.'

His voice was calm and deep and Mags closed her eyes and allowed herself to sink into him. He smelt good. Of man and honest fresh sweat. She hadn't known she was so tired. Or so lonely.

'I want you lass, and I think you want me. And as far as I can see there are no obstacles in our way except the stupidity of our charges.'

'James and Mary, you mean?'

'I do. The lad is as much a son to me as Mary is daughter to you, I reckon. But leaving them aside, we have our own lives to lead.'

'How did you come to be with him?'

'Ah lass, there hangs a tale. I was married once. To a lass called Ruth. My Ruthie. She gave me two big louts of sons, then died when the youngest was ten. The boys and I, we managed and it was a good life. I was a blacksmith and content but the boys decided to listen to a recruitment sergeant and take the shilling. Well, I wasn't letting them go off without me, so I joined up alongside them. Made sergeant in a matter of weeks, much to their disgust. Their aim had been to outrank me and lay down the law to me for once in their lives,' he gave a low chuckle. 'Then they both died in India. One day there, next gone. Fair broke me. I walked away from the army. Technically I am probably a deserter on someone's files. Anyway, I cadged a lift on a ship to bring me back home. I wasn't at all sure I could be bothered to live, but I had to be somewhere. At the quayside I found young James. All of seventeen and a lieutenant at the time and more dead than alive. He reminded me fiercely of my eldest and I decided that I wasn't going to let him die if I could do anything about it. It was a bad place, India. Men died like flies. I did what was needed and he pulled through. Sometimes out there it didn't take much to swing the pendulum over from death to life, just a bit of care. Once he was back on his feet I took on the job of his sergeant and valet. He simply put my name on the pay roll and I was back in the army with a different regiment. I reckon they can't shoot me for desertion as I have drawn pay all the way down the line. Be interesting if they ever try to court martial me,' again he chuckled. 'Could make for an interesting case.'

'So you are courting me with a death sentence over your head?' she asked softly.

'Aye lass. You ought to know what you are getting into.'

'And what am I getting into?'

'A warm bed and a wedding ring as far as I am concerned.'

'Hmm,' she murmured. 'I barely know you.'

'You knew me and I knew you the minute we set eyes on each other. Don't try and tell me you didn't feel it too.'

Mags drew in a deep breath. He was right, and she knew it. When she didn't speak he said,

'So what is it to be? Do I let you go or kiss you thoroughly?'

'I think we will go for the kiss,' she told him and reached up to pull his head down.

. . .

The following day Mary remained in her room. Mags brought her some soup to sip and salty water to rinse her mouth with. Mary refused to speak to her and maintained a solid sulk. Mags ignored her and hied off to find Hal and enjoy a cuddle. She was used to Mary; she would come around.

With no lessons, Jack found he had time on his hands. James found himself being regarded by two keen eyes though this time they did not belong to the cat. James had been dozing in the kitchen in his stolen chair but was beginning to feel the need for some exercise. On sitting forward he spotted Jack in the shadows under the big kitchen table that sat in the centre of the room.

'I used to do that,' he said.

Jack emerged into the lighter shadow at the edge of the table. 'Do what?' he asked.

'Hide under the kitchen table. Cook used to pass down morsels for me to eat. So did my mother at times.'

'My mother doesn't cook. Mrs Gibson does that.' Jack emerged into the light.

'My mother was French and she would make some tiny cakes she called 'cat's tongues'. When I was little, much smaller than you, I refused to eat them as I thought they were made from kittens.'

'That was silly,' declared Jack and stood to face James properly. Then, tilting his head to one side, he regarded James. 'Were you ever small?'

'Not for long. My family has a history of very big men. My brother, Lucian, on the other hand, is of a more normal size.'

'I'd like a brother. I wouldn't mind a sister if she would play chase and ball, but I would really like a brother.'

You need company, James thought, remembering the rough and tumble he had enjoyed with the local village children. There was no village near Swann Manor. He wasn't sure at the moment that there were any villages at all in Lincolnshire. No wonder the lad wanted a brother or sister.

'Do you have any toy soldiers?' James asked.

All he received was a sharp nod and the sound of scampering feet. When Jack returned he was clutching a polished wooden box.

'These were my grandpa's,' he explained.

James eased himself to the rag rug and shoved the rocking chair so that it was wedged against the wall so that he could prop his back against it. The toy soldiers were mostly made of lead, but some were of carved wood, and it was beautiful work. As he and Jack spread them out Mrs Gibson strode over and stood with hands on her hips.

'And how am I supposed to get to my ovens?' she demanded.

James grinned up at her, 'Either we move, or we hand you what you want?'

'Hah, it's a good thing I have nothing but a slow roast in there today.' And with that she moved back to work at the central table. So James, along with General Jack, repeated the battle of Badajoz. With far less blood.

When Mary arrived they were told firmly to move into the sitting room where Tom had lit a fire. With shared grins, the two warriors moved their battle out of the way of food production. Mary watched them go. The big limping man and the small boy clutching his precious soldiers. She raised her eyes to meet those of Mrs Gibson. Neither said a word, but much was understood.

Two days later Mary rose early to journey to a village she was concerned about. The farms there hadn't been checked for far too long and her conscience was bothering her. She had been worrying about them ever since their last rents had come in. Now was as good a time for an unexpected visit as any. With the snow most people would simply remain at home, perhaps repairing tools or making something, but on the whole would be waiting the weather out. Her jaw was sore, but the cold would be welcome and might make it hurt less and the skin around her eyebrows had returned to its normal colour, except paler where the sun had not caught it last summer. She would venture forth and see what she could discover. Unexpected was always good with tenants, she had found.

She wasn't speaking to Mags, but knew that her sulk would have to end soon. At the end of a cold journey would be a good time. By the time Mags had fussed over her and warmed her up then all the bad temper between them would have evaporated. She wasn't in the habit of gazing into mirrors, but had been peering into the mould-flecked one inside her cabinet a lot over the last two days. She was shocked at her appearance. She looked normal. Ordinary. Everyone around here was used to her appearance; she had grown into her odd looks in front of the whole estate and there were plenty of women who looked worse than her around. May Brooks over at West Hill Farm had a goitre and warts all over her chin, but she had a husband and three sullen sons. A tooth and thick eyebrows hadn't seemed too much of an impediment to getting on with life. However, now they were both gone, she was shocked to discover how secretly pleased she was with her looks.

As she checked her saddlebags she became aware that it wasn't only her grey cob that was saddled up, but the huge black Satan as well. She turned to find James standing close.

'Are you leaving?' she asked.

'No, coming with you.'

'Why on earth would you do that?' she demanded. She definitely wasn't used to company when she was working. 'You are still frail.'

'The fresh air will do me good.'

She recognised an uncompromising position when she met one. And she had no power or authority over him. Annoyed, she continued her preparations for a day on horseback.

It was surprisingly pleasant to have his company as she traversed the iron hard fields and lanes. The snow had let up for a while, but everywhere was a mix of black and white where it had settled in some places and not in others. Perhaps when it came again the whole world would go white, but for the moment the landscape was piebald. He didn't speak, no change there then, but settled beside and behind her so that she and the grey mare led. Satan seemed quite content to let the grey lead, which surprised her. She had wondered if the huge horse might want to take charge, but it seemed like his master he was content to follow for the day.

James for his part was quietly horrified that the woman was heading out for what was clearly planned to be a long journey on a bitter winter's day, when daylight hours would be few. They had ridden away at first light with the dawn only just fighting its way through the night dark. Now the sun was a hazy light low on the horizon and didn't look set to be any brighter as the day drew on. Too many clouds and too low. He personally suspected a whole lot more snow was on its way. At least she rode astride and was well wrapped up in sheepskin clothing; actually, probably better wrapped up than he was.

Meanwhile Mags was stirring in her bed beside Hal. His body was large and warm and infinitely comforting. She had thought she wouldn't sleep with a strange body beside her, but in the end, she had slept long and deep. The energetic love-making they had indulged in had helped, of course. She found his bright blue eyes regarding her.

'You alright, lass?' he asked.

'Never better,' she told him. And wondered that she could have known the man for a day and was content to start planning a lifetime with him. As she leaned across to kiss him, she found she had no doubts whatsoever. He would do. He would more than do.

Mary and James stopped in a hollow she clearly knew and had been heading for and slipped from the horses to rest them and eat and drink a little. They both had some bread and cheese in their saddlebags and washed it down with some small ale corked into salt-glazed bottles. Neither spoke, but then nothing needed saying. After the rest stop, they headed on again and he was relieved to realise that the village they were headed to was only over the next field. He guessed that Mary had stopped as she hadn't wanted to need to take refreshment from the farmers in the village. Why he didn't know. Perhaps they were terrible cooks.

The village as it emerged was a huddle of cottages with one or two scattered out rather separate from the central core. There seemed to be no mill or any other artisan activity, just the cottages in amongst the fields. One or two trees acted as some kind of windbreak on the seaward side, but they were spindly and bent. Mary rode up to one of the largest cottages and dismounted. To James' eyes the cottage seemed well maintained and sound. Evidence, he suspected, of a decent landlord. And as that landlord was Mary he wasn't too surprised. He hadn't taken her as incompetent or greedy.

They were welcomed inside and instantly James' hackles rose. Something was wrong here. Eyes skipped away instead of boldly gazing; bodies shrugged low instead of greeting with gladness at having the tedium of winter broken. He felt that Mary read the situation the same. She was reasonable and her questioning pertinent. But the responses tasted in the air of guilt. But of what, he could not make out. After a while, having warmed themselves by the glow of the fire, they took their leave. Mary headed out to visit the other cottages and he tagged behind keeping his eyes open. At last, they had greeted and discussed the concerns of the coming Spring with all of the cottages except one. Flakes blew in their faces and stung; the weather had worsened while they had been inside. Mary was standing looking around as if confused and he nodded silently towards the cottage he had noticed she had missed.

They trudged through the snow leading the horses. There was no evidence of either light or fire gleaming through cracks in doors or windows. It was probably deserted, yet Mary had no record of an empty cottage around here. Mary knocked and called, but there was no answer. James stepped forward and shoved the door open. They stood together in the doorway and peered into the dark. Then there was a soft rustle and some movement. James shoved the door further open so what poor light remained fell inside. There was a heap of something on the floor. Mary strode in and peered down, then walked around the heap so that she was not blocking the dim light. James heard her gasp as she crouched down. He crossed the small room to join her. In a mess of blankets on the floor in front of what should have been a fireplace, was a woman. They both knew there was no hope, but James pushed his hand forward to try to find a pulse. She was far too cold for life and, he suspected, had been dead for a while.

The sound came again and they both turned to the far corner of the room. By now their eyes had become more accustomed to the interior gloom. Crouched down was a small child. Mary stood fully upright from where she had been bending over what was presumably the mother and gazed at the child. Then she moved forward and bending down, lifted her up.

'It's a little girl, I think,' she said softly. She began to chat gently to the child, but garnered no response. 'She is bitterly cold,' she told James.

'Let's get her out of here,' James instructed. 'She needs food and warmth.'

Outside, he reached for the child. Mary looked at him for a moment. 'I will take her,' he said. 'I can wrap her inside my cape. Meanwhile, you need to find out what had been going on here.' All Mary did was nod before relinquishing the small body. It was instinct that caused them both to remount. Mary moved her grey forward as one of the far doors opened and a family could be seen standing in the light thrown by the fire inside. A large man stood outlined for a moment, before coming forward.

'Martin Dunlop,' Mary called to the man, 'what do you know about this woman and child?'

'She's a witch!' he called across. 'And her spawn.'

'Why do you say that?' Mary demanded.

James noticed that some other men had begun to leave their homes to come and take part. Some of them carried brands, small branches bound together and dipped in pitch that burned and threw an uneasy light over the scene.

'Look at the weather we have been having! Solid rain and now this snow,' Martin declaimed.

'It is winter, you fool, and Lincolnshire. Wet autumns and cold winters are a normal part of life. How exactly is witchcraft involved?' Mary asked.

'Been worse since she arrived here with the brat,' Martin insisted.

'Where did she come from?' Mary asked Martin, but it was another man who answered, younger, and presumably outranked in this village by Dunlop.

'She said she was a widow and wanted to find work,' the younger voice interrupted. Mary turned to view him.

'Alan Foster, what do you know of this matter?' Mary asked him.

Foster stood foursquare and faced across the space towards Dunlop. 'Martin told us not to go near her. When Giles Cobb did, he beat him badly for stepping out of line. Martin wanted that cottage for his eldest and wanted the widow gone. Giles has been laid up for eight weeks now; the beating weakened his chest. With this wet weather he is having trouble breathing still.'

'And why did none of you contact me about all this? Nor mention anything when I arrived? You do not decide who lives in any of the cottages, I do. You do not beat each other up without my permission. What is it about that none of you understand?' Mary's voice carried clearly and anger vibrated throughout it.

James saw one or two heads hang, but mostly the crowd were watching Martin Dunlop. Clearly, when Mary was not around, he was the law in this place. And a rough and cruel law it seemed to be.

'So, because of you Martin Dunlop, Giles Cobb is injured and unable to work for me and a woman lies dead, apparently of starvation. That is assault and murder.'

Mary's voice was emphatic, but Dunlop was not going to take her verdict. He moved forward. Satan shifted under James. He could stand stolid beside a cannon as it fired, only responding with a shiver in his muscles to show he had heard the roar, but moving fire was something he took exception to. A static fire left Satan unconcerned, but any fire that moved around he considered it only his duty to attack it and stamp it out with his huge hooves. Now he shifted under James towards Dunlop and James didn't reign him in. The horse moving without his instruction was less obvious to the edgy crowd that had now gathered in the falling snow than if he took the reins and deliberately moved the horse forward.

Dunlop was now menacingly close to Mary and he had ignored James, taking his silence as an indication he was nothing to worry about. As Dunlop's arm moved up to pull Mary from her horse James struck. All Mary saw was a slashing movement and Dunlop's cheek opening up to pour blood down onto his jerkin.

Mary leaned down from the saddle, 'You are out, Dunlop. I do not need you or your kind on this estate.'

She sat taller in the saddle and sought out Alan Foster. 'How is it the child still lives?' she asked him. Beside her Dunlop spat on the ground. James kept his eye on him; he didn't anticipate trouble from any other direction.

Foster's reply rang out clear across the heads of the people now milling closely around the two horses and riders,

'Because I have been putting milk and bread in the cottage every morning,' he said, and his words were clearly a gauntlet thrown down to Dunlop. Inside James' coat the child began to wriggle; she was warming up it seemed.

'And in doing this you felt you were putting yourself in danger from Dunlop?'

'Aye, my lady, I did.'

The reply was unequivocal. For the first time James felt the mood of the crowd move away from Dunlop towards Mary. He could completely understand how a thug on the ground was more influential than a landlord some miles away who visited a couple of times a year.

Mary once more leaned down from the saddle to face Dunlop. 'Out,' she said, 'now.'

Dunlop's face snarled, 'You can't put me out in the snow.' His tone was uncowed and threatening.

'Can't I?' Mary counter challenged. 'You should hang for what you have done. Pack what you can carry. You and all your family are out.'

'I have six young'uns,' he complained.

'You should have thought about that before you tried to starve a woman and child to death and beat a man to near death.'

James watched to see if Mary weakened. He wasn't much surprised when she didn't. He had already worked out that the Swann Estate was huge, and that she ran it alone, and probably well.

Dunlop marched back to his cottage followed by a murmur of gossip that to James' ears didn't sound in Dunlop's favour. It seemed there were other grievances against the man being aired. Some of the men came over now to 'encourage' Dunlop to go. The family eventually emerged each of them carrying a bundle. The whole gang of them headed out of the village and began to take the seaward road. James was glad of that as he and Mary, along with the child, would be heading inland. Mary was sitting thoughtfully staring at the Dunlop cottage. She called one of the men who still held a flaming brand in his hand over.

'Fire it,' she instructed.

'The cottage, ma'am?'

'Yes. Do it now.'

The man didn't hesitate, he threw the brand up onto the thatch and even with the wet of the snow, it began to glow. The thatch underneath that was still dry caught suddenly, then the air was full of the crackling light of the whole cottage going up in flames. Mary and James watched for a while before she led the way out of the village and out onto the road that would lead back to the Manor.

When they were some distance away James pulled up alongside her and asked,

'Why burn the cottage?'

'Didn't you see? They took nearly nothing with them. They intended to walk down the road, then when I had gone, return. I wasn't having that. Don't feel too sorry for them. I know his wife has family about eight miles away who will take them in. They won't sleep in the snow tonight.' She paused then added, 'We need to turn off the road in a moment to go to the local church. That poor woman needs to be buried. Once I have handed the problem over to the vicar we really can push for home.'

The journey back to the Manor was made in a blizzard of horizontal snow. All James could think was that the sooner he was out of Lincolnshire, the better. He had nothing but admiration for the woman leading the way who worked this county and kept it safe, and productive. Men like Dunlop were a like a disease. The polluted their communities with their self-serving bullying. He was lucky she hadn't sent for the magistrate and had him hung. James doubted he would feel lucky, however. He was more than likely fomenting a reprisal. He hoped Mary was up to coping with that. Men like Dunlop tended not to fade quietly away.

When they arrived, James rode Satan up to the kitchen door and made him jump his front hooves onto the cobbles twice. The noise of his huge horseshoes clanging on the stones was as loud as a church bell. As expected the door came open and Mrs Gibson looked out. In the swirling snow and dark James reached his bundle down to her arms.

'Shave her head, then burn the hair and all of her garments.'

Mrs Gibson didn't fail him, she took the bundle into her arms and with no questions returned quickly indoors. Once in the stables, Mary and James helped Robert to brush down the horses and hang their tack up onto the relevant hooks. Cold as they were, the horses had to come first and the more they helped, the quicker they could all settle down in front of a warm fire.

Finally they were sitting around the table with hot food in front of them. James' feet were still like ice and he suspected Mary's felt the same, but good food and mulled wine would help to thaw them out. The day had done nothing to improve his view of the county, however. Nothing on God's green earth would cause him to ever make his home here.

He was well into his dinner before he became aware of a change in atmosphere. Looking up he found himself glancing between Mags and Hal. He was looking more contented than any man had a right to look and Mags had developed a becoming blush. He looked at Mags thoughtfully. He had been too caught up with weighing Mary up to pay attention to her companion, who seemed to spend her daylight hours running the house and her evenings silently concentrating on her embroidery or mending. Now he looked more closely and what he saw was a plump and pretty woman of about forty. A glance shot across the table between the two and Mags once more concentrated on her plate while her blush deepened. Hal, meanwhile, caught and held James' eyes. James gave a nod to show he understood. Well, it seemed Hal's army days were well and truly over. He had found a woman he wanted and James knew that meant his old friend was settling down. Better not be in bloody Lincolnshire, he thought to himself, or visits from me are going to be far and between.

All four were settled around the fire in the small sitting room as usual when Mrs Gibson carried the little girl in. Her scalped hair and thin little face gave her the appearance of a newly-hatched baby bird, all eyes and bare skull.

'Did she manage to eat?' Mags asked.

'Enough I think of bread and warm milk. Her little tummy won't take much as yet,' Mrs Gibson reported.

To everyone's surprise the child found James and reached out for him to take her. Giving a gentle smile James lifted his arms and took her into his two big hands. The girl gazed up at him with huge blue eyes and then snuggled into James' embrace and closed her eyes as if settled down to sleep.

'Has she spoken yet?' he asked Mrs Gibson.

'Not a word, sir. Not even to cry.'

Mrs Gibson then returned to her kitchen domain and James stretched out his legs and closed his eyes. The day had exhausted him. And whether a cat or a child on his lap, it made no difference.

Mary sat quiet and watched the big man with the small child. He had a faint smile on his face but looked sound asleep. He hadn't complained once during the day, but she had been aware every time they had stopped that he was in pain. He had impressed her deeply with the way he had accompanied her but never tried to take over.

His only real input had been to be at her side when she had entered the dark cottage where they had found the woman, and she had been grateful for his support then, and again when he had slashed Dunlop across the face making the man think twice about laying hands on her. She sighed, Dunlop was an unresolved problem. She would need to find out who in that village was strong enough to stand against him should he try to return and to give him her support. She began to run some of the farmer's sons who were getting to an age to want their own place through her mind. A couple of them placed in the village might tip the balance. Meanwhile there was her house guest. She was surprised she was beginning to warm to him. And Mags seemed to be doing her own warming. She had a suspicion that fewer sheets would be going down to the laundry this month. If she wasn't mistaken those two had come to some kind of arrangement together. Well, Mags had been on her own for forever and Hal appealed as a solid and reliable man. It certainly put pressure on her to find her own husband. If Mags was moving on with her life, then it was time she did the same. She felt no surprise when the two of them murmured a quite good-night and disappeared while it was still early.

James stirred from sleep when Mrs Gibson retuned for the child. They had both been fathoms deep.

'Her name is Elfie,' Mary heard James tell Mrs Gibson softly as she lifted the little girl into her own arms. With a nod, the cook left.

Mary watched the fire for a moment then looked across at James. His eyelids were half closed, but his eyes glittered darkly in her direction. She swallowed. She didn't want to cause offense, but she had questions.

'Does Hal always,' she paused, 'I mean, does he always, when he meets a woman …' her voice trailed off.

'Seduce her within five minutes? No. I am as surprised as you are. What about Mags, does she take every man she meets into her bed?' His voice was unjudgmental, but the comment was as blunt as she had come to expect from this man.

'Far from it, Mags has never before shown any interest in a man and I have known her since I was ten.'

'Hal likewise, I know soldiers have a reputation for whoring, but not Hal. He has always remained true to his dead wife, and she went a long time ago.'

'How could they ...' she wasn't sure what her question was exactly or, more to the point, she wasn't sure how to word it.

'Perhaps for some people it only takes a glance. Now it has happened, well, we assume it is happening, I am not surprised. They seem more than well suited.'

All Mary could do was nod, before asking, 'And did you?'

His dark gaze was amused, 'Did I do what?'

'Go whoring? I mean, if that is what soldiers do.'

He gave a bark of a laugh, a short sharp sound that made her smile in return.

'Once. I took the shilling at eleven and claimed, as I was large, to be sixteen. I was placed firmly under the wing of a Sergeant Harris, a grizzled old campaigner if ever there was one. The army often knows facts it chooses to ignore. He kept me alive for the first few years of my service and made sure I knew how to be an officer as my brother had turned up and bought me a commission. When I was fourteen some of the men enticed me away from my sergeant's ever-sharp eyes and got me drunk and took me to a brothel. I was horrified and, I will now admit, terrified, so I vomited everywhere. Messed up two dresses, spilt wine on top of a table, the carpet and at least three uniforms. I can't tell you the names I got called. I maintain it was all their fault for giving me far too much gin and brandy. They were happy enough to hand me back, *virgo intacta*, to Sergeant Harris. He smiled at the memory and closed his eyes and Mary wondered if she had lost him again, but he had more to say. 'They did me a fair turn. Put me off brothels for life.' He chuckled, 'Hasn't done me any harm.'

'When did Elfie tell you her name? I didn't hear her.'

James opened his eyes to regard her again, 'She didn't tell me. I named her. Do you know her hair stubble is a soft as a cat's fur?'

'Did you think it would be as rough as your beard?'

James raised his eyebrows and ran a hand over his face before giving her a disarming grin. 'I suppose so. I haven't had much to do with children.'

'Where did the name Elfie come from?' The question was nagging at Mary.

'It's short for Elfrieda. A good Anglo-Saxon name. I named her for my companion. She was a good woman. I like the idea of her name being carried on.'

Mary chewed this information around in her mind for a while before blurting out, 'You mean you have named her for your mistress?'

James again opened his eyes and gazed thoughtfully away up at the corner of the ceiling. 'I suppose that is what most of my brother officers would call her. But only behind my back. To me she has always been my friend and help-meet; a companion on the road.'

Mary wasn't sure what to say so sat frowning at him. He watched her face for a while before seeming to decide to explain a little more. 'When a man dies the men usually take lots to see who will take the wife, and any children, on. Without that, the woman would have to become a whore or possibly a washer-woman, though we usually had too many of them, or starve. The men would know the woman and would usually see that she was tucked under the wing of one of them, unless she was thoroughly disliked that is. Elfie's husband had been a Sergeant in another regiment. Hal had come to know her and brought her home for me.'

'Just like that?' To Mary it seemed incredible. While she knew women were chattels, it seemed particularly brutal to think of them being passed from hand to hand like old clothes that were considered to still have a bit of wear in them.

'Just like that. I was lodged in a one room-cottage at the time and I came home and she was sitting by the fire sewing. She was quite a bit older than me, but I was comfortable with that. I had found up to then that most women my age avoided me. I was too large and my manners too blunt, apparently. Elfie didn't mind either fact. We dealt well together for a long while.'

They sat quiet for a time and Mary found that now the exhaustion of the day had lifted she was wide awake. 'What did you do in the army?' she asked.

He didn't bother opening his eyes but just said, 'Infantry.'

'Does that mean guns and cannons?' She read the newspapers, but the army was another world to farming the Lincolnshire fens.

'It does. Then one day someone turned up with a Baker rifle and I fell in love. Nothing like decent artillery to excite an infantry man.'

'What is a Baker rifle?'

This time his face was full of amusement and he did open his eyes. 'Rifles up to then were tubes of metal a bullet was exploded along. The bullet could, and did, go just about anywhere. The Baker was a revolution. The barrel is bored into spirals. This means the bullet spins as it travels along the tube, so by the time it emerges it is heading in a single direction. It meant accuracy. For the first time we could aim at something and have a reasonable hope of coming close to the target.'

'And that is a good thing, I suppose.'

'You said you could teach your son to shoot, so you must know something about guns.'

'My father had a decent pair of pistols and taught me to use them. It is hard to be accurate with them. I became as good as he was, but it wasn't unusual for the bullet to land some way from where we aimed. He always predicted that someone one day would improve them.'

'Well, he was right. He would have enjoyed using a Baker. Mind you, some of the riflemen lay down flat to shoot and he might not have enjoyed that.'

'Lay down?'

'Hmm. They lay on their backs, cross their ankles, and rest the barrel between their boots, so the gun is laying down the length of their bodies. I have seen a man take out an enemy at over one hundred yards doing that. It was an amazing shot.'

'Is that what you did?'

'No. I tried it, but I preferred to get closer and rest the gun on a rock or tree to steady it. I was good at standing still. If you don't move, it is possible for the enemy to look right at you and not see you. What the enemy is looking for is movement. I was one of the first to prove the usefulness of the Baker to the army, and one of the first to persuade the army it was worth paying a premium for them; they don't come cheap and the army watches every penny. It is likely the only thing in my life I will do that was worthwhile.' He had a wry grin on his face.

'What is the army like, really?'

'Thinking of joining up?' There was something in his face that made her feel self-conscious; not an emotion she was familiar with. 'I tell all the lads who ask that question, it is drillin' and killin'. Nothing more. Nothing less.'

'It can't be as simple as that.'

He had closed his eyes again, 'Oh it can. I promise you, it can.'

'James, why did we really go to war with Napoleon?' Mary prodded.

Two intense blue eyes held her gaze. 'There were many reasons. At first, because he was there. Later when the scope of his ambitions became apparent, because he terrified people, me for one. In life, the person who wins is often the one who wants the prize the most simply because others are content with what they have. Bonaparte wanted too much, and if he hadn't been stopped, he would have controlled the whole of Europe. Damn him, I wasn't sure where Russia was; Bonaparte not only found it, he attacked it!' With that, he once more closed his eyes.

Mary sat and watched him as he dozed, letting herself sink back into the cushions and relax. She didn't do enough of this. Just sit. The fire spat and crackled and the soft chatter of its noise was soothing. Light from the fire and the candles threw a soft gold up onto the walls until it was subsumed into the shadows that hung under the ceiling. For a while she didn't think, didn't worry about all of the challenges she knew would meet her on the morrow, she let a sense of safety surround her. Then, she shook her head. This peace was not real. Reality was endless problems.

Eventually she went up to bed, leaving James the fire. She made no attempt to undress or plait her hair, instead she stood by the window, hugging herself. Her thoughts were once more whirling; the man downstairs, what she should do with the child, Martin Dunlop, who she was sure would try to retaliate, Mags' reaction to Hal and his to her, and then back to the man downstairs comfortably settled by her fire in her house. He confused her utterly. When he had grinned at her, something inside had lurched, and her cheeks had flushed pink. When she touched him by accident, sparks as if from a fire shot along her skin, and when he had told her about his mistress, or companion as he called her, she had felt rocked sideways. Did he consider himself free to marry? She was honest enough to admit, if only to herself, she was strongly attracted to him. Honest? She lusted after his very bones! The idea of being held in his arms, touched by those huge rough hands that could hold a small child with tenderness, to lay across that big, strong body, made her ache! She deeply envied Mags. She had taken one look at Hal and he at her, and presumably a question had been asked, and just like that, only one bed was needed! Mary had no idea what the question had been, whether this was a liaison for the length of Hal's stay or something more, but Mary suspected that it was something very real for the both of them. Which raised even more questions. Might Mags leave her?

The air by the window was cold so Mary began to pace. James was clearly suffering from pain; the black thumb-sized marks under each eye and the way his mouth went white and thin at times told her that. Yet he had ridden here from London on a horse that few men would have the strength to manage. His Satan reminded her more of the huge destrier war horses knights had once ridden, which, now she thought about it she supposed Satan was, than the hunters men normally owned. The beast had been quite calm in the midst of shouts and turmoil until some idiot had waved a flame in its face and then it had only shown a slight reaction in shifting out of the way. Yet when James

The Army's Son

had edged it closer it had moved with silence and stealth so that James could flick his blade at Dunlop's cheek and protect her. That Dunlop had planned to haul her off her horse she didn't doubt. And that was another thing. James hadn't interfered. He had allowed her to make decisions. Every other man she knew would have assumed control and taken matters into his own hands, ignoring her, especially when the crowd of villagers had looked violent. He had asked why she had fired the cottage, but he had sounded interested, not condemnatory.

And Elfie! The way he was so tender with the child and the way he was so patient with Jack's endless army questions. She paced faster. This was not just a man she would like in her bed. This was a man she thought she might want for life. But he had given absolutely no indication that he thought of her as anything other than a woman he was honour bound to help! Finally, she went to bed, still confused and now doubly exhausted as well.

The following day by unspoken consent everyone stayed inside and hugged the fires and did little. Mary was still tired from such a long journey in the snow and it made her wonder how James felt considering he still wasn't well. She couldn't work out what was wrong with him. Certainly his left leg troubled him and when Jack had knocked him on his thigh once when running past James had gone quite white with pain. James spent the day dozing with Elfie on his lap or playing soldiers with Jack and his lead models. It took all of his gentle persuasion to stop Elfie sucking them as then the paint came off and no one would be able to see which army they were in. Mary watched him and wondered at such unfailing gentleness from a man whose existence since early childhood had been infused with 'drillin' and killin'.

They ate early and both Hal and Mags slid out of view with no fuss and no acknowledgement of anyone else. Mary settled into her usual seat and caught James' eye.

'Hmm,' James murmured, 'I wondered if it would flare and burn but it seems it is still ongoing.'

Mary smiled without humour, 'I wondered the same. Whether something begun so quickly could have any substance to it.'

James was watching her keenly. 'Perhaps sometimes it really does take just takes one look.'

It was Mary's time to sigh, 'Well, they are both independent adults. According to Mrs Gibson he follows her around like a shadow and they can be found folding linens together or turning mattresses or whatever other tasks Mags fills her days with and talking together all the time.'

'Spying on her?' His accusation was full of amusement.

'Not deliberately.' She felt a little prickled with guilt. She hadn't exactly avoided Mrs Gibson's gossip.

'Well,' James began, 'I have seen couples go through conventional courtships who have probably spent less time together than they have and no one thinks it unusual. Add up the minutes a sheltered girl and a conventional man spend together before they head for the altar and it isn't much. Society's rules don't allow a leeway for getting to know the other person; most couples who marry, in my view, marry as strangers.'

'I was certainly a stranger to my husband,' Mary declared with feeling.

'Jack's father? How did you meet him?'

Mary didn't answer for a while, but simply gazed into the fire. As far as she knew, only Mags knew her story but she felt safe with James. Perhaps she was being a fool, but thinking it through she couldn't see that he could harm her if she told him the truth. The law was the law and gossip couldn't alter that. 'He was a friend of my father's,' she began. But it was hard to go on. To go back and revisit those times.

'Older than you, then,' James suggested, after a pause.

'At least 70. I was sixteen.' It sounded even worse stated baldly like that. James was watching her, all signs of dozing gone. 'Mother died when I was four. I screamed the house down every time my father left home, so he took to carrying me up on his saddle with him. No doubt I was spoilt, but it was the best thing that ever happened to me. I grew up knowing all of the tenant farmers and their families and my father and I grew closer than is usual for a father and daughter. He employed Mags to care for me and eventually to teach me to read, write and do my numbers, but I still rode out with him often. He died suddenly three days before my sixteenth birthday. His will nominated Giles Brewer as my guardian. I think he must have thought that, as Brewer was a landowner whose property abutted ours, he could keep me safe until I reached marriageable age. It would be in his interests to keep an eye on our lands. Insurrection here might bleed across to interfere with his interests. It made a kind of sense. But Brewer had his own plans. On my birthday we buried my father at eleven than re-entered the church and Brewer married me. He had spent the three days since my father died obtaining a special license from the Bishop of Lincoln.

'The vicar didn't know what to do. The will clearly put me under Brewer's control. When it came to, does any man know any reason this marriage should not take place, he asked twice and waited ages. I could hear the mutterings behind me. A lot of people didn't like what was happening, but many thought it made sense for me to be settled with a man to take care of me as I was still a child. The congregation was split pretty much in two from what I could hear. When it came to, do you take this man, I said 'no', but I was so terrified by everything that was happening I whispered it. The vicar ignored me and carried on.'

'Buy surely, he didn't expect a real marriage?'

Her laugh was bitter. 'Oh he did. That night I tried to hide, then to run. For such and old man he had a hefty arm on him. He simply slapped me hard and told me I had no choice. And he was right. It is the smell of him I can't forget. He stank of old age and to me it was foul. But when it came to it, I was pretty sure he was failing in his aim. I knew how it worked with the animals and penetration was necessary. He tried now and then, but I don't think he had the energy to force me into his bed that often and I was fairly sure things were not going the way they should when he did.'

James' soft curse was like a benediction. 'Anyway, a year went by and I by now was running not only my father's estate but Brewer's. It was a lovely summer morning and a man arrived. He was on a crutch, had lost his left leg below the knee and his right arm below the elbow. How he was managing I couldn't imagine. He was looking for work. I asked him if he could clean out a stable and he said yes. I took him over and showed him where the tools were and left him to it. Half an hour later I took him some cold meat, bread and ale. He was doing a good job, but was clearly embarrassed at having me see how he struggled, so I went away again. By the end of the day the whole yard looked better than it ever had. I asked him to stay for a while, but told him it would not be a permanent position.

'He had dark eyes and long dark hair and beard and his skin was dark brown from the sun. The third night he was here I climbed up to the loft he was sleeping in and asked him if he knew how to get me with child.' She gave a huge sigh. 'And he did. And as I had suspected, Brewer had been way off the mark. By then his mind was going and the man who should have been running the stables was caring for him pretty much day and night.'

'What was his name?' James asked softly.

'Thomas. I never asked for more. He was kind. And gentle.' She gave a laugh, 'And grateful! He said he had never dreamed to find a billet like ours.'

'What happened to him?'

'As soon as I thought I was carrying I gave him a hefty purse and told him I never wanted to see him again, and I haven't.'

They sat quiet for a while before Mary blurted out, 'Do I disgust you?'

'Because of Brewer or because of Thomas? Because nothing you have done disgusts me, or should anyone else. You are a practical and pragmatic woman. You could have shut yourself up in a room and sobbed for years, but you didn't. No, what I feel is admiration. You found yourself in a difficult position with no one to protect you and you got on with your life. And Jack is a son to be proud of, whoever his father is. Will you tell him?'

'One day, I hope. The difficult part will be deciding when.'

'What happened to Brewer?'

'His mind kept fading in and out. He died when Jack was two. He simply stopped eating gradually and no one could force him to. We tried. After he died, the man who had cared for him wanted to go back to his homeland of Wales. I paid him off well as he had had a fairly dreadful time caring for a difficult old man. Brewer wasn't a nice man with his mind and didn't improve with losing it. He had hit the man often. That was when Tom and Robert came to work for us. They are cousins and younger sons. They have been a terrific help and it has been wonderful to have young people around in the house.'

They sat in silence for a while until Mary rose to go to her bed. James had once more closed his eyes and seemed oblivious, so she was mildly surprised when he spoke.

'I'll make the fire safe and come up in a while.' She turned and moved towards the door when his voice stopped her again. 'And Mary, you were beautiful with the tooth.'

She turned to find his dark blue eyes gazing at her. His words made her frown and he saw it. 'You should see the Spanish women. They have a ferocious beauty that can attract a man like iron to a magnet. They have strong features and teeth that go every which way, but somehow that only adds to their attraction. They also have interesting facial hair,' his smile was wicked and wide, and then it faded. 'When you go husband hunting, don't sell yourself short. You are lovely and strong and clever. There is a man for you somewhere, I am certain, and he will be a lucky man indeed.'

She gave him a small nod, then said, 'Don't sleep down here. You have a bed upstairs.'

His eyes were shut again and he gave a huge contented sigh. 'Yes, with feather mattresses and a hot brick. A soldier's idea of Paradise.' She couldn't help but smile.

As she climbed up into her bed she couldn't but think about James. She knew she spent far too much time doing exactly that. He had said he still missed his Elfie. Did that mean he had loved her? Had been in love with her? And would that be present or past tense? What did 'being in love' mean? As far as Mary could tell, it meant sixteen-year-olds becoming rather too acquainted in the Spring. Which resulted sometimes in wedding bells but more often in the girl's mother making room around her hearth for a cradle she hadn't expected to need again for a few years yet. Followed by downcast eyes for a while until everyone became adjusted to the new family arrangements. Clearly he couldn't have married her as his status as an officer would not have allowed that, but if he could have done, might he have done? She had the feeling the answer would have been a 'yes'. So did that make him more, or less admirable? And why was she so set on admiring a sleepy army officer anyway?

And what exactly was wrong with him? She had a feeling he was in constant pain, yet he never mentioned it and had managed a gruelling ride in filthy weather without a word of complaint. But he looked white and pinched around the nose, in a way she recognised from others she had treated for broken limbs and the like. And the journey in the snow had exhausted him. He had hardly moved all day. Then she remembered the spoonful of opium Hal had poured down her throat after he had removed her tooth. Was James using that to keep going? She suspected not. The syrup had a sickly-sweet smell and she was sure she would have smelt it on his breath or seen evidence of constant use. She had a feeling Hal would not tell her what ailed him, and she was certain James wouldn't. It would have to remain a puzzle. But at least when they left now, they would be leaving in a coach and James would have Hal to look after him. And where would that leave Mags? With whirling thoughts she finally gave in and slid towards sleep. And just before she let herself go, she remembered that James had said he missed his Elfie, but had fallen in love with the rifle. For some reason that made her smile as she finally let the day go.

The following morning Mary rose and, slipping from the warmth of her bed, moved over to the window to see what the day was doing. She had slept late, which was unusual for her. Settling in the window embrasure she hugged her knees and looked out. The sun was brilliant and the sky a sheet of blue that stretched away forever. Beneath, the snow glinted and shone. It would be impossible to keep Jack indoors today, she thought, and smiled. She had a warm feeling inside that felt

The Army's Son

unusual and made her leave getting up properly for the moment, while she thought about it and tried to identify it. Then she realised it was what James had told her the previous night. The words that hummed inside were, 'ferocious beauty'. And he had compared her to strong Spanish women. Oh, she liked that. She had always felt dour, somehow, as if her unattractiveness didn't allow for smiling and laughter, unless she was with Jack of course. He still thought her the most beautiful person in the world. She hadn't realised how she had been dreading him viewing her with adult eyes and judging her against all the pretty women that he would see.

She still would never be a dainty, pretty thing. But she didn't want to be. She had lived as a man for too long to pretend to be other than she was, a capable adult. Perhaps there was a man out there somewhere who would want, what had James called his Elfie, a helpmeet and companion? That sounded exactly right. But she was surprised how much his compliment meant to her. Deriding herself as a fool she finally headed down to breakfast.

As they all ate she informed everyone she would be heading out to the Home Farm, run by the Smiths. She suspected that the village where Elfie and her mother had been found would close ranks and plead no knowledge of either the woman or the child if she returned to ask more questions. Betty and Ted Smith tended to know most of what went on in the area, so she would ask them if they had heard anything. 'But first,' Jack demanded, 'a snowball fight.' She had been surprised to find that both Hal and James had already been outside and that their coats appeared damp in places, presumably from an earlier foray into the snow with Jack. She smiled her thanks and listened in to Jack's questions about soldiering. Both Hal and James were deriding the military for a career, stressing having to stand still for hours, 'What not moving at all?' was Jack's disbelieving question. When he was stood beside Hal to see how long by Hal's pocket watch he could keep quite still as if on parade, he lasted less than two minutes. When James told him about laying in wet grass, or even a bog, or worse under a beating sun, absolutely still in order to wait for the enemy, Jack's enthusiasm for becoming a soldier appeared to wane. Mary breathed a sigh of relief. She had read the numbers of dead in the newspapers after each battle. Salamanca had been dreadful, as had Badajoz and Ciudad Roderigo.

Instead of a fight, as honours appeared to be even, they all built a snowman, complete with an old cape, a top hat and a clay pipe. It was almost eleven before Mary kissed Jack farewell, sent him inside, and headed for the stable. She wasn't too surprised when James followed her and silently prepared Satan to go out.

'Is there a reason you are following me about?' she asked.

'Of course,' he replied. And said no more. Mary stood beside her grey mare and frowned at him, her lips pursed. He glanced around and saw her face and broke into a soft laugh. 'I have never seen you pucker up so!' he declared.

'Well?' she pressed.

He gazed passed her out across the flat fenland and shrugged searching for an answer that she might accept. 'I thought I might pick up something about how to run an estate from watching you. It isn't something I know anything about. All I am, all I have ever wanted to be, is a soldier. But all knowledge is useful.' Her frown deepened and for a moment he thought she might argue, but finally she mounted and they prepared to ride out. As she swung into the saddle he commented, 'That man, Dunlop, he isn't going to go away.'

'No, I know. I will need to work hard to bring that community around. They are ashamed and leaderless and they have been led by a bully for more time than I realised. But if he turns into too large a problem, I will call on the magistrate and have him accused of murder, inciting riot and propagating witchcraft. The threat of hanging by the neck should get rid of him.'

James raised his eyebrows. He was becoming more impressed by Mary as landlord as each day passed. He wasn't always sure, however, how much woman was left inside.

Home Farm was spotless and neat. The yard had no rubbish in it, the barns were well maintained, and what stock he could see looked bursting with health. Even the hens scuttling around seemed to have had their feathers groomed. James didn't want to be so impressed, but he was. He knew what effort and proficiency, 'clean and tidy' took.

They ate bread and cheese with hot, dark brown, tea, and then James left Mary to chat with Betty Smith while he was shown some of the farm by Ted. They were standing outside, leaning companionably on a fence while Ted sucked on his pipe and blew smoke rings up to the sky when James found himself saying, 'I had a sister once, a clever girl, she told me the horizon at sea was about twenty miles before the curve of the Earth fell away. I think this land is as flat and a man can see just as far.'

'She died?' Ted asked.

'I have no idea,' James admitted. 'We were separated when I was eleven and she fourteen. That was over ten years ago. Now I am home I want to see if I can out what happened to her.'

Ted turned and looked at him but made no comment. James was finding him comfortable company. Then Ted asked, 'What is the Peninsula like?'

'Varied. There are green mountains and places as dry as dust for miles.' He looked up to the heavens, 'The last time I was in snow with such a crystal sky I was in the high Sierras in northern Spain.'

Ted gazed at him and then said, 'Bad, was it lad?'

'Bad enough,' James admitted. If the nightmares ever stopped, he would be surprised. He changed the subject. 'Is the estate profitable?'

'Oh aye!' Ted told him with a laugh. 'She is a skilled landlord and fair and knows her stuff. But think on. Most estates this size have a man running them. A man who goes to London and gambles. Who wants a new coach with four matched horses pulling it, and who pays off his mistresses with gems worth a ransom every so often. Mary does none of that. She makes Mags darn her skirts when she tears them! It isn't only that she is good at what she does, she is frugal and we have all benefited.'

James hadn't thought about that. Now he did, he was amazed at how small Mary's household was. Two experienced women, three youngsters, the cook, and Sally. Yet the estate seemed substantial. Another question was buzzing in his head.

'Was Brewer really seventy?'

Ted gave a snort, 'Might have been eighty, for all I know. It all happened so quickly. None of us knew Brewer; I don't think he had been friends with the Earl for all that long. News went out about the death and the funeral was arranged for three days later. It all felt rushed, and some areas, such as people he had done business with in Lincoln or Hull, hadn't heard about his death before the funeral was done and dusted, so they never got the chance to pay their respects.

'We were all standing around the grave and young Mary was there as white as a new sheet and looking as though she was still in shock, when the vicar herded us all back into the church. Word was going around that there was to be a wedding. Now, some girls of sixteen are set for marriage, but some aren't, and Mary wasn't. She was still a child, we all knew that. She stood at the front looking pale and thin and as if she was in a nightmare she hoped she would wake up from. Brewer was next to her and, honestly, I thought he was to give her away. It never occurred to me he was the groom. Then the service began and a murmur went around the congregation. By the time the vicar asked if there was any just cause the wedding couldn't go ahead, we all sat there looking at each other. Betty and I didn't know what to think, but we assumed that as she was so young and had no relatives he was putting a ring on her finger to keep her looked after and safe. It never crossed anyone's mind the filthy bugger would lay a finger on her. When it was clear she was with child, well, the women went wild. They blamed the husbands for not speaking up, but what could we have done? We all went to Brewer's funeral for Lady Mary's sake, but I know I wasn't the only one who wanted to dance on his grave. The only good to come out of it is her little lad. He is a fine one and a son to be proud of. That she dotes on him is clear.'

They stood again in silence as Smith refilled his pipe and James thought over what he had learned. Gradually they became aware of a figure racing over the rutted fields towards them. Ted stood upright and moved across the yard towards the figure. Then Mary and Betty came out of the kitchen door. Mary spun on her heel and was clearly beginning to make haste to leave. James headed to join her. They had the horses packed and ready as the lad reached them. Gasping the child blurted out,

'It is Auntie Annie, my lady!'

'So I guessed,' Mary called to him. 'Did your uncle send you?'

'Aye, my lady, I came as fast as I could.'

'I will get there as quickly as possible. Go in and get warm before you head back.' At that the lad looked ready to collapse with the relief that his task was done.

Mary turned to James, 'Go back,' she instructed.

'Why? Where are you going?' He was beginning to hate her roaming around alone more and more.

'To deliver a baby,' she glanced over her shoulder, 'and this is one is not likely to go well.'

'You deliver babies?' he called, but she was gone, leaning over the neck of the grey and racing over the iron hard ground.

He didn't catch up until they were scrambling into the yard of a small farmhouse.

'Mary, why did they come for you?'

'James, go home. This is my twentieth babe. There will be no room for you here and nothing to do.'

James ignored her and shooed her in while he saw to their mounts.

When he entered the farmhouse a sheet had been strung on a rope across the room to divide it in two. Behind the sheet he could make out the shadows of a bed with people around it. The fire was roaring and he was glad of it. A man emerged, shirtsleeves rolled to his elbows and looking worried. James introduced himself and the man immediately fetched a bottle of brandy and slumped in a chair facing the sheet. James sat opposite and accepted a glass.

'Got any bairns?' the man, who had given his name as Geoffrey Folstead asked.

'No,' said James, with his fingers slightly crossed.

'Aye well. This is our fourth. Lady Mary says that is good. First babies are the hardest for the mother to deliver. Late ones are a bit easier.' James looked puzzled. Seeing his expression Folstead added, 'Babies come out head first, if you are lucky. This one is showing the world his arse first.'

James licked his lips then frowning asked, 'Is that bad?'

'Aye,' said Felstead taking a large swig of brandy, 'I could, probably will, lose both of them.'

'Ah,' said James.

At that point Mary appeared with a willowy young girl beside her.

'You are right Geoff. The little one hasn't turned the right way round and Annie is well into her labour.' The girl beside Mary looked white but determined.

'I need her moved, Geoff, will you help? Before you pass out from the brandy,' she smiled. 'Carol here is being a great help. Are the other two with your sister?'

Geoff nodded and made to move behind the sheet and obey Mary's commands. When he returned James asked,

'What is Lady Mary doing?' He asked the question wondering if he could do more than just keep Folstead company.

'She has moved my Annie to the end of the bed. She says it will be a slow do.'

James nodded and sipped some more brandy. He had heard women in labour before, but had never sat this close, or watched the agony on a man's face as he grappled with the fact that the outcome was unlikely to be a good one.

It took twelve hours and Mary didn't rest once. For all that time he heard her voice reassuring, informing and comforting. Annie grunted and groaned, but James was grateful did not scream. And then at last there was an unmistakable cry. Folstead, who had been asleep in his chair shot upright and headed behind the sheet. James sat forward and twisted round. Eventually Mary appeared and he leapt up as she swayed on her feet.

'How are you?' he asked softly. And she burst into tears. He wrapped her in his arms and let her sob. She felt small and fragile against him and he felt a rising anger that this woman carried so much on her shoulders. That she wanted a companion made perfect sense. Half a dozen might make even more!

It was not yet dawn, but James was certain he knew the direct way to Swann Manor. He prepared the horses, who were not keen about moving from their stable, and tied them by the farm door as Mary appeared.

'What are you doing?' she asked when she saw her grey tied behind Satan.

'Come up on Satan and let me carry you home.' He watched as she opened her mouth to protest, then said,

'My father used to carry me about like that.'

Getting on and comfortable wasn't easy, especially with his leg, but the ride home across the moon-lit fields and tracks with the snow all shadows and sharp edges, a field of stars above, was both soothing and peaceful. The only noise was the creak of the saddle leather and the breathing of the horses. It was as if they were the only two people in the world. James felt more relaxed and contented than he believed he had felt in years. Mary had crystallised into a real woman with her sobs, as had his feelings for her. The relief her tears had given her he could understand, having felt similarly at times, especially when after the stress of battle men, or women, he had known and cared about had died. He let his mind float and concentrated on the feel of her warmth in his arms and wished he could keep her there and never let her go. It was time to leave, he realised. He was going to find not seeing her every day painful and he needed to go while she was still indifferent to him. He hadn't intended to become fond of her, but how could he not? She was one in a million and his respect had grown day by day. He'd like to know exactly how Lady Mary of Swann Manor became a midwife though! There was definitely a tale there.

He and Hal had decided to stay one more day and then leave at daybreak on the next. James would write the letter of introduction Mary needed as soon as he was back in London and ensure it was delivered by hand. That way there would be no delay and no mistake. James longed to ask Hal what the situation was with him and Mags, but kept his tongue behind his teeth. Hal would let him know in due course. Certainly, he and Mags seemed more than fond of each other if the glances they shared were anything to go by.

Mary felt decidedly out of sorts. The morning had flown by; James had taken Jack to help him groom the horses and Hal and Mags had simply taken themselves off somewhere private. Elfie was eating a little more than she had and the terror in her eyes was easing, though she still hadn't spoken. Mary strolled into the parlour after lunch, ostensibly hunting for a book, but actually seeking out James, when she came upon the tableau of James sitting in the chair he had during his stay appropriated for himself with Jack leaning his forearms on James' thigh, his face cupped in his hands and one leg bent as he swung his foot back and forth. Something hit Mary hard in the chest and then she spotted Elfie, cradled in James' left arm, small body pressed into his. James was chatting to Jack and then he turned to Elfie to include her. Elfie's eyes lit up with adoration and a small hand gently reached up and stroked James' cheek. The smile he gave in return nearly broke her. What might it take to make him look at her like that? Then James realised she was there. His dark blue eyes caught at hers, and the look in them was so intent she felt herself gasp, and then his face smoothed out to a blank. Shaken, Mary fled to her study to do what she ought to have been doing in the first place.

Once there, she doubted herself. Had she interpreted that look correctly? It had been so quick, a mere moment. For that brief instant she had thought he had shown the same longing that ached within her. The bridge of her nose prickled and her chest constricted. She knew she was close to tears, for really, no reason at all, but she was Lady Mary Swann; she never cried. Accounts had never felt like such a welcome escape before.

. . .

They were about to leave. James had little to pack, but equally, did not wish to leave anything behind by mistake; he never wanted to be forced to have any more contact with Swann Manor. Satan was going to have to be tied behind the coach, something he was definitely going to have strong ideas about. He was leaving his room when he bumped into Mary going towards hers. She stopped. The upper landing was gloomy with little light from anywhere and bitterly cold. She was wearing a woollen shawl over her shoulders and one side had slipped down. They stood in the itchy-eyed light and neither spoke. Then James reached across and gently returned her shawl to her shoulder. His hand rested on her and he found he couldn't bring himself to move it. Ah, he thought, war. It took more than was ever visible. She was a cruel mistress. Mary didn't move, she just stood in front of him until her head tipped forward and she rested her forehead on his chest. When she breathed his name, James, he had to swallow the emotion down. He ran his hand down her arm to her wrist and gripped. Moving slowly, he pulled her hand across towards his groin and pressed her palm flat against the front of the fall of his trousers.

'Sweet lass,' he whispered, 'you need a man, not a eunuch.'

Her face lifted to his, questioning as he dropped her hand. Then he stepped back and moved past her.

The minute James and Hal had been waved away, Mary walked briskly to the study to find her father's dictionary. She hunted for ages before giving up. She was fairly sure what James had meant, but didn't have one clue how to spell 'eunuch' and wanted to be certain. She searched the 'U's with increasing frustration. Eventually she rode out to find the curate who was Cambridge educated, so surely could enlighten her. He had been keeping the church going since the vicar who had married her had died. Mary had attended his funeral and muttered all through the interment, 'I said no'. The curate rambled on about 'tales of the East' and how more people ought to be interested in them, but Mary came away more perplexed than ever. She would just have to trust James. He hadn't taken her hand and pressed it where he did for no reason. She would have to assume that more had been lost when the injury that caused his limp had occurred. The very idea made her want to first be sick and then cry and beat her fists at the heavens.

In the coach, James had turned his shoulder on Hal and was staring out at the flat fields, patterned still in the black and grey shapes and shadows of drifted snow and sodden mud. Hal allowed half an hour to pass and for Satan to stop muttering his objections and get his head down to the business of following quietly, before he said,

'Ignoring me, are you lad?'

James gave a great sigh and fell back against the squabs. 'Ignoring the whole bloody world, if you want the truth, old man.'

'Old man, hey? You are in a bad mood. What I want to know, is just how bad?'

James turned and frowned at him, 'What do you mean?'

'Bodies heal, lad. Yours has over and over again. Don't give up yet, in fact, don't give up ever.'

James' look became intent. There was little light in the carriage, but Hal felt that look like a sword at his throat. He added, 'You can't keep things from me. We have been together too long and lived through too much. Your rod doesn't work, does it?'

James threw his head hard back against the squabs.

'No,' he spat out. 'And yours clearly does. And if you think I am bitter about that, you are right. I don't mean to be, but I am bitter about every other bloody man who can bed a woman.'

Hal sat quiet for a long time. He had had his suspicions, but he hadn't wanted to push the matter. He was full of a sick fear. James meant more to him than any other man and he was determined to help him to come to terms with this. What worried him, was whether any man could? Any man like James; young, determined and, he suspected, half way to being in love. That was the cracker. Without Mary in the picture, the whole problem became one of time. But that woman was one in a million, they both knew it, and she and James would almost certainly have suited. Hal suspected a woman like that came along once in a generation and the thought didn't cheer him. It was James who broke the silence.

'She needs a husband. And I won't do.'

There seemed nothing more to say, so Hal sat on his fear. How he was going to convince James that life was worth continuing with, he wasn't sure. It was going to be a damnable task, but he had to try. He and Mags could wait, James couldn't. Not just now.

Chapter Seven

Mary arrived in London in the pouring rain of Spring 1816. And the rain was filthy, as it wiped soot and smoke out of the air. She wondered if she was so fed up with the wild openness of Lincolnshire that this really might be an improvement? At least the air there was clean!

She had rented a small three-bedroomed terraced house with room in the attic for the few servants, a couple brought with them, some hired, that they might need. She didn't want to cause any kind of stir in London. Not yet. She wished to be socially invisible for the time being. Mags set to, to improve both the comfort of the house and its cleanliness, while their own servants wandered the local streets to find out where decent meat and vegetables might be found. They all returned scathing about both the quality and freshness of both.

It wasn't difficult to find both a lady to improve Mary's speech and crisp up her Lincolnshire drawl and a man to teach dancing. The dancing she found relatively easy; altering her speech much harder. Besides, she was who she was, she didn't want to pretend to be someone or something she wasn't. However, she had to admit, she didn't want to be mocked for her country ways. James had said she needed some polish and she was determined to work hard to ensure her trip was a success.

Some things in London were better, she had to admit. She had ensured she was fitted for some better gowns, but with a back-street modiste not one of the well-known ones the rich used. She wished to be 'London fashionable' but not give away who she was or why she was in London, not yet. Mags too had to be provided with some fresh dresses, but she was as grumpy as a cow in labour with the whole process and Mary let her wander off with one of the footmen that came with the rented house and explore, instead of remaining with her and waiting. Which proved fortuitous. Mags came back with all sorts of small items that made life more comfortable, and fun. Mary had always thought her dry, flaky skin was due to being out of doors so much, but when she bathed with some 'French milled' soap Mags had found, her skin became much finer and softer.

'About as French as Wandsworth,' Mags muttered.

'I don't care,' Mary said, kissing her cheek, 'I love it. Go out tomorrow and buy a huge box of it. We will send it home. I don't ever want to wash with Lincolnshire soap again.'

'Getting too high for the rest of us,' Mags said shaking her head, but her eyes were laughing.

The days slipped by and every time James came into her mind she shoved the thought away. It simply hurt too much to think about him. She had a strong sense that he would have been perfect for her and he seemed to have buried himself deep inside her heart, but she would use him as she had used all her hurts. Meeting him, having feelings for him, had convinced her she really did want a husband. Jack needed a man and so did she. She would go hunting; but first she would arm herself. And, she thought, she would smell nice doing it!

They had been in the small house a month when quite late one night there was a scatter of stones on the drawing room window. Mary and Mags lifted their heads and frowned at each other. It was Mags who was nearest and therefore moved to the window.

'It's Hal!' she exclaimed. And shot out of the room.

Mary looked down into the dark street below to see Mags run to Hal and receive a hasty kiss. They parted and were clearly whispering intently. Mags swung around and vanished, while Hal looked up to Mary and gave a wave. Mags burst into the room, 'James is dying. Hal wants us to come and be with him.' Without thought they both grabbed outer clothing and hurried out into the street.

James and Hal had rented a similar small terraced house, only two streets away. Mary wondered if that had been deliberate, but didn't ask. She didn't want to know; any answer might hurt. James was in a side room to the kitchen, the door open so the kitchen fire could warm him and was laid out on a bed that might have been intended for a housekeeper or cook. At first glance Mary thought he was already dead. She rushed over and gazed at his face. He seemed unconscious and was coated in perspiration. His pallor and his white lips terrified her. With one swift movement she swept the sheet back to look at him. He was naked and what caught her eye was the dark black mark high on his left thigh. Crossing to that side she peered down at it.

'What is that?' she asked.

'Shrapnel,' came Hal's incomprehensible reply. Mary turned to look at him. 'A cannon blew apart and some of it buried itself in his leg. The surgeons refused to amputate as it was so high on the thigh, but gave him a couple of weeks to live. Bugger refused to die and just kept going. He seemed to be better, well, managing the pain, but two days ago he began to fail and when I looked the metal seemed much closer to the skin. I think it has moved.'

Mary ran her fingertips gently over the surface of what she could see pushing against the skin. She turned to look at Hal.

'You are right. He is dying. I have no doubt of that and have seen it all too often, as have you.' Hal nodded. 'What do the doctors and surgeons say now?'

'I have had three to him,' Hal told her. 'They all wanted to bleed him, which I refused, then said they could do nothing more for him.'

Mary stood thinking for a moment, then she turned to Hal,

'You are a blacksmith,' she stated, 'how sharp can you make a blade? Can you sharpen an edge to shave hair without even grazing the skin?'

Hal nodded.

'Can you do it twice?'

He nodded again. Then without a word turned and left the room. Mary picked up a beaker and with her fingers moistened James' lips.

'What are you going to do?' whispered Mags.

'Cut it out. While it is in him, he will certainly die. If I remove it, he will have a deep wound that he may recover from. When it happened I can only assume the metal was so deep the army surgeons could do nothing. Since then it has moved through the body to the surface. I have seen it happen once before. A miller had a piece of wood as large as my palm in his calf. He was in pain, but I didn't think I could do anything for him as it was so deep. Two years later he sent for me as it had risen to just under the surface of the skin. A surgeon in Lincoln had cut it out and he recovered. One calf was always thin but he said the pain was much less. I was glad for him. He let me examine the healed wound. It is a slim chance, because fever will likely take James, as it could so easily have taken the miller. But he lived. And now I can only try.'

'If he dies, you could hang for murder.' Mags' voice was certain.

Mary grinned at her, 'Then marry Hal and look after the children for me,' and she began to strip off any non-essential clothing. At least her dress was navy blue. It was a good colour for not showing blood.

Mags put two pots of water on the fire, one small and one large and then whisked out to find blankets and clean linens. Mary wiped the sweat off James' face, moistened his parched mouth, and whispered to him that she was going to hurt him but she was determined he should not die and that he had to fight hard to survive.

James had lost so much weight in a handful of weeks that they found the three of them could lift him onto the kitchen table. That was now covered in two costly wool blankets that were about to be ruined and a linen sheet that while clean looked fit to be disposed of anyway.

Mary laid him out as she wanted him and then began to wash around the wound and shave the hair away from his thigh.

'Why are you doing that?' Hal asked.

Mary answered without looking at him. 'I have delivered twenty babies and so far, all have lived. The woman who taught me, Betsy, asked me if I would eat a cow pat. I felt sick, and said of course not. She said that it was possible to eat filth and live, because the stomach was used to all sorts going into it, including dirt on badly washed vegetables and so on. But, she said, the body doesn't take in food from through a woman's private parts, so we shouldn't fill it with grime or dirt. So whenever I deliver a baby, I do exactly as Betsy taught me, I wash my hands and any tools I need to use. So I shall do the same here. Skin keeps dirt out, so logically, I shouldn't put dirt below the skin. And I get rid of dirt by washing.'

Hal thought about the battlefield surgeons who would use the same saw all day for amputations on man after man and were not unknown to drop pipe ash or part of their lunch into the wounds. Most of those men died. He was content to let Mary do what she wished; he suspected it was all nonsense but he saw no reason to make her change her ways.

Mary had the fire at her back and was soon sweating as much as James. Removing the metal didn't take long but repairing the hole in his thigh took ages. She sewed tissue where she could. Tied cotton thread around anything that seemed to leak too much blood and eventually poured a bottle of brandy in the wound and then sewed it up. The sun was up and she was swaying on her feet. James wasn't dead. Yet.

'I am accustomed to splinting broken bones and with help can put a shoulder back in place, but I have never cut into a body before,' she told Hal.

'You two lasses get home. I will send news as soon as I know how he is doing. If he is going to die, I think it will be soon.'

Mary gave a tired nod and then she and Mags slipped away from the house. A house they would have to swear they knew nothing about if James did indeed die.

The notes came every day, always addressed to Mags. And every day James lived. Well, he breathed and was occasionally conscious. Then, for a few days, he had a fever and it seemed he was lost to them, but then he began to rally. Both Mary and Mags lost weight without trying and begun to look as gaunt as James had. Mags always blushed when she opened the notes and Mary was well aware there was more written on the paper than just information about whether James was alive or not.

'When are you two going to marry,' she asked.

Mags looked at her. 'Well, not before James is well. He is like a son to Hal. Has he told you how they met?'

'Not really. Hal arrived with the coach when James was with us at the Manor. We didn't get around to discussing much of their past together.'

'Well, he and his two sons joined the army and they were all sent to India. When both boys died, Hal deserted and went looking for a passage home. What he found was James, sick with a fever. He nursed him back to health then joined a new regiment as James' sergeant and valet. So, he could be shot for desertion but he never actually left the army! He and James have been together ever since.'

Mary was thoughtful, 'It is clear they are devoted to each other.'

Mags looked at her, 'As I am to you. And when James is well and you are married, we will marry.'

'I don't want you to wait that long.'

Mags smiled, 'And you don't have a say in it.'

'Is Hal really serious? Do you believe he genuinely wants to marry you?'

'Yes. I believe him.' And with that Mags went back to her sewing.

Six weeks flew by and Hal came in person. He came to say James was much better and that they were heading out to stay in the country, taking things slowly with the coach. Mary took herself out for a walk leaving Hal and Mags to make their farewells. She had asked to go and visit James, but Hal said James had already refused her. Why, he didn't elaborate. Mary felt hurt and angry and frustrated. She longed to see him, but it was clear he didn't want to see her. The turmoil of her emotions was giving her a headache. Eventually she sat down on a bench in one of the parks and accepted that James was right. They had no future together and the pull they felt for each other was exhausting and fruitless. Only yet more hurt could come of being in each other's company. How the hurt could be greater than the one she was currently feeling she wasn't sure. She hadn't realised how much hope she had been fooling herself with. Well, she had never been a fool before, and it wasn't time to start.

As she sat on the bench she allowed her mind to go where it willed. Somewhere behind her, beyond a belt of trees, early riders could be heard thundering up and down and calling to each other. Apart from that, no one seemed to be around, but Mary wasn't in London inside her head, she was in Boston. She had been walking along the port, tired after selling grain in the Guildhall. The men there were now used to her and, although many of them still hated dealing with a woman, she was generally treated with respect. It was exhausting, though, dealing with their prejudice and not for the first time she wondered about employing an agent. The problem was, however tightly she managed a man, she would never trust him. She had tried twice, but both times the men had tried to cheat her, thinking that she wouldn't notice. She had fired a pistol at one to get rid of him. Not for the first time she wondered if she should have kept Jack's father on, but Jack's existence would have given him a hold over her. And she would never risk Jack's future by admitting Jack wasn't her husband's. Much like now, her thoughts on that waterfront had been whirling.

She had felt his gaze on her back. She had turned and, amidst the masts and rigging and sails and activity of a busy port, she had seen him. He had been standing about ten feet away, quite close. He might have been Spanish, a lot of Spaniards worked on the ships coming into the harbour. His skin was dark golden brown, his hair black, and he was wearing nothing but a pair of breeches. Dark hair spread wide across his chest and arrowed down to his waist. But it was his eyes that caught her. She had gazed back. His eyes spoke to her. He wanted her. She had felt it in a rush of warmth right through her guts. She had stood completely still as a fine rain blew in gusts across her bonnet and knew in her bones, that if she had walked towards him, he would have taken her below decks and banged her as hard as a hammer banged a nail. And she wanted it.

She had swallowed and, completely involuntarily, had licked her lips and instantly known that she had given herself away. His gaze had become more intense. Instead of walking towards him, she had turned and walked away. In her mind she had returned to the incident over and over again. It had felt so real, yet how could it have been? And she knew deep in her soul, that the real reason she had walked away was that she had no personal confidence. One of the reasons she could move among the men in the Guildhall was her personal ugliness; her tooth shoving out of her mouth into the air, her huge thick eyebrows running across her face, and her skin weathered from endless days in the saddle riding her lands. The sailor had been beautiful, she had not. She was sure she had read the situation correctly, yet how could she have done?

He wasn't the only man she had felt a flare of attraction towards. It happened now and then, never so intense, never in so strange a circumstance, nor with such outright lust. A flicker of heat as a hand briefly caught the skin of another, a gleam in an eye. That was all. Like a mare coming across a stallion, just a flicker that a mating might be acceptable. Always she had quashed it. Self-control had got her a long way. She had no intention of being a Mary Queen of Scots figure, destroyed by her own desire. But now she had got to the stage of wanting to find a mate. Jack was growing up fast. He had doted on James, nagged him every moment he could for tales about soldiering, about how to ride such a huge horse as Satan, clearly hero worshipping him. James' masculinity had called to Jack. For the first time there had been a man in the house he could model himself on. Mary wanted that for Jack; a man to guide him to adulthood. And she wanted to be that piece of wood that got hammered! And she wanted more children; lots of children. Her life was so lonely and up until now she hadn't minded; she had been working for Jack. Now they both needed more.

She walked back to the house determined to go back to Lincolnshire. She couldn't face the ballrooms yet. She needed time to turn herself into the kind of woman who might attract the type of man she wanted. And besides, she needed to outgrow the nightmares about that first incision into James' thigh. And what followed. Hard as she considered she was, that had taken her to her limits. The sight of his opened body, the blood, the terror that she might murder rather than help him. Nausea still swept her when her mind was unguarded at times, even in company in broad daylight. She would take Jack and Elfie and go home. Once her wounds were well and truly licked, she would return in full armour.

The summer flew by and both Jack and Elfie grew like weeds. Jack loved having a little sister to follow him and play with and Mary was relieved that her decision to keep the child as her own seemed to have been the right one. Gradually Elfie was coming out of her shell enough to say the occasional word and she was becoming tanned and rosy in the long summer days. She looked fair set to being a lovely child and young woman and Mary frowned wondering how she could give the girl a come-out into society when she hadn't had one herself. Despite her enquiries, no one seemed to know who her parents had been, or how her mother had come to die alone in the cottage.

Mags received regular letters from Hal but Mary never enquired about their contents and Mags never told her what was in them.

James meanwhile not only lived, but began to recover. After long months on his back, first with fever and then with healing, he began the process of hauling himself out of bed and beginning to move. As the days grew long and then short again, he marched up and down the drive of the house he had rented in the country with Hal, and then as soon as he could, lay across the back of a docile horse called Carrot. He was a shell of his former self. Muscle and sinew he had taken for granted all his life had wasted away. It shamed him deeply. More than he expected.

The Army's Son

He worked until he was exhausted, then slept, woke, and worked again. He chopped logs, walked and marched, eventually with a weighted pack on his back and rode for as much as his healing leg could take. At the same time he thought about Lucian, his elder brother. James wasn't rich and the rent on the house was eating into his funds whereas Lucian had inherited the estate they had grown up on. Surely he could stay there while he finished healing and discovered if the army wanted him back or not? As soon as he could manage the days on horseback it would take to get to Wiltshire and Causton; he would go and see.

Some of his colleagues had been in India fighting another Maratha war and yet others were out in the Americas. He longed to have his life back. He had no future except in the army. Mary he would not think about. He wasn't right for her. He had only his army pay and she needed a real man, not man whose rod remained stubbornly limp. He could think of a dozen reasons why he wasn't right for her, but she still frequented his dreams and his longings. He knew he would never meet a woman like her again. She would have made a wonderful army wife!

Hal found him one day as he was heaving an axe into logs with a regular rhythm sending chips flying hither and yon. He stood with his hands on his hips and his legs spread and regarded James, clearly wanting to interrupt him. James shot him an irritated glance then eventually stopped. 'You messed up my swing,' he protested, and then stood upright to mirror Hal with his hands on his hips and legs wide, just to annoy him. Hal gave a wry grin to indicate he knew what James was about and James relaxed his stance. 'What is it?' he asked Hal.

'You are well enough. Looks like you have chopped enough fuel for half a dozen winters. I want to marry Mags.'

James shielded the sun from his eyes and sighed. This had been coming for a long time. 'Go and marry the woman. I don't know why you have left it so long.' Hal didn't dignify that with an answer.

As Hal left he looked James over and instructed,

'And don't go opening that leg up again. The wound was deep and it will take a long while for that leg to strengthen.'

They both knew the minute he was gone James was riding for Causton.

'Where are you going to live?' James asked, to deflect him.

'No idea. Lincolnshire probably until young Mary is married off. She doesn't strike me as the kind to live the life of a nun all her days.'

James laughed out loud. No, Mary wasn't the nunnery type. Exactly why he wasn't for her, he thought wryly. 'Stay in touch,' James said. Which could be, they both knew, translated into, thank you for all you have done for me and I will miss you.

'Will you come to the wedding?' Hal countered with.

James frowned. 'If I do,' he said, 'I will stay at an inn.'

Hal nodded. They both knew that was wise.

With Hal gone there seemed no further point in remaining in the rented house. Now he could manage Satan it was time to be on the road. He took the journey slowly, revelling in the early Autumn weather. The trees were beginning to go gold at the edges and birds rose in clouds, smudges of pink and yellow, as they sought early hips and haws. Eventually, James rode around what had been the outskirts of Causton but was now row upon row of cottages. The village he had grown up in was now a town and James wondered at Lucian allowing so many people to build on what had been good farmland. He came to the Dower House first and paused. He could now identify it as a pretty Queen Anne, with a moulded gable at the front and four windows below and five above, giving a pleasing regular appearance.

It had been sadly neglected, however. Beech trees had grown up in front so it was almost invisible from the road and brambles heaped up as high as the tops of the ground floor windows. Miss Buckley had lived there. She had taught him the rudiments of reading, writing and arithmetic, but he had bored her. He hadn't found it easy, or perhaps it had seemed pointless and therefore dull to him. She hadn't been bored by his sister Chantel, who had soaked up everything Miss B had said and demanded more. He remembered one day watching her do arithmetic without numbers. At that point he really had given up. For some reason, he couldn't remember why, they had stopped going to the Dower House and Miss B had come to the Manor. He turned Satan, who was restless with standing still, and he and the big horse moved into the drive that led to Causton Manor, his childhood home.

Lucian was lying out in the late summer sunshine on cushions and rugs, yet more rugs heaped on his legs. He felt the cold acutely now. That was what he dreaded about death. The cold. He rather hoped he would go to hell, at least there it might be warm. Knowing his luck, he'd go to bloody heaven and freeze his balls off. He heard the horseman as soon as he turned into the drive. It was quiet here now with only him and Simon and that is how he liked it. Even the pond, which had once throbbed with frogs and clattered with ducks was silent now it had filled in with weeds.

The horseman came round the curve and into view, but by then Lucian had rung the bell by his side for Simon. He wasn't up to meeting strangers; Simon could do the honours. As the horseman slid from his mount and strode over, Lucian experienced a moment of utter panic. His father had risen from the dead and was coming for him. Finally, his time, which he had convinced himself he welcomed, had come, but he wasn't so sanguine now the moment really had arrived. The man stood before him, legs apart, hands behind his back, his thick rather long hair far too bright to be his father's. Surely William's hair would be grey by now? Panic retreated when the man said softly, 'Ah, Lucian. I find you at home then.' Lucian stared and then began a bout of coughing. When he could finally speak, and Simon had mopped the blood from his chin, he took in a breath to try to form the question,

'James?'

'At your service, big brother.'

They sat over the fire and a decent brandy for a long while. Lucian slipped into sleep sometimes, then awoke after twenty minutes or so, and continued. He wanted to know where James had been and what he had done. That he had made Major, clearly made him proud. The lad Simon spooned soup into him when he could and mixed the brandy into hot milk with nutmeg and honey. Neither of them discussed the fact that Lucian was clearly dying. At last, as the embers glowed and they all agreed to retire, Lucian grabbed for James' hand. 'Look after Simon when I am gone.' James nodded. Simon blushed beetroot and said nothing. 'You will be Lord Causton then,' he muttered. James frowned and went to find a mattress and some blankets to wrap himself in. The house was a ruin, with birds nesting in many of the rooms that were smothered with their droppings. Mice and rats had eaten holes into just about everything and woodworm had riddled the stairs and balustrades that James thought he could remember his mother polishing with beeswax and lavender. As he fell asleep he thought, 'Lord Causton. Damnation.' He had forgotten that with Lucian's death, he would have a title.

Lucian had no idea where Chantel was and had made no attempt to find her.

'How could I explain Simon?' he asked, as he kissed the back of one of Simon's hands softly.

James said nothing. He had seen too much to care who his brother, or anyone else, loved. That there was care and affection, was all that mattered. Death came all too soon, in his view, to worry about something that for many men was clearly natural. In the ranks secrecy ruled but everyone knew who the couples were. Officers could be more blatant, though the army didn't attract many of that persuasion. Why pay for a commission to be in an organisation that held countless people who could shoot you in the back surreptitiously if they didn't like your leanings? Often the ranks had not had that choice, but had been conscripted from poverty or the jail.

'Start at the school,' was all the advice Lucian could offer about Chantel. 'I sent her there, but she might have walked off like you did.'

James had three days with him before he died. He had him buried quietly by the local vicar and as the service ended, Simon vanished. James had impressed upon him that he took his promise to Lucian seriously, but the lad clearly just wanted to get away and grieve. He stood alone by the grave and gazed up at the clouds scudding above. Where the hell was Chantel? And how was he going to find her? But first he had a wedding to attend.

The church was full by the time Mary arrived, but she had wanted to stay with Mags until the last moment. Her intention to 'give Mags away' in place of her long-dead father had been met with initially spluttering indignation by the new young vicar and then silent entrenchment. Under no circumstances was a woman giving the bride away. Mary's insistence that he show where Church Law, the Gospels, or English Law forbade her to do it was met not by argument but by utter refusal to enter into a discussion. He wasn't having it, and if Mags wanted to be married by him, then she needed to find a man to fulfil the role. Mags had bitten her lip and kept quiet. She didn't care who 'gave her away', in her mind no one was and all she wanted to do was be Hal's wife. In the end, Ted Smith was delighted and honoured to be asked to fill the role.

It was gloomy inside and Mary stood for a moment to let her eyes adjust. Mags and Ted Smith were immediately behind her and she needed to reach her seat right at the front quickly. As she stepped forward she could now see the two men down by the altar, but it was only one she gazed at. Hal had not said a word as to who would be he groomsman and Mary hadn't asked. She had hoped, and dreaded, it might be James, with a whirl of emotion she had been determined to quell. And now, there he was, looking straight at her, his intense blue eyes never leaving hers as she walked quickly forward towards her place. She couldn't look away and felt her chest constrict and tears threaten. He looked magnificent.

A head taller than most men he was broad shouldered and deep chested with narrow hips and the light from the window behind and to one side him lit him clearly. She had never seen him in his best regimentals, but had always vaguely assumed they would be the scarlet jacket and white breeches she had seen soldiers in when she had been in Lincoln or Boston. Instead he was in darkest green. His jacket had black frogging across the front and his trousers, or overalls as she had heard them referred to, had leather running up the inside, to give wear on long rides she assumed, which fed into mid-calf boots that curved in at the top in two sweeping lines into the centre. On one shoulder was slung a pelisse, again of dark green, trimmed with brown fur and held with a silk cord across his chest. His sword in black and silver, huge and with a dangerous curve, was laid beside his shako on a stool. The hat was an exotic shape being rather like a bell, with a large black cockade at the top. Whoever designed the uniform was a master. He stood like every woman, and man's, dream warrior. Mary knew her late arrival would go unnoticed. Not an eye would see her; every pair would be on the glorious male standing facing them.

Mary reached her seat and bowed her head to hide her flushed face. His gaze had burnt her to the core. How she wanted him! And how could there be a God when such a man was impotent! If she had doubted in the Grace of God the vicar repeatedly banged on about, Mary now knew to the core of her being it didn't exist. Or if it did, not for her.

She didn't hear a word of the service and unashamedly glued her eyes to James throughout. She didn't care if people noticed. She may never see him again and if this was the last time she saw him she wanted to drink her fill. When it was over and the happy couple walked back up the aisle Mary followed as she had to. She felt James's eyes behind her burning into her back and knew that he wanted her as much as she wanted him. But she had to smile and nod and play the hostess. And when James vanished as invisibly as he had arrived she was not surprised. They had not spoken a word and did not need to.

That night she lay staring upwards, unsleeping, in too much pain to cry.

. . .

James headed straight for Bath. Or as straight as the winding muddy ditches that often passed in England for roads allowed him. When he saw a toll gate he unashamedly crossed country. He had bugger all money to his name and had no idea how long it might take to hunt down his sister. Having watched Lucian die, he had a knot in his gut about Chantel. The idea that she might be in trouble or dead bothered him. And the fact that it did made him twist with guilt. At eleven, with dreams of becoming a soldier, he had seen Chantel at fourteen as a grown-up. Now, an army Major with years of battles behind him, he was wondering at which point he should have begun to consider her situation. Surely at some stage he should have realised that he ought to at least be in correspondence with her, shouldn't he? Life had flown by like a river, one day flowing smoothly into the next. Either there were battles to train and prepare for, men to command and care for, or wounds to recover from, always something. But what on earth had happened to Tilly? How the hell could Lucian have discarded her in that way? Could he, should he, have done better?

The thoughts whirled right up to the school gates. Yes, Chantel had finished her schooling there, yes, although they didn't know her whereabouts exactly, they could hint him on his way. She had married the Duke of Daughton. James was speechless and unaccountably angry. Married to a bloody Duke! How did that happen? What was she playing at? She couldn't be a bloody Duchess! Except it seems she was. He sipped tea with the headmistress and two of the teachers as politely as he could all the while being relieved he had worn his best regimentals, even though the pelisse was a bloody nuisance to keep in place, as it occurred to him that his visit had made their whole year and in his well-worn riding clothes he would have ruined their idolised view of their ex-pupil!

Not only had they plied him with tea and cakes, they had owned a Debretts. He now knew where the site of the old Daughton Castle was, and the new house called The Court. It was closer than the ducal home in London so he decided to begin the next stage of his hunt there.

It wasn't hard to find. When he was still miles from his destination he could see it, high on a swell of land dominating the area. As he drew closer, planning all the while how a siege might take place and what defences the place might have, just as personal amusement, he told himself, he began to realise it had the appearance of Badajoz. After the army had blown it to pieces. Now he was again wondering exactly what had become of Chantel.

The house was tending towards a slum; the grounds unkempt. It was the kind of place the army might bivouac in because a regiment could bed down there and no one need worry about the damage caused. James found the duke a surprise too. Daughton was a fair-haired unprepossessing man with an uncertain manner. The army didn't do uncertainty. He didn't appear clever either. James had never thought that his wild and happy sister would sell herself for a title, but it seemed that was indeed what she had done. After a brief introduction, Chantel let him deeper into the house.

James stood inside the study gazing around, before walking forward and taking a seat. Chantel lifted her chin defiantly, as if guessing why he was there. What came out of his mouth was crude and insensitive. He hadn't intended to be so crass; perhaps it was the discomfort of his realisation that he had probably let Chantel down over the years and the thought that she had possibly had to sell herself in marriage to survive.

'I believe you have something of mine. The Causton patrimony.'

Chantel flinched. If she had ever had time to wonder what meeting James again might be like it wasn't this bald attack. His voice was quiet and deep and measured. Chantel found herself looking into eyes as hard as flint. Gone was the little boy who had whooped his way around Causton Hall wielding a wooden sword; gone was the boy who sat at dinner every night with curious eyes, saying little and missing nothing; gone was the small body with icy feet who crept for comfort into the bed of his big sister. What she now faced was a stern-faced battle-hardened warrior. Who was not pleased with her. She almost wished she had Joshua beside her to support her but pride made her lift her chin even higher.

'Lucian gave it to me.'

'And I would like it back.' His gaze didn't falter. 'You have done well for yourself. I never dreamt my sister might aim so high.'

Chantel felt her cheeks warm. She hadn't aimed to be a duchess. She had aimed not to have a boring life consisting of nothing more than gossip, new clothes, and wasting money.

'It has all gone,' she said, and was ashamed that her voice was uneven. This man, this man who was the closest relative she had in the world, frightened her. And men never frightened her.

To her surprise James seemed to slump a little and rubbed his hands over his face as if exhausted. Then he sat up straight again. 'Well pay it back.'

'Why do you want it?' she heard herself ask.

For the first time there was a tinge of a different emotion in the words. 'Causton needs it. And I don't have enough. I need the patrimony.' He paused before asking intently, 'Have you *seen* Causton?'

'No,' she admitted, 'I was forbidden to go there years ago and have never gone back. Why would I? It was Lucian's responsibility.'

James just looked at her. A long cold gaze that caused her blush to deepen further. Why should she explain herself? She had been thrown away like so much rubbish and left to fend for herself.

'What did you do with it?' he asked.

Chantel swallowed and wondered how to answer. Eventually she said, 'I invested it into two and a half houses to rent. The third is still being paid for over a fifteen-year agreement. I had responsibilities; people who depended on me.'

'Well, you are married now, sign the houses over to me. I will collect the rents and continue the agreement.' Surely, he thought, the duchy cannot be as impoverished as this house suggested.

Chantel wished she felt a little braver. 'I have mortgaged them,' she almost whispered. She knew she had done wrong. The patrimony was given to her to support her, not for her to use to support a bankrupt duchy.

James' face didn't alter. He just sat and held her eyes with his. Then he said blankly,

'Liked the good life did you?'

Instead of fighting back, Chantel almost collapsed. 'Lucian forbade me to go back to Causton as he knew I would take over running it. It was my dream to carry on the work of father and Sam. I was not a success on the marriage market and Joshua inherited unexpectedly. We agreed to a 'white' marriage. His brothers, father and grandfather had bankrupted the whole duchy. All he had inherited was a title and a mountain of debt. I promised to try to turn the duchy round and make it pay and he agreed not to interfere, but instead to live off an allowance. He has kept his word and I have kept mine. I have the challenge I have always longed for, and he knows I will keep him from dropping into the shame of being a duke who ought to be debtor's prison. He knows his rank would protect him, but he would be a social outcast. Because of the entailment, the land still exists, though poorly managed and everything that could be broken is, but we are beginning to turn everything around.' She tried to see if her words had had any effect. She could hear the exhaustion in her voice when she said, 'I rise at five-thirty every morning and begin work, I stop at ten to wash and eat, and then work until I drop. Then I nap and start again. Day in. Day out.'

For the first time James seemed to soften. 'I see,' he said slowly. And then he said,

'We don't know each other, do we.'

'Stay for a while,' Chantel blurted out. To her horror two tears slipped down her cheeks. 'I don't cry,' she said, 'ever.'

James gave a gentle smile that softened his features. 'Of course not,' he said. Luc was dead. There was now, out of that bustling Tudor manor house that had been the heart of the Causton estate, only the two of them left. It didn't seem possible, but there it was.

Chapter Eight

Mary and Hal were in a coach travelling to visit a duchess. Well, Mary was. Mags had woken up feverish and with a streaming head cold, so Mary was on her way to introduce herself to the Duchess of Southwald on her own. Well, not quite on her own. Hal had insisted on travelling inside the coach with her, and then there was her coachman and guard, both of whom she hardly knew as she had had to employ them from Lincoln. They had proved excellent however, cleaning and repairing the coach in the week before the journey to London and she was beginning to trust them. Whether Hal did, was another matter. Did he think they might run off with the coach if he wasn't there? She had decided not to ask.

'Nervous?' Hal asked.

'A little. Rumbustious farmers who think women don't have brains I am used to. Duchesses, less so.'

Hal chuckled, and Mary felt better. She let silence fill the coach for a while, well, apart from the yells and cries from the street and the constant clatter of horseshoes on cobbles.

'He still isn't thinking about marriage?' she ventured. They both knew who she was asking about and what physical impairment she was referring to. And it wasn't his weak leg.

'No lass,' was the quiet reply.

Mary turned away to gaze out of the window. There was no point in regrets. There was only the future and a son who needed a stepfather. And she would lay down her life for her son.

'At least it isn't raining,' she thought, as she climbed the steps to hand in her card and ask for the Duchess of Southwald. She had been as good as James' word and had declared herself willing to sponsor Mary for her husband-hunting season. Although letters had been exchanged, and Mary wasn't going to admit it but she had checked every one of her own words with the dictionary, they had yet to meet. Mary took in a deep breath, gave a quick glance back to Hal standing by the coach, and stepped into the hall. It was a wide and lovely space and Mary looked around and up with appreciation. It was white and pale blue, with beautiful plaster work and a pale green and white marble floor. A mixture of large green plants and white statues stood in large niches. It was only as she was gazing around she realised that beside the footman standing beside her there were five others in a full livery of deep blue and gold by each door. They all stood with military precision facing straight ahead. Not one turned his head to view her.

A woman came walking towards her. She had fair hair swept up in a smooth style and was wearing a dress of dark blue silk. 'She matches her hall and footmen,' Mary thought and hoped her face showed nothing except polite gratitude.

'Lady Mary Swann?', the woman said, and gave her a welcoming smile that settled Mary's nerves somewhat. After exchanging greetings the duchess escorted Mary to a downstairs room. As they approached the door, the footman on duty leaned forward and opened the door for them, once they had entered he, presumably, closed it again. Mary stood for a moment staring at the shut door. 'What a waste of a man!' she thought; she would have rather had him ploughing a field or making a wheel. Not for the first time, London made her feel out of joint. She felt a flutter of panic, how would she find a husband here?

'It was more than kind of you to agree to help me,' Mary began. 'I really do not know anyone in London, or elsewhere, who might help me.'

'Well, Captain, or rather, Major Causton once did my husband and I a serious favour. We are grateful to him. My husband rashly invited him to ask if there was ever anything we could do for him.'

Mary felt her cheeks go pink. Ah, not a particularly willing favour, then. 'I don't actually know what that favour was?' Mary enquired.

'No, I suppose not. He appears to be a somewhat modest man. My husband assumed he would ask for money.'

Mary felt a swell of rage on James' behalf. How dare this woman say such a thing. Something must have shown on her face, because the duchess quickly added, 'He carried our only son to a surgeon. He found him buried under a pile of the dead the day after a battle. Our eldest son had died of the measles and we had not had time to ask Gervaise to return home.'

'I hope your son is well?'

'He has had an arm amputated.' The woman turned to look past Mary out of the window. For the first time Mary saw the grief. She had lost one son and then had another return damaged from a brutal war.

'Many men have returned in such a state,' Mary said softly. 'I had a man request work once. He had lost both a part of his right arm and his left leg. He stayed for the summer to work in my stables and was excellent. He impressed me.' And then she added, 'I have a small son, which is why I wish to marry.'

Something in the woman softened. 'I see. You did not explain that in your letters.'

And the very air changed. Mary became not a burden to entertain when the woman was still coming to terms with her losses, but just another mother. They would not become friends, Mary thought, but they would deal together amicably.

. . .

Once back at home, Mags asked through coughs and sniffles, 'What was she like?'

'Reserved, I think, rather than unfriendly. She has lost her eldest son to disease and her second lost an arm in the war. I am not sure she would trouble with the London season this year except that James has requested it of her. She said she was to host a ball and she would put me in the receiving line. I didn't dare ask if she would have bothered holding a ball if it wasn't for me. I was too scared of the answer.'

'Did she have any advice?'

'Oh yes, better clothes, I am to call and collect her dresser tomorrow and she will introduce me to the correct modistes. Also, I have to try and lose even more of my 'provincial accent', I did have the nerve to ask about that one.'

'What did you say?' Mags sounded aghast. She had known Mary a long time.

'I merely suggested that it might appeal to a provincial man seeking a wife.'

After a huge sneeze Mags asked, 'How did she take that?'

'I think, well, hope, she liked me the better for it.'

'And what is a dresser?'

'A servant whose job is to help the duchess dress and undress and maintain her clothes in good order.'

'Is that a whole job? I do that for you when you need it and also run the house!'

'Yes,' Mary leant forward and kissed her forehead, 'but you are a pearl above rubies.'

Mags frowned, 'Have you misquoted that?'

Mary grinned, 'I may have done. Now, get well so you can join in the fun soon. Hal isn't going to like being dragged around Burlington Arcade and Regent Street by me, now is he?'

Mags gave a huge sigh and Mary tucked her under the covers and left her to sleep.

It was the first time in Mary's life that she had been free to enjoy herself. And she found it hard. She found she was worrying about what was happening on the estate and how the children were. It hadn't seemed wise to bring them with her. She missed them, both of them, with a keen ache. Jack still translated Elfie's wishes into words and the two of them seemed to have an almost supernatural understanding of each other. But as she began to sink into the whirl of shopping and afternoon visiting, she began to make, if not friends, then acquaintances who would make her more public social events that were to come more comfortable. And shopping for clothes; clothes that need not last forever, that need not be warm and sensible, that need not be in dull colours, became a joy that Mary revelled in. The duchess's dresser, a dour woman called Enid, had found her one modiste whom Mary adored. This woman skipped straight over the pale colours and swirled out vivid blues, greens and reds.

'You, I think, are a vivid woman. You need the vivid colours,' she had declared. She was also the only modiste that Mary believed was French despite the claims of the others. She was spending a fortune, and for the first time, didn't care, admitting to the worrying part of her brain that she could afford it.

The following Spring the Duchess of Southwald's ball came around all too soon. Mary had rented a far larger house complete with a full staff. The consequence of the house boosted her confidence along with her wardrobe. She now had an array of dresses in glorious fabrics and colours and felt fourteen again.

'The green or the dark red?' she asked Mags.

'I really like the cream. The lace is so beautiful.'

'Girls out of the schoolroom will be wearing white, so I need something different.'

'Dark blue?'

Mary gave her a look. She knew Mags was hinting her away from the red. She held it to the light and swung it from side to side. Hanging straight the silk was a deep dark red, but when the fabric moved it caught the light and became a glorious orange-scarlet. It flowed around her as she walked and slithered suggestively over her limbs. The bodice glinted as tiny gold beads flickered in the light and drew attention to her breasts. The waist was under her bust and the sleeves were tiny and puffed. Above all, the colour made her feel strong and wonderful and the cut was superb. The whole dress showed itself to be the work of a master, or rather, a mistress!

Mags sighed. 'It is going to be the red, isn't it?'

'I may as well arrive as I mean to go on. I am no shrinking violet, now am I?'

Mags helped her slide into it so that her hair was undisturbed. Mary had uninhibitedly copied the duchess and her dark hair was arranged in a smooth swirl high on her head, with the addition of a curving tail dropping down her back to her shoulder blades. The fashion was for curls, but Mary's hair dropped a curl faster than a gutter snipe dropped his 'h's.

'No one without your height could wear that dress,' Mags told her, standing head on one side as she reviewed her.

'Good,' said Mary. 'I am unique. Why not celebrate the fact. I have no intention of trying to be something I am not.'

Mags sighed again. 'You are going to have all the wives worried sick.'

Mary gave her a 'look'.

The duchess had invited Mary to dinner before the ball.

'The invitation says supper,' she declared. 'If I present a dinner, the men will eat too much and fall asleep, and the women will drink too much and get lost doing the gavotte.'

Mary swallowed a smile at the dry tone. They had attended various small afternoon events together and the duchess had made it plain that they were nothing more than temporary acquaintances. It made Mary feel horribly guilty and so she had made it plain that with the ball the duchess's responsibilities would come to an end. The sad thing was, she thought, she personally rather liked the no-nonsense woman under the silk and would have enjoyed being closer to her.

As the duchess was personally sponsoring Mary, Mags would not

The Army's Son

be invited. Mary wasn't sure how she felt about that, but did not question the decision. She was aware of having to be on her best behaviour so that she could be socially independent as soon as possible.

She descended the staircase from the room and maid she had been allocated for the night, dressed, coiffured, perfumed and with a borrowed necklace around her throat and her back as straight as possible. Her stomach roiled with fear, but she balled it up, hid it deep, and presented as calm a face as she could possibly manage. If tonight went badly, she would be heading back to Lincolnshire still single! It was no different to selling her wool fleeces or her corn; only this time she was selling herself.

The receiving room below was steadily filling with people, some arriving from the front door and many also descending the stairs. The house, which had seemed like a mausoleum when she had arrived earlier, was now bustling with people and all six footmen seemed to be busy taking garments and escorting people about. Mary took in a breath and hoped she wouldn't be forced to enter the crowded room alone. The duchess was, however, as good as her word. She immediately greeted Mary and taking her arm, walked her around the room introducing her to people with the agreed lie that she was a distant cousin, come to stay for a while. 'Yes,' Mary thought, 'one night!' but she smiled, and curtsied, and nodded politely and instantly forgot most of the names.

She always took notice of tall men. Being tall for a woman made her keenly aware of men whom she considered suitable for her to stand next to; being taller than a group of four or five men made her feel like a broom handle rather than a woman. And men seemed to resent it. Her fleeting glances spotted an attractive sandy-haired man by the fireplace. He was taller than most of the other men but unlike James, who was solid, appeared too thin with a markedly pale complexion. What caught her eye also was that he had a huge blade of a nose, thin and beak like. She smiled to herself; he wouldn't grow into that nose until he was fifty, and then it would make him wonderfully distinguished, and, attractive. Life really did give all the good things to men. At fifty she would look old and worn out, no doubt!

When they eventually reached the man, Mary was surprised to discover that this was the younger son, the man James had rescued. She had no idea if he knew how it had come about that his mother was sponsoring her, but decided not to mention the fact.

'Gervaise, my son, Lord Alton.' The duchess's tone was flat.

'Ah, you must of course be Lady Mary. Delighted, to meet you at last.' His smile was warm and his eyes twinkled. The left arm of his jacket was pinned up, empty.

Mary responded to his warmth with her own. With a wide smile she said, 'I have to thank you for lending me your mother for a while. She had been beyond kind to me.'

His eyes switched to his mother's and if anything, his eyes twinkled more and his smile became wicked.

Just then a footman slid through the room and came and whispered in the duchess's ear. With a muttered apology and every indication of annoyance she turned and left them. Gervaise watched them go in great amusement. Mary frowned, wondering about the undercurrents she could sense, but not understand. Until it hit her.

'Oh!' she said.

Laughing light blue eyes met hers. 'Indeed,' he murmured.

The duchess had a son of marriageable age and she, a widow of uncertain provenance, was seeking a husband. And the duchess didn't want the resulting sum of one plus one to make two.

Mary pulled her lips inwards hard and thought. 'Will you dance?' she asked him.

'I fear not,' he said, motioning with his empty sleeve.

'I am sure we could waltz.' He gazed down at her. 'Oh, I am so sorry. I just ...' she petered out without finishing.

'Hate being judged?'

Mary was afraid she might have tears in her eyes, of both hurt and anger.

'My dear girl, I now definitely believe we should waltz. Furthermore, I intend to escort you into dinner, although mother tells me it is to be a 'light repast' I am not convinced her chef and she are in alignment on that one. I am certain you will prefer my company to the elderly admiral she had lined up for you. I also am somewhat offended.'

'I don't have ...' Was she ever to complete a sentence with this man?

'Intentions? Respectable or otherwise?'

'Oh! I feel mortified.'

'Do not, my dear girl. Instead come and talk with me over the filet of sole and the ptarmigan. I believe we might enjoy each other's company.'

Mary nodded her agreement. She thought so too, and for the first time felt truly comfortable with someone within London society.

The women at dinner fell into three clear groups. Some pretty girls, invited she guessed for Gervaise to look over, a few young matrons, all of whom wore such low necklines once at the table they looked almost naked, and a few older dowagers of a similar age to the duchess. She hid her concern at the way Gervaise had rearranged her seating position by keeping her face utterly blank of expression. Gervaise shot his mother a wicked, intense grin. Mary, meanwhile, kept her eyes on her plate during the interaction.

Gervaise let her tell him all about Jack and Elfie, which was breaking numerous social taboos, without looking bored once. When she asked about his own childhood, he, in his turn, spoke about playing with his adored elder brother. There were no sisters.

'I rode off to war, but he ended up dying of a childish ailment,' he said sadly. 'I miss him, but no one else wants to mention his name. It's as if they believe saying his name will make it worse, but it doesn't, it just suggests that they don't want him to have ever existed.'

'You know that isn't true,' she said quietly.

'I do. But I can't tell you how pleasant it has been to share my memories of him with you.'

They shared a smile. If the duchess saw, Mary didn't care.

. . .

After dinner, Mary stood at the Duchess's side at the entrance to the ballroom as she greeted her line of guests. Each guest was introduced to her cousin, Lady Mary Swann. Mary curtsied and shook hands for what seemed an interminable time. If this was society, then she was heading back home as soon as her search was done! She was hot, bored and her back was beginning to ache with standing still for so long. Eventually the Duke, who had appeared only as dinner had, and Duchess appeared to feel they had completed their duty and they all moved towards the ballroom.

At first the Duchess introduced her to some of her own friends, but then Mary began to look around, needing to explore and find her own feet. She would keep her word and did not intend, would not, cling to the Duchess. Once again she wished she could have brought Mags with her as companion. Even here amidst the noise, Mary was missing Jack and Elfie with a wrenching ache.

The room was stuffy, over lit, and horrendously noisy. The duke had reappeared to murmur something to the duchess before he again moved away. Mary gazed around the room and realised with some surprise that she did not feel overwhelmed. On the contrary, she felt rather irritable and completely equal to the situation. Most of the men looked soft, even the younger ones. Equally, most men seemed to glide from their noses into their throats. Chinless didn't describe it. The women were overdressed in flounces and frills and few looked clean. Hair was teased into bird's nests of frizz and curl while skin appeared grubby beneath jewels that glittered and shone. As someone who had ridden every day of her life since being a small girl, Mary knew she was lean and lithe and, as a fairly tall woman, she had always refused to bend her shoulders or back to appear a dainty little thing. James may have called her small, but he was two yards and two in his stockings. And she thought, remembering, he was rarely in his stockings! He had been a full six inches taller. No, she most certainly did not feel cowed by this motley assortment of the best society could provide.

As she gazed around she became aware of a lithe-looking man leaning against the opposite wall gazing back at her. He was all in silvery grey, with light hair to match and a lean, lined face. At least he had a chin! He looked rather sly and dissolute, but interesting. Either the initial babel of noise had dimmed or Mary had become more used to picking out individual sounds as she clearly heard a high-pitched, rather nasal woman's voice discussing someone who was provincial and new to town. 'Well, that is like me,' thought Mary. But then the voice began to insult the topic's height and style choices, saying she was 'out of all style'. It was when the voice began to defame the lack of curl in the topic's hair, Mary drew in a breath and slowly turned to her right. Her eyes met those of a young miss, seventeen or so, with English good looks; golden ringlets, china-blue eyes, soft peaches and cream cheeks and a pink rosebud mouth. The pretty blue eyes were full of venom and antagonism as they met Mary's, while the mouth was twisted into a moue of distaste.

Swinging her right arm across to the left of her skirts, Mary swished the heavy satin around and to her right, with the glorious sound of expensive silk. She then took two steps forward, which brought her nose to nose with the girl. Mary looked down, using all of her extra inches and stared into the girl.

'Your manners, chit, are appalling. Your mama should keep you at home until you learn better.'

With that she swished her skirts again, using them as a weapon, and turned to her left where two of the girl's friends stood. Using the cold look she has successfully used on Lincolnshire farmers for years, farmers who were misogynist to their core, often ignorant and built like their equally unintelligent bulls, she waited for the two girls to move apart so she could walk between them. The girls lost their cruel smiles, glanced at each other, and both began to blush hotly and unattractively. They moved apart and Mary swept between them heading for the man in grey across the room.

She strode through the room using all of her long-legged gait, knowing she was fit, healthy, and in her prime. She may not be beautiful, but she had confidence and presence to spare. Under no circumstances was she going to mince along like a ninny as some women did.

Either the ton took to her as she was, or she was going home. She reached the man and he stood away from the wall as she drew so determinedly near.

'Lady Mary Swann,' she greeted him. 'You were staring at me.'

'I was,' he agreed. 'What did you say to Lady Penelope?'

'That her manners are appalling and her mother should put her back in the schoolroom. Or words to that effect.'

He laughed, showing rather long teeth like a wolf. 'Excellent,' he declared. 'Sir Sebastian Silvester, at your disposal.'

'I hope you mean that, as I would like you to promenade me around the room.'

'I should be delighted,' he said with another grin and held out his arm.

So they did exactly that, moving around the room, Silvester nodding to acquaintances but introducing her to none. Mary said nothing. She was here to meet people, men, men she might marry and Silvester was not at present playing his unwitting part. But at least she was not stuck against a wall alone, so she sighed inwardly and smiled and made the most of being on the arm of a presentable man. Certainly, she was being noticed. It occurred to her that it was he rather than her that was causing a minor stir. She slanted a glance up at him and he returned the look with raised eyebrows and a wolfish smile.

'I rather assume you have appeared from the depths of Lincolnshire for a reason. And,' he paused to nod at a tall dark-haired man over the ostrich feather plumed heads of some females leaning in to gossip, 'I can't imagine it is female attention you require.'

Mary thought for a moment, then asked carefully, 'Should I take exception to that remark? Not all widows are open to affairs.'

'Indeed,' was his bland reply, 'and that gives me my answer. You are here to marry then.'

'You sir are impertinent. Beyond rude.' Mary stiffened and began to pull away from his arm, but he moved his free left hand and fixed it over hers that lay along his right forearm so she either created a scene or remained in place.

'Now then,' he murmured. 'If I am right, then introducing you to the married set will not serve your purpose,' he gazed into her eyes, 'now will it?'

Mary wasn't sure whether to hit him or laugh. He watched the indignation play across her face and returned to look over the crowd. She was more woman than this fashionable set were used to. He would be beating them off with a stick before long if he was any judge of character, and he was vain enough to know that he was a good judge, a very good judge. The married ones would be a definite problem, he mused. She was right, widows were seen as fair game to a man wanting an affair rather than a commitment, though why he did not know. Widows could fall pregnant as easily as virgins, unless they had reached the age of becoming grandmothers. He, however, when hunting for pleasure, had always targeted the young married-off to men they despised. The minute the rumour mill whispered at pregnancy, he had descended, he liked to imagine, like an eagle falling upon unsuspecting prey. And news of 'interesting conditions' was always discussed in the clubs. The despised husbands were always only too quick to boast of successfully impregnating their far younger wives. Ah, the ton. To a cynical mind such as his, it provided endless entertainment. And now he had Lady Mary to escort. It was looking to be an interesting Spring.

They were continuing to process around when a young man stepped back suddenly right into Mary. He span around, his face still alight with laughter. He was of medium height but well-proportioned with a mop of tight dark curls atop a face smothered in freckles enhanced by dancing brown eyes that Mary thought would find remaining serious a problem.

'My sincere apologies!' he said with a low bow. Even the bow was full of self-directed laughter, she thought.

'Stevens, you are an idiot,' Silvester commented calmly. 'Lord Giles Stevens, may I present Lady Mary Swann.'

'Honoured ma'am,' he murmured. He and Silvester chatted about people she had never heard of for a while and then with a smaller bow Stevens addressed her directly.

'The next set is a waltz, Lady Mary. Would you care to be my partner?'

'I should be delighted, Lord Stevens,' Mary replied. He was lovely, but far too youthful. But waltzing with him would be a delight.

As they took their places she thought it only fair to warn him, 'I do know the steps, but this will be my first public waltz.'

'Then we will take it slowly,' he smiled back in response.

He was as good as his word. At first they remained at the edge of the floor taking the turns gently and keeping clear of the other couples, some of whom Mary was somewhat relieved to notice appeared to gaze upon them warmly. Stevens was clearly a well-known character and well liked too, no doubt. The waltz was to be in a set of three. For the second Mary began to really relax and enjoy swirling around in the arms of a fine young man. Stevens upped the pace, twirling her in and out of the other couples with increasing confidence that she could remain with him. During the third, they were for the moment out on the edge of the floor near to some alcoves whose seats were for the moment empty. Suddenly Stevens shoved his thigh through Mary's skirts so that her groin was firmly on his warm and muscled leg. She shot a shocked glance up at him, her mouth falling open in horror at him doing this to her, as he spun around sending her feet flying as she wheeled in a dizzying circle until her feet found the ground at last. He was laughing. It had been skillfully done, but Mary knew she was heading back to Lincolnshire unwed. She would never live this down.

They glided to a halt. He bowed, she curtsied, and they made their way back to Silvester. As they drew near she could see Silvester's face was rigid with anger. As they stopped in front of him he glared at Stevens and said in voice that was low but intense enough to be heard by other's nearby,

'I ought to whip you to within an inch of your life, puppy. Now get out of my sight and call on Lady Mary tomorrow and grovel for her forgiveness.'

Mary watched, knowing her face was flushed with discomfort, wondering if Silvester really could handle this. He bent forward and hissed so only Stevens could hear, 'Now leave. And look suitably chastened or I really will run you through.'

The lad left. He was brave enough to take his embarrassed face through the onlookers looking neither left nor right. Silvester, meanwhile, raised his voice so that she was sure the all-ears crowd around them might hear. He passed it off with,

'It is entirely my fault, Lady Mary. I should have realised the boy was too foolish to have entrusted you to his care. Come, we will walk a little.'

Mary swallowed. No one had died. It wasn't the end of the world. But she had delivered over twenty babies and patched up burns and breaks on men and women for years. Ladies, and society en-masse, were far more delicate and she could not afford to lose her reputation. Especially not on her first night! She would ask Silvester later if the boy would be alright. She didn't want his youthful prank to cause him to be ostracised from society. And it had been masterfully done!

So she did what she always did and always had done. She hid her feelings and lifted her head high and tried to look as proud and remote as possible. Within a few steps Silvester hailed a man he called Forrester. Geoffrey Forrester was a portly man with a full head of silver hair and the ruddy cheeks of the outdoorsman. Mary smiled into his twinkling blue eyes and liked him immediately. Too old, she thought.

He was kindly and Mary warmed to him even further. They chatted for a while and then he requested her hand for a set of quadrilles and Mary accepted gladly. Here, she would be in safe hands she was sure. As with the waltz she knew the steps but this was to be her first performance where it mattered. To her relief it all came back to her, all the practise up and down the hall and the drawing room, all the counting in her head. They were doing so well until Mary inadvertently turned the wrong way. Two strong hands gripped her shoulders and gently shoved her in the right direction. Laughing, she caught herself and swung back into the rhythm. She wasn't the only one to step wrong and the mistakes made it all so much more human, so much more enjoyable, and she hadn't expected enjoyment. She certainly hadn't expected fun.

Geoffrey returned her in due course to Silvester and to her surprise she found she was glad to have someone to anchor to; a port to head home to. She would need to ask him how he considered his role, and whether he minded, but for now it was her first night and she was more than content to rely upon his support. Silvester in his turn welcomed her back and tucked her in beside him as if she had known him for years instead of a few hours. A tall dark man approached. Bowing low, he introduced himself as Sir Lionel Jessop. Both Silvester and Geoffrey appeared to know him.

'I have taken the liberty of introducing myself so that I may apologise for manhandling your person,' he began.

'Oh,' said Mary, 'thank you so much for rescuing me. If you hadn't all might have become chaos.'

He smiled, she smiled back, and yet another friendship, or acquaintance at least, was begun. They danced the next set and Mary thought her sore feet would fall off. Riding in a blizzard was far less tiring.

Silvester continued to play his part and introduce Mary to various people, all of whom appeared perfectly willing to also make her acquaintance. They had turned away from meeting a woman called Cassiopeia when Mary blurted out, 'I hate my name. Mary is dull, dull, dull. Boring and dull. Why couldn't I have been called Sarah or Emma? Something pretty to offset my plain face.' She turned away from him idly watching the room and he gazed at her. Plain! She was almost, but not quite as tall as he, with dark hair that gleamed with health, piled onto her head and coaxed into natural waves in contrast to the over-ironed desiccated curls girls such as the chit Penelope boasted. Her hazel eyes gleamed with intelligence and were set off by arching brows with no hint of soot flaking around them to indicate they were anything but naturally dark, while her oval face could be as remote as a statue and as alive as fire. And her mouth. Her rather wide and thin-lipped mouth had already suggested to some deep secret part of his brain that he rarely examined that she could take in a man and suck him dry while enjoying the act. He swallowed and admitted to himself that his neck was somewhat red with a heat he hadn't admitted to or allowed since he was a callow youth.

'I don't know,' he murmured, 'I wouldn't be too hard on yourself. I find you acceptably attractive.'

She shot him a quick, sharp, smile and he swallowed again, feeling that he had dodged out of that one quiet well. Then something shifted in her eyes, and he wondered. And there was nothing more sexually alluring than a woman who could make a man wonder. For the first time in a decade his jaded soul wanted to laugh. Minx.

When Mary left Silvester's side for the promised dance with Gervaise, she was aware of Silvester's surprise and interest. She could almost see the calculations going on behind his eyes. Gervaise led her with his one arm to the side of the dancing area and stood looking at her.

'I do like a man who can look down on me!' Mary declared.

'You, my dear, need to learn to prevaricate.'

Mary gave him a wide and wicked grin. 'But friends tell each other the truth.'

'Indeed. And how are we to manage this feat? I have to inform you I have been instructed by my mother not to dance.'

Mary tipped her head to one side feeling uneasy. 'She really has been kind to me. I should not go against her; that would be quite wrong.'

'Ah, but there is a young lady here whom I wish to show that I can dance. I wish her to begin to realise that I have lost only a part of an arm, not more important parts of my person.'

Mary shot him a glare and said, 'Does your mother know about this young lady.'

His, 'Certainly not,' was crisp.

'Then put your right arm firmly around my waist and I will put my l left arm on your shoulder and hold my right behind my back, out of the way, and we shall see how we manage.'

'You have given this some thought.'

All she did was smile.

They stayed at the edge of the dancers and at first stumbled over each other. And then, magically, they found a method, and were swinging around and amongst the other couples. They smiled up at each other in companionship and friendship, but not in lust. When at the end of the set Gervaise returned Mary to Silvester his eyes turned towards a lovely blonde dressed in a rich-cream dress. Mary raised her eyebrows and he gave a tiny nod. As he turned to leave Mary mouthed, 'Good luck.' He kissed her hand and left to circulate amongst the guests.

'You are a dangerous woman, Lady Mary Swann,' Silvester commented.

'I am glad you know it,' Mary retorted briskly.

The following morning Mags was alive with interest. 'What was it like? I have never been able to really imagine a ball.'

'Well that is not going to last!' she declared. 'You are coming with me in future. Tonight was different and I had to be introduced, but if I am going to suffer all this, then you can too. Anyway, to answer your question, loud.' For a woman who had spent most of her life riding the flat and remote wilds of Lincolnshire with nothing but the snort of a horse, the jingle of a bit or the wind for company, the noise level had been exhausting. 'I had no idea human beings en-masse could be so loud. It was like shoving your head into a huge bee hive. And glamorous, with the chandeliers twinkling above and all the colours and jewels sparkling. But not very clean.'

Mags snorted with laughter. 'How do you mean?'

'Well, some of the dresses were stained when the light caught them and people smelt, but different to farmers.'

Mags hooted with laughter now. 'Oh do explain!'

'I am not sure I can. Farmers and their wives can be grubby, or downright filthy sometimes, but it is recognisable dirt along with the sweat of honest hard work. This was different. Some men smelt as if they had applied a different perfume every day for a week and never washed in-between. And the clothes, some looked decidedly grubby and stank of stale perspiration. The thing about being hard-work dirty is that you have to wash most of it off, I suppose, because it is so extreme, but these people smelt as if they put on the same clothes over and over again without ever letting fresh air get to them. It was different.'

'You aren't too convinced by the life of the London rich then?' Mags asked.

'It is enjoyable, but I shall not hanker for it once I am again settled on an estate. It is pleasurable for now, or even occasionally, but not as a way of life. It is clear that for some people this is their life and they make sure it is a constant social whirl, but I know I would tire of it. In fact, I suspect many of them do too, but they lack the resources to make any other kind of life for themselves.'

Mags made a 'hmm' sound, but gave no further comment.

'I really do need you to come with me,' Mary told her.

Mags' eyebrows hit high up her forehead. 'Seriously? Me?'

'I don't see why not. A lot of women had companions with them, especially older widows.'

Mags gave her a look, and another 'hmmm,' but let her opinion remain at that. Mary guessed the idea had not found much favour. She moved to the window and gazed out. 'One thing I did not have, was jewellery. The Duchess leant me a necklace.'

'Did your mother have any?' Megs enquired.

'I don't really know. I think I have a memory of a pearl necklace and a heavy gold chain with an enamel picture hanging from it, about the size of my father's thumbnail, with shiny stones around it. On the grounds my mother would never have worn paste jewellery, I assume it was ringed with diamonds. There is nothing in the house of that nature now, and for the first time, I am wondering if there was and Brewer took it. Surely father would have bought mother something but there is nothing. Not even their wedding rings.'

'Perhaps they were buried with them,' commented Megs.

'Possibly, I suppose.'

'And?' pressed Mags.

Mary turned to her with a bright grin, 'I am going shopping. Tiaras seem to be popular. I have decided I should like one. And a necklace. I can't stand the idea of anything in my ears, I think hanging jewels from the ear lobes a horrid idea, so I shan't bother with them, but possibly a bracelet. A collection Jack can pass on one day. The estate can well afford them and I am feeling like throwing years of frugality out of the window for a while.'

Mags grinned back at her. 'May I come?' she asked, and they both fell about laughing for no reason at all.

Hatton Garden was full, it seemed, with people skilled in taking the dull rocks of diamond and polishing the planes until the light flew around inside, quite trapped. Mary and Mags began early as the shops began to stir and by early afternoon had found a tradesman they felt comfortable with, with goods they were attracted to. Mary was fascinated to discover the tricks the cleverest of them used to make multiple uses of one jewel. It could dangle from a tiara catching and throwing light with every move one made, or be detached and hung on a chain to settle in one's cleavage, or be pinned to a garment (along with a safety chain) to be worn as a broach. She and Mags arrived home quite exhausted, but well satisfied with their day's work. Silvester arrived not twenty minutes after they arrived home and, looking at the clock, Mary realised it was the conventional time for 'morning calls'.

She welcomed him into the drawing room with a smile and an inward sigh. What she really wanted was to kick off her shoes and sink back with a pot of tea, or two. He had young Giles Stevens with him, who had his arms overladen with roses. Mary put on her best polite face and tried to greet them graciously.

'You are tired,' Silvester said abruptly. 'We will not stay long.'

Mary gave a soft laugh and sank down into her chair.

'Oh come in, take some tea and rest with us for a while. I am tired, too tired to stand on ceremony. A ball last night and shopping all day, I am quite drained.'

Stevens stood grinning from ear to ear, 'But I need to make my apology first, my lady.'

Mary cocked and eyebrow at him. He sobered, 'Seriously ma'am, I am most dreadfully sorry. It seemed like such a lark to whirl you around. I had no thought for what it might have done for your reputation. I will lay these flowers as an apology with your staff and take my leave.' His ears were quite scarlet.

'Place the flowers on the table and I thank you for them and for your apology, then come and relax with us. And we none of us will admit to lacking decorum and in not sitting all prim and proper to anyone outside this room. Mags, do be a dear and ring for more tea while I introduce you properly.'

They stayed an hour, much longer than was proper and there was much laughter. Stevens was a bright and wicked raconteur and Silvester added his comments like salt to a meal, spicing the story with the odd word that revealed more than one might think possible to the tales of the great and the good, and the not very great, and definitely not very good. As they left he enquired of Mary,

'Do you attend the musicale tonight?'

'No, I have been invited but had already refused. I am used to early mornings and alongside them early nights still. I am not dissolute like you.'

To this he arched a single narrow eyebrow, 'The theatre tomorrow night then? May I collect you at seven?'

Mary gazed at him a while, 'You are choosing to be my escort?'

'For the season if you will let me. I anticipate pleasure from the ordeal.'

'I won't be your mistress.'

'Madam, you are presumptuous, I didn't ask you to be.'

Mary laughed, 'No indeed. As long as you understand that, I should be most grateful for your company.'

Stevens butted in, 'I can be presumptuous. Will you be my mistress?'

'Absolutely not,' Mary told him, and batted him on the arm.

He gave a defeated sigh, 'May I also escort you though.'

'Again, that would be delightful.'

They saw the two men off and settled down to a quiet evening and an early night. As long as no one else knew of their unfashionable habits of reading and sleeping, no harm could come to their public personas!

Despite her reservations about 'the high life' Mary began to enjoy the lovely clothes she could now commission as all she did in them was walk in parks and spin around dance floors. There would be nowhere to wear them in Lincolnshire she was quite certain. But for now, fun was the order of the day, along with, of course, husband hunting. She really did want Jack to have a father figure and she was more than ready to cease sleeping alone. But why, oh why, was that part so hard?

To her surprise Silvester became a firm support. At every event he was there, watching, introducing and giving her the inside information on gambling habits, insane relatives, and any other particular he felt she ought to know. He seemed as keen on finding her a husband as she was and appeared to be enjoying the challenge even more. For her, frustration was the order of the day.

They were at yet another musicale, the most dreaded of social occasions in Mary's book when a tall dark and not-quite handsome man Mary had spotted quite often in the distance or in crowds came to be introduced to her. Why he wasn't handsome she couldn't work out, his nose, eyes and mouth were all in the right places, but his face was merely masculine, while missing by the slightest amount being that of one of male beauty. Perhaps because of that, she was attracted to him all the more. His name was Maximillian Dowding, and he was a Lord and heir to an earldom. He carried an uncompromising aura that was seriously attractive to her; a male earthiness that most men in the ton seemed to lack. She gazed at him as she ducked her curtsy and he bowed and found herself flicker with interest. She could feel Silvester's eyes burning into her back.

The Army's Son

Later, as they made their way home in Silvester's coach, she could feel that he was brooding. 'What is it?' she asked.

He took in a deep breath. 'You liked Dowding?'

'Yes. Very much so. He is attractive, personable and the right sort of age. He is the first man, apart from you dear Silvester, whom I have thought I might enjoy becoming friends with.'

'Friends!' He gave an inelegant snort through his nose. He went quiet for a long while until they had almost reached her house. Then he interrupted the silence with, 'How would you feel about a detour?'

In the darkness of the coach Mary frowned. Silvester had always behaved with strict propriety, was he about to attempt to ravish her? She rather thought not. She had come to believe he preferred men; it would explain a great deal about him.

'Detour where?' she enquired.

'Down towards the river, to sit in the dark for a while.'

'You intrigue me, but I admit to being nervous. Where and why Silvester? I will not have you make a fool out of me.'

'Actually, it is in the hope of you not being a fool that we will make this strange errand.'

'Very well,' she agreed. If she didn't trust Silvester, what was she doing going home alone with him in his coach in the middle of the night?

Silvester stopped the coach and hopped out to converse with the driver. Then he climbed back in and they set off again. Mary was aware of a flicker of unease. They did indeed head down towards the river and Silvester was silent the whole way, which Mary found oddly reassuring. She would have felt more concerned if he had chatted away as if nothing out of the ordinary was occurring, when it clearly was. The coach finally drew to a halt under a huge oak that must have seen some changes in its life and the carriage lamps were put out. They were parked on the flat, and the ground to their right, on Mary's side of the coach, rose up gradually to a large square house that had a straight front path to the door and two casements on either side. The house appeared to be well maintained from what she could see in the dark of the moon with clipped shrubbery around. No doubt it had its own mooring on the river, Mary mused. Silvester still said nothing, and Mary set her head back against the squabs and dozed.

She was nudged into full wakefulness by Silvester. Another coach had arrived at the side of the house and a man was being let out. All Mary could make out was that he was tall. He strode around the side of the house to the front and the coach drew away. The door opened as if he were expected and as the light flooded out onto the path. Mary murmured, 'Dowding?' She felt rather than saw Silvester's nod. A woman with pale hair was waiting for him and all Mary could make out was her wide smile. Dowding reached her and drew her into his arms as a boy barrelled into them both. Dowding turned and lifting the boy swung him around in the moonlight, before ruffling his hair and kissing his brow. Then they all disappeared behind the closed door. Silvester banged on the roof and they moved off gently for a while, before stopping again. Mary could hear the coachman scramble down and light the lamps, before they were turning and heading for her home.

'His wife?' she asked.

'A difficult question to answer,' Silvester mused. 'Rumour has it he is in the market for a wife, a legitimate one, but he spends as many nights as possible, so it is said, here.'

'Won't he give her up when he marries?'

'What do you think?' Silvester asked.

'I suspect not.'

'Exactly. I suspect the same. What he is probably shopping for is a woman to leave in his draughty Hall or London house, get a heir and a spare on her, and let her get on with her life. As long as she provides a boy and the child is his, he can ignore her. He will probably pick a chit straight from the schoolroom who will not have the character or maturity to move him from his course. Meanwhile, he will continue to spend the majority of his time here, with a woman and children he clearly cares for, in the comfort of a small modern house.'

'Why doesn't he marry her? The woman he went to tonight?'

Silvester sighed, 'I have no idea. They have, it seems, four children,

The Army's Son

that would be difficult to pass off, and presumably she is from the lower classes, again a tricky obstacle. And then, perhaps she doesn't want the life of the ton. Neither of us really enjoy it, do we?'

'I see,' Mary murmured. And the problem was, she did. 'Well, he was too high for my touch. I need a father for Jack and a man to run the estate. A man who is heir to an earldom wouldn't have time for us. Find me a younger son, Silvester. Those are your orders!'

Silvester chuckled, but Mary couldn't get the image of the man and boy, limned in candlelight, their hearts so close, as the man had whirled the boy around and kissed his brow. She felt almost faint with longing. She wanted that for Jack so achingly badly, and she wanted more children, and it all seemed an impossible day dream at present.

They were at yet another ball and Mary was beginning to tire of the social whirl. There was a sameness to it all. She had excused herself from Silvester and was making her way to the Ladies' Withdrawing Room when she was forced to pause and let a pair of somewhat foxed men blunder past. She was desperate to pass water and thought she might burst if she didn't reach the room fast. The wait forced her to stand by a group of three unknown ladies. The elder was tall and dressed in maroon satin that was quite high-necked with a matching turban with black feathers; there was a young girl of similar height on one side dressed in the white of the newly out who had to be her daughter; and the third was a girl of a different sort altogether. She was quite small, with fair hair that appeared to curl quite naturally and unlike the other two, was extremely pretty. Mary vaguely noticed that her dress was nothing like the quality of the other two, but her physical need was too imperative for her to notice more.

In the Withdrawing Room she took one of the narrow jugs that sat on a shelf and retreated behind a curtain. Lifting her skirts out of the way, she set the jug high between her legs and relieved herself.

'Do you require help, my lady?' came a voice.

'No thank you,' Mary called through the curtain, thanking the fates that she had not been born poor and therefore likely to have to do this girl's job or similar.

She left the jug for the girl to empty into the bucket and re-entered the main room. Sighing with relief, she went to the mirror and checked her hair. Exchanging greetings with some of the women she was acquainted with she hurried out as she was promised for the next set.

She returned the same way and again waited by the same three women in order to make her way back to Silvester. The tall young girl turned, her face now towards Mary and a picture of spite. Mary blinked as she reached and pinched hard on the soft flesh at the back of the shorter girl's upper arm. When she let go, Mary could see a whole set of new and old bruises; clearly this was not a solitary attack.

Nausea kicked in Mary's stomach. To witness such bullying, when there seemed no provocation, felt dreadful. Mary wondered what the girl's life was like. Looking at that arm, quite possibly a living hell.

Her set was with Stevens. She slipped in between him and Silvester.

'Ah, I thought you had left me dangling,' Stevens told her with a grin.

'No.' Mary took his arm but held him in place. He looked down at her. 'Would you mind finding two glasses of champagne? But you are not to drink yours.'

Stevens made an ironic bow, 'Your wish is as always my command.' He moved off to obey.

'What are you about?' Silvester asked. Then, looking more closely added, 'What is the matter, my dear?'

Mary nodded her head, 'Perhaps nothing. I have a small play I wish to act out. I will explain later.' Silvester's concern surprised her, especially as it appeared genuine.

When Steven's returned with the champagne, Mary took hers. 'And now what are we to do, if not to drink these,' he asked. 'Throw them at someone?'

'Yes,' Mary told him.

He grinned. 'I knew I liked you them first moment I saw you.'

'Now lean down so I can tell you my plan,' Mary scowled at him. His grin just got wider.

They strolled, Mary's arm on Stevens', as dozens of other couples were doing. When they reached the trio of women, none of whom seemed to be being asked to dance, Mary stumbled and, jogging Stevens' arm, caused him to spill his champagne down the side of the blonde girl's dress. Mary immediately addressed Lady Plum, as she had mentally named the older woman.

'Oh, I am most dreadfully sorry! That was entirely my fault.' She held out her hand, a cool smile on her face, 'Lady Mary Swann. I will of course ensure the dress is cleaned.' Mary's true feeling was that if plunged into a wash, the dress was so poorly made it might simply fall apart. Meanwhile, Steven's was charming the little blonde girl and asking her for a dance. The girl shot a terrified glance towards the other women.

'Of course you must dance with him,' Mary opined loudly. 'Off you go!' She made a shooing motion with her hand. 'Your daughter, ma'am?' she asked stepping into the way so that Stevens and the girl could slip away without anyone reaching a hand to stop them. The older woman, blinked, outmanoeuvred. Credit to her, thought Mary, she didn't let it show if she recognised it or not.

'Lady Billington, and my daughter, Vanessa. Miss Grace, Silvia, is my niece.'

'Ah, you are lucky to have a lovely daughter,' Mary gushed. Clearly the girl was as plain as a pikestaff compared to her cousin, but Lady Billington blushed with pleasure and simpered. Oh dear, thought Mary, it was going to be a long half-hour. She smiled and set about making conversation.

Stevens accompanied Mary and Silvester back to her house. Once there they sat around, the two men drinking brandy Hawes her rented butler had acquired, while Mary sipped port. She had been careful not to ask about the provenance of either.

'I understand she is called Silvia,' Mary commented. 'Not a by-blow of yours Silvester, is she?' Silvester narrowed his gaze and didn't deign to reply. 'What did she say about her aunt and cousin?' she asked Stevens.

'Not a thing. She seemed impossibly shy at first, but then began to converse a little. I found her utterly charming.'

'Are you smitten?' Mary's voice held a laugh, but then she raised her eyebrows.

'I think I may be,' Stevens admitted.

All Mary could say was, 'Oh, Giles.' Then, 'Surely you cannot be in love after one set of dances.'

'Why not? She said nothing against her aunt, except how grateful she was to be given a home when her parents died. Mary, the stitches in the neck at the back of the dress were the size of my thumb-nail, even I know that is not right. I cannot even see the stitches in your dresses, or my shirts. I intend to send a note to her uncle tomorrow to request an interview with him.'

'You can't marry her because you feel sorry for her!' Mary was horrified.

'Why not? She is pretty and seems sweet; my mother would love nothing better than to dandle a grandchild on her knee. I have to marry someone, why not her?'

After he had left Mary sat silent by the fire. 'Stop worrying,' Silvester instructed.

'What have I done?'

Silvester smiled, 'Nothing. He longed to rescue a damsel and you provided one. That is all the boy needed.'

'How old is he?' Mary was chewing the side of her thumb.

Silvester sighed, 'Older than he looks. About twenty-seven. A good age to marry.'

'Can he afford to?'

At this Silvester gave a laugh. 'Mary, he is the catch of the season. His family are fabulously wealthy.' At her look of surprise he laughed again, this time without humour.

'He could have been yours, you know. He is quite smitten with you.'

Mary raised her eyebrows, 'Silvester, dear. That would feel like marrying my son.'

He laughed again, this time with warmth. He rose and kissed her hand, then allowed her to accompany him down the stairs to see him out. As he fastened his cape and collected his hat and cane he stood quiet for a moment just looking at her, then he gave a small smile and left, leaving Mary frowning at the closed door. Wishing the night footman a quiet night, she headed up to bed and the waiting maid. Finally, lying gazing out at the lightening sky she realised it was almost dawn. In Lincolnshire she was used to getting up at dawn, not retiring to bed then. She had a nagging concern about Giles Stevens. He seemed so young! And rather silly! She couldn't see her James spilling wine down a girl's dress, however she badgered him. Her James had a gravity and authority she couldn't imagine Giles Stevens ever acquiring, yet in calendar years he was younger. Well, she knew which one she would like to yoke her life to. She wished he really was 'her' James. Yet, what did she really know about him? They had really had only a few days together. But she did know him, she believed, knew him in her bones. And thinking about him got her nowhere. But it didn't help that all other men seemed, well, so insipid beside him. Exhaustion claimed her and she sank into sleep with relief to be away from her thoughts.

James was in her thoughts the moment she awoke. And she remembered how he had made the stand for Sally, how he had supported her when she had been faced with Martin Dunlop, how he had stayed when she had been birthing the breech baby and carried her home after, how he had silently reassured her when Hal had wrenched the eye-tooth from her very bones. She did know him, she did. And to say finding another like him was proving difficult was an understatement. She breathed deep and pushed her shoulders back. If Giles Stevens could find a bride, then she just had to work harder to find a husband. If nothing else, he and his little Silvia had perhaps emphasised that she needed to look amongst the widowers, perhaps. Or the men who had been pursuing a career and not had time to think about settle down. Where did senior army officers go for entertainment? Newly determined, she decided to have a discussion with Silvester. She would not pine over a man she could not have. She would not. Who she was trying to convince, was a moot point.

With Silvester, mild mannered Geoffrey and Lionel Jeffreries who had saved her from destroying a quadrille, Mary found moving amongst the ton both easy and at times enjoyable. She seemed to have made a friend in Charles Dowding, enjoying his conversation, and often walked in the parks with Stevens and his charming fiancée. Every other day she wrote to Jack and included little pieces of embroidery created by Mags. Skillful Mags was making tiny pictures in embroidered silks of the birds they were used to seeing at home, minor miracles of art, created to amuse him and Elfie. She missed Jack with a raw longing and wondered if it was really worth remaining in London. And once a week she sent a whole piece of foolscap to Elfie that she had smothered in small cartoon figures, walking, falling over, sitting in puddles, alongside ducks and puppies and kittens. Jack would 'read' the pictures to Elfie and she would trace them with her finger for a whole week until another page of little pictures arrived to amuse her. Her heart felt sick; the weeks were slipping past, the children were growing, and she was still no nearer to finding a mate. In the dark hours of the night she thought of James, but fiercely shoved him out of her mind. Wanting him made no sense at all.

 Then one night as they were arriving at her house in Silvester's coach they enjoyed some minor city excitement of a different kind. They had drawn up to her house and after the coachman had lowered the steps Silvester stepped down to help her out as he always did. Perhaps that was the problem. They were following a routine. The street was dark as pitch and would remain so until Hawes opened the door and held aloft the candelabra. As always, Silvester helped her, and her skirts, down and turned to check his coachman had by now exercised the knocker. Hawes was, bless him, waiting as he always was and the door began to open. Suddenly a hand clawed out, reaching for

The Army's Son

Mary's neck, presumably to grab at her new necklace. Shocked and surprised she inadvertently cried out. Inadvertent, because she did not see herself as a woman who required defending, but as one who would instantly fight back. Instead Silvester was there and, in the gloom of the street, the only light there was gleamed along a length of silver. The assailant was not to be deterred and swinging around made another grab, the light gleamed again and at last there was a grunt, the assailant doubled over and ran off.

'Did you spear him?' Mary asked.

'No, kneed him.'

'I didn't know you carried a sword stick.'

As the light from Hawes' candles reached them Mary watched as Silvester slid the lethal blade back into its plain-looking back lacquered housing. She had always assumed it was simply a walking cane carried as an affectation. Clearly not. Silvester reached his arm around her shoulders and turned her to move her up the steps towards the house. Hawes had clearly witnessed what had happened and was heading towards them alongside two footmen with cudgels.

As Mary reached the top of the steps she eyed Hawes, 'We own cudgels, do we Hawes?'

'Indeed, ma'am,' he murmured and the two men slipped out to check that the assailant really had vanished.

'Tea,' insisted Silvester to Hawes. 'Lady Mary may require something stronger, but I am seriously in need of hot tea.' Mary shot him a look of amusement then led the way up to the drawing room.

They entered the room to find Mags still up sewing away as usual so they regaled her with the tale of their assailant. It was only then Mary realised Silvester's cuff was stained with red.

'Him or you?' she asked sharply.

'Me,' he offered with a wry grimace.

His eyebrows shot to his hairline as she drew a small wicked knife out and let it clatter onto the side table. 'It was in my cloak pocket. You don't think I ride around Lincolnshire undefended, do you?' she asked as she shot out of the room. Silvester opened his mouth to comment but she had already gone. Mags regarded him. 'She knows what she is doing with cuts. And she would not let anyone else treat you.'

'Madam Margaret, I am quite discomforted at causing her trouble.'

Mags laughed, and for the first time, considered that Silvester might not be all bad.

Mary returned with a bowl of water and clean linens. Within seconds she had washed and bound a slash in his wrist. Mags watched Silvester keenly and worried. She wasn't at all sure he was the right man for Mary, or for Jack, who she missed almost as much as Mary. Mary seemed convinced he was not looking for a wife, but there was a softness in his gaze as he looked down on her bent head that worried her.

'My own fault,' he insisted, 'I wasn't quick enough to respond.'

'Nonsense,' Mary retorted firmly, 'you were like lightning. It was a dark night tonight. No one could have moved faster.'

Gently he lifted the heavy dark hair that lay upon the back of her neck having fallen from the pins that had held it high on her head. Mary froze and Mags watched keenly, wondering.

'Your neck is hurt,' he murmured.

Mary returned to her ministrations, but Mags could see she had blushed. Not something her tough-shelled Mary was prone to. 'It is nothing a night's sleep will not cure,' she retorted firmly.

They drank the tea and left the brandy Hawes had brought untouched.

'I am becoming a Puritan in your company, Lady Mary,' Silvester drawled.

'Do you good,' was her snapped response. But she shot him a swift grin.

'On that note,' he added, 'it is time to leave. Away from your company I may once again engage in my usual vices.'

'I am beginning to believe you are all talk Sebastian Silvester,' Mary told him calmly as she rose. 'I will see you to the door and once again I thank you for your quick action.'

At the door, with Hawes and the two burly young footmen once more on duty in the hall, Silvester caught Mary to him in an awkward one-armed hug. Silvester never hugged. And never did anything awkwardly. Mary found her nose stubbed by the pin in his cravat and her shoulder pulled painfully into his grasp. He kissed her quickly on the forehead and released her. 'Keep safe,' he muttered and only then let Hawes pull the heavy door open to let him out into the night.

Mary stood for a while wondering what that had all been about and then turned and ran upstairs calling her thanks to Hawes over her shoulder. Hawes meanwhile shook his head and absorbed the look Silvester had aimed his way. He didn't need instructions, unspoken or otherwise, about keeping his young and headstrong mistress safe, but he appreciated the sentiment. Perhaps they should keep the footmen outside rather than in when Lady Mary was out, so that they could keep an eye on the pavement outside. He would talk it over with the lads. They might need some heavy overcoats for the cold, and gloves. Planning, he made his way to the back of the house and his own bed.

Chapter Nine

James arrived in London and found some cheap lodgings. He longed to find Mary, but she might be planning to marry someone else by now and Hal would not know what was buzzing in her head, nor where her heart lay, and he had no idea if he would be a welcome visitor or not if he went to her home. His plan was simple. He would attend as many social events as he could in the hopes of 'innocently' bumping into her and take it from there. It was the first time in his life he had considered courting a woman and he was feeling out of his depth. What had flared between them in Lincolnshire had been a long while ago now and it had been stillborn at birth. And perhaps he had been imagining it, and it had no reality outside his own desire. But he would try. She was the only woman he had ever met whom he had wanted as his own, but the reality was, he was probably far, far too late.

He was standing at the edge of a ballroom gazing out over the dancers. He knew Mary had grown to love dancing and had ambled out tonight to consider whether it was something he could manage now. As an army officer he had been forced to learn the steps, but twirling around had always seemed a daft way to spend the time. It made a man out of breath though, he had to admit, and concentrate; neither of which were bad things for a soldier to do. Now, as he watched the pretty young misses and older married women he reconsidered. All those bouncing garrottes were still not to his taste, but the waltz now, the idea of holding Mary in public or in private definitely held appeal.

He looked down to discover he was being accosted by an old man leaning heavily on a stick. Like most of his age he was rotund, but not as much as most. James' own stick was behind his back.

'Major Causton?' the man enquired. James nodded his assent. 'Howard, Earl of Fyte.' James nodded his respects.

'I was wondering if your wife were here?' the old man began.

'No sir, I have no wife.' As yet James thought and, as always, wondered.

'Ah, it is the military wives I am seeking out.'

At James' slightly raised eyebrow and wry smile the old man gave a bark of a laugh, 'No lad, I am not seeking to satisfy a peculiar taste! I had a son, Lieutenant Colonel Douglas McCloud, did you by any chance know him?'

'Not know, but I did meet him a time or two.' James did indeed remember the man; he had appeared to be yet another of the loud-mouthed drunken braggarts the army specialised in.

'Ah, in that case did you meet his wife? Or even see her?'

James frowned, 'I am afraid not sir.'

'Ah, another dead end,' the old Earl muttered. His disappointment was palpable and he looked far too old and tired to be hanging around the edges of ballrooms. James frowned. He suspected there was more to the man's enquiry than happenstance.

'I remain a serving officer,' he told him, 'why don't you explain what it is you need and I can certainly see if I might help.' Besides, talking to the old man would give him something to do.

By mutual agreement they moved along the outer corridor to find a quiet place to sit and talk. At the door of a side room they spotted two large leather chesterfields and an established fire.

'Ah, that is more like it,' the old man said, with a grateful sigh.

James looked behind and spotting a footman idling, swung his cane to catch the boy on his calves. 'Brandy and two glasses, lad,' he commanded. The boy went bright red and ran off, but by the time James and the earl had settled had returned with a decanter, two glasses and a tall pie-crust table to stand them on for convenience. James thanked him and slipped him a coin.

After a few minutes settling into comfort and enjoying the fire James prompted, 'You said you had a son. Is Lieutenant Colonel Douglas McCloud dead then? If so, I didn't know.'

'He died of the flux some years ago. The army was busy at the time and I am not sure how widely reported his death was. I live in Scotland and used the Scottish papers to post his demise, but I had assumed, I now believe incorrectly, the army would post the news in the London papers.'

'Ah,' James said. Many soldiers died of the flux. It was a slow and gruesome way to go; the bowels turned to water and the pains could be horrendous. The army was quick to boast of men who died gloriously in battle, but could be a mite forgetful of those who died just as much in service of their country but not in a way that could be promoted as 'gallant'.

'We were estranged,' the Earl went on. 'He had a temper and so did I until age burnt it out of me.' Age burnt a lot of things out of a man in James' opinion. 'I was, of course, informed of his death,' but that was that. The years went by and I began to wish I had known more about his army career; I mean the every-day matters, not the stuff the army tell you. He was my only surviving child. His mother and I, we buried four others. Anyway, I began to engage in York society somewhat, I live in Scotland you see, and the officers I met there seemed to have had little to do with his regiment. In York I engaged in making a nuisance of myself every couple of years or so bothering officers about tales of my son. Never gave a thought to the women.'

At this rather obscure comment they both gazed into the fire and sipped their brandies. James was moved to ask, 'How did women come into it?'

'Ah, you may well ask. Many years had gone by and I had begun, not to lose interest, but to feel I was not achieving anything, when purely by chance, when in York, I asked a chap, a major, if he had met my son. As it happens his wife was there. The man had and told me some tales about Rupert I absolutely knew were gilded. They were fawning over me because of my title and I was becoming disenchanted when the wife interrupted by asking after his wife. Well, that was the first I had heard that he had one, but I couldn't bear to let that be known at that point, so I muttered something innocuous and moved on. But I was shocked. I then made enquires and discovered that he had indeed married; the army gave me the date and her name, but that was all. I returned home thoroughly bad tempered. Mostly that this information was known by such an unpleasant couple and not by myself!' He gave a bark of a laugh against himself and James began to warm to him.

The Earl continued, 'Well, of course I wondered about the woman, but as she had not turned to me when Rupert died for what she was perfectly entitled to in terms of property and income, I assumed the worst; that she was some lightskirt who had married for status and a comfortable life and had found another protector. More years slipped by and a lieutenant who had heard somehow that I was asking about my son approached me at a function. Naturally, I had been enquiring amongst the majors, colonels and generals about Rupert, I hadn't considered the lieutenants.'

Such unthinking snobbery was not unknown to James, nor unusual, but every so often its utter blindness hit him anew, like a slap in the face.

'From this woman I learned not only that Rupert had married, but more about whom he had chosen. It seemed that she had not been a lightskirt but a respectable girl whose father was a major and who had grown up within the army. Now, this did surprise me, as the fact that she had not come begging for her rights seemed now extremely strange.'

James wondered if a woman, a widow, claiming what was rightfully and legally hers, should be referred to a 'begging' but kept his own council.

'Even more extraordinary was that the woman appeared to have known the wife well and that she had left Rupert long before he died. Now she was quizzing me on what had happened to her, as if her running away was something to do with me! Or that she might even had run to me! Well, I was astonished. But it was as she was turning to go and she asked if the child had been a boy or a girl that utterly surprised me. On further questioning, it seems the woman was with child when she left Rupert. If that is so, and if the child lived, I might have an heir. That did bring me up short. So I headed down to London and have been enquiring here, and that is why I especially seek out army women. They, it seems, know a deal sight more than the men.'

This was of no surprise to James. Army women were a force unto themselves. On the whole, what they didn't know, wasn't worth knowing, from troop deployments to the ration situation. 'What was your son's wife's name?'

'Louisa Kilburn, I understand.'

'Why exactly do you wish to find her?'

'I hold assets in her name. Once I die, it will be far harder for her to claim them and I should like to hand them over.' He sighed, 'And once I had got over the shock, it occurred to me that Rupert may not have been an easy husband. If the girl grew up in the army and still ran away, it is unlikely it was army life that frightened her off. I'd like to meet her.'

'To force her back to Scotland?' James enquired.

The Earl chuckled, 'Oh no, I am long past the age of forcing women to do anything.' He gave a huge sigh, 'No, I should like to hear what she has to say, ask after the child, see if it lived. There is a title to inherit; and a girl may want a grand come-out. I can't die and not know, do you understand?'

'And you have been asking around yourself?' James remembered how hard he had thought finding Chantel would be and of all the agencies he had considered he might need to call upon.

'Oh no, not now I know there might be a child. I have hounded the Lords, Parliament, magistrates and have hired an army of enquirers. But I can't help remembering how my first information came to me so casually, so I continue to badger people.'

They sank back in silence and relaxed, while the pounding of feet and chatter of voices continued, but at a pleasant distance. James let his head fall back and closed his eyes. He couldn't get out of the army habit of sleeping when possible and eating when there was time. Wellington had ordered the battle of Salamanca in the middle of sitting on a rock eating his lunch. The French general had split his troops and Wellington had thrown his meat on the ground and leapt up saying, 'By God I have him', or some such. And that was the end of any rest for the troops for some brutal time. You never knew what or when you might be thrown into action. But as he dozed companionably by the old Earl, he began to frown. Exactly who had Chantel said her house guest was? The woman had had two daughters, though he couldn't for the life of him remember their names. The elder had been the image of Samuel and had to be his brother's so definitely not Lieutenant Colonel Rupert's. But what had Chantel said about why the woman hadn't married Samuel? He hadn't been paying much attention. But primarily it was because she had had a husband, who had inconveniently died rather too late to be of any use. He had a nagging feeling the woman might had been called Louisa. In truth he had ignored her existence.

He opened his eyes and glanced sideways at the Earl, who also had his eyes closed and now began to snore softly. If the woman was this long-lost daughter-in-law, could this old man do her any harm? On consideration, he thought not. There was no male child involved, so no inducement to whisk a child away from his mother, and the girls were grown enough to have their own opinions. And besides, Chantel was a duchess and her husband a duke. The woman would have plenty of protection there. Perhaps he would write to Chantel and tell her about this conversation. He would find out where the old boy was staying before he left. As far as he was concerned if the woman was who the Earl was hunting for, if she wanted to stay hidden that was up to her, but on the other hand, she might want what was due to her for her daughters' sakes. A letter wouldn't hurt. With that he settled down for a companionable nap.

The following night was a ball. Mary was loving the dancing. She was no longer concerned with turning the wrong way, though Jeffries still teased her about her first night. Now he was a regular partner of hers. Practise had made her if not perfect, then at least as good as everyone else. Now she could fly over the floor and smile at her partner without giving a moment's thought to her feet. It was a glorious feeling. She had been in London for seven weeks and it felt like a lifetime. She was beginning to consider returning home. Parliament would break for the summer soon and London would empty. Not completely, but it would be noticeable. And still no men seemed appropriate husband material. They were too young, or two old, or too fat, or too rich, or too much in debt; there was always something. And not one had stirred her blood. And then, as these rather lowering thoughts were moving from the back of her mind to the front, she caught a sight of a head of dark blonde hair looming above the crowd. Her stomach lurched in a quite different direction to the direction of travel with her dancing partner. Mary's hands were suddenly uncomfortably hot and her face felt cold. All she could think was, 'It can't be. Surely it can't be.'

Watching from the sidelines Silvester asked Mags, 'Who is that?' and gestured towards where the tall man was standing. Mags, who was there on her sufferance as she found balls too loud and too hot and too full of people she didn't have time for, turned to gaze where he was indicating.

'Oh my!' she gasped, 'It can't be! Can it?'

'Margaret, you are a sensible woman, so make sense,' Silvester snapped.

'I can't really see from here, but I am wondering if that is James?'

'Who is James?' he asked, his voice once more smooth.

'He is an army major. It was he who arranged for the duchess to introduce Mary to London society. He once rescued their son at great risk to himself. The son, I understand, lost an arm but is well, and most importantly to them, alive.'

'A hero then,' Silvester's voice was like cream flowing over a table.

'Oh yes. His father and Mary's were at school together.'

'Of course,' he murmured. Wasn't that how all this worked? Endless connections?

As the dance stopped, Mary could be seen leaning forward to talk to her partner. Instead of returning to Silvester and Mags, they could be seen moving towards the part of the room where the tall man stood holding court. Mags watched Silvester's face as Mary moved away from him. Then it closed into his usual cynical demeanour.

Silvester saw the moment Mary knew that her suspicion was correct. Her face lit up as if a fire had ignited inside her. Even from here he could taste her delight, sense her intense excitement. And for the first time since he was a raw-kneed thirteen-year-old, he felt intense emotional pain. How could he have been such a fool? As he watched her lift her face to the man he almost wanted to laugh. He had found the only woman who might have satisfied him, in character, intelligence, courage, let alone sexuality, and he had let her slip away like water down a slope. He could have, now he realised, should have, tried for her. She was lonely. She longed for companionship and a male partner. She wanted the chance of more children and perhaps most of all a mate she could bind to and trust. And he was not as old as she thought. His hair had gone prematurely silver when he was twenty-one. He hadn't challenged her assumption that he was past forty; in fact, he was only thirty-two. He was comfortably wealthy but had no huge estate tying him to a place far from Lincolnshire, he was more tired of London entertainments than he could express, yet he had never once considered altering his life, until now. He could have lived in the country, helped Mary with her estate and been a father to the boy. Now he felt it was beyond his grasp it all flashed into his mind at once. He looked at Mags and beamed his most cynical smile at her. Mags eyes told him she was not in the least bit fooled.

James was surrounded by a gaggle of young men. He was standing, as always, with his feet slightly apart, his hands clasped behind him, and his back straight. Behind his back he held a long black-lacquered cane horizontally that she could see had a large silver head on one end. Mary wondered if the knob was the only weapon or if the cane, like Silvester's, also held a blade. He stood taller than most men, broader than most men and he didn't hide the fact. He wasn't looking at her but she knew that he knew she was there. 'I've told you lads, soldiering is drilling and killing. Nothing more.'

'But nothing less, I'll wager,' commented one of the young men.

'Lads, run along. I wish to speak to the lady.' At the gentle admonishment, they all turned and bowed to Mary and took their leave, their voices quiet but excited.

'Lord Causton,' she murmured.

'Lady Mary,' he returned.

She bobbed a curtsey, he bowed from the waist. They gazed at each other.

'You have admirers, I see,' she said. She was vaguely aware of her previous dance partner melting away, as did the other onlookers who had been wishing to capture a little of the glamour of a war hero by catching his attention.

'Mary,' he said softly. And he smiled. That gentle smile that was his and only his. 'Waltz with me?' he asked. The musicians could be heard retuning their instruments.

'Can you?' she asked.

'Try me?'

How could she resist? He turned and with the smallest nod gestured one of the many footmen running around with silver trays and champagne flutes towards him.

'Be a good lad and look after this for me,' James asked. The footman seemed as smitten as any of the other young men that had clustered around him. He appeared thrilled to be asked to hold the black cane and Mary had to raise an amused eyebrow.

As they stood waiting for the music to begin, James asked, 'Are you married?'

Mary tipped her head and looked at him. 'No.'

He frowned, 'Engaged?'

Again came the answer, 'No.'

His frown deepened, his eyes on the jewels around her neck. He felt uncomfortable, unsure he should continue. She was wearing a tiara with sapphires and diamonds and a matching collar with a tear-drop diamond of considerable size pointing enticingly down towards her desirable cleavage.

Mary read his mind. 'Ah, yes. The whole of the *bon ton* is wondering. There is a book somewhere that gives ten to one that a friend of mine, a Charles Dowding, who happens to be an Earl, gifted them. Silvester, who accompanies me everywhere is 25 to one. He is vastly insulted. In fact,' she paused, 'I bought them myself. One day, hopefully, Jack's wife will inherit them.'

James' face broke into a broad smile. 'Well done. You don't need them, though. You are stunning just on your own.'

Mary glanced up, then away, as a rose pink filled her cheeks. Her blush gave him a little confidence. The dance began and he took her into his arms. She fitted as he knew she always would. He wasn't sure if after the dance she might drift away, perhaps never to be seen again, so he tried not to allow his grip to tighten or to pull her too close. She had made friends, found her feet, and had a new life far from the one he had shared for a while in Lincolnshire. And what was he? A somewhat battered army major currently on half-pay and with no fortune at all. In fact, not far from being in queer street.

When the set of dances ended, James escorted her over to where she indicated Mags was waiting. Beside Mags was a slender man of average height with attractive silver hair. As James made his bow he was aware that the man's face was completely shuttered. Mags however, received his kiss with delight, and took both of his hands.

'Oh how lovely to see you. And you looking so well!' James gave a small nod. 'Hal is still at Swann Manor with the children! We have been talking of going back to Lincolnshire! How glad I am you found us, we might have been gone.'

James turned to look at Mary, but said nothing.

'Did you arrive in the carriage?' Mary asked James.

'I did.'

'Well, I have danced enough for one night. Why don't you take me home. We can catch up on gossip on the way. Silvester will see Mags home, won't you?'

James took in a breath. He was being manipulated, which he was perfectly happy about, but Silvester looked frozen into immobility, which suggested he was far from pleased with the suggestion.

'I will indeed ensure Madame Margaret is returned home safely,' Silvester said gracefully over Mary's hand.

For Mary, seeing James had settled everything in her mind, and now she could hardly draw breath with the stress of it. Her chest felt tight and her stomach was like ice and her thoughts were a blizzard of confusion. He was back. And looked well. And she wanted to laugh and cry and dance and run, all at once. They stood side by side and silent until James had retrieved his cane. As their cloaks arrived James asked, 'Did you arrive with Silvester?'

'Mm, yes.' Mary's response was evasive enough to suggest she knew she was behaving badly.

'Will he forgive you?' James was curious about this friendship. Clearly it was one of some long standing.

Mary sighed, 'He doesn't own me.' Her voice held a snap of irritation, which made James smile.

He ensured her skirts were well away from the wheels as he helped her into the carriage and received a warm smile in response. Once inside however, embarrassment cloaked them like a heavy weight. Eventually Mary asked softly, 'Why were you at the ball?'

There seemed no point in prevaricating, 'I was looking for you.'

'Why?'

'Ah, lass. I needed to see you again. Just that really. My eyes felt hungry for the sight of you. I didn't mean to interfere in your life.'

In the dark Mary tipped back her head and opened her mouth. My eyes felt hungry for the sight of you. Dear god. The man could say such things as if they were the most commonplace comments, but her heart was beating so fast now she could hardly breathe. 'Are you well?' she whispered.

'I believe so. But like all ordnance it needs testing.' He gave a soft laugh. 'But I can't see that happening any time soon.'

Mary sat silent, her emotions in turmoil. But she had learned never to let an important moment slide past, she might never get another one, so she turned to him and found his hand with her own. His fingers curled around hers and gripped.

'Lass?' he whispered. And then he turned in his seat, and without thought she turned in hers, and their mouths met, softly, sweetly, and with hesitation on both sides. When James slid his arms around her she gave him her weight and leaned against his chest, his coat buttons digging into her breasts, but she didn't care. She wanted to cry and laugh, all at once. A fire ripped through them. What had been tentative became hard and demanding. Mary was gasping, her arms tight around his neck, her gloved hands desperate to be bare so she could filter his hair against her skin. By the time the carriage slowed Mary was almost laying on top of James, their mutual need rising with the power of a summer thunder storm. As they pulled apart Mary whispered,

'James?'

'I want you.' It was all he said. And it was so like him. Like his eyes being hungry, he said what he felt. Tears clenched in Mary's chest.

'Then come inside,' she invited.

The two footmen with cudgels were waiting at her steps. James reviewed them both and gave a nod of approval and Mary felt like laughing as both stood taller. 'Good lads,' James told them quietly. Hawes ushered them inside and asked if they would like tea in the drawing room. 'Not tonight', Mary told him. The thought of sitting opposite James and sipping tea was unconscionable. James handed over his cape, shako and cane and Mary headed up the stairs with James beside her. She didn't even attempt to fox Hawes at the top.

Instead of heading straight into the drawing room she turned immediately left towards her room with James close behind her. She was wild to be in his arms and the sense of his urgency was driving her need higher.

They walked through the door to Mary's room and James caught at her shoulder, kicked the door closed and slammed her hard against the wall. Her face was full of fierce glee and she reached towards him and kissed him hard. He thought he might devour her; kisses had never been so wild, so desperate. Heat roared through him and he was struggling to find the fastenings at her back as she was hauling his jacket buttons undone. He pulled the dress down but it only trapped her arms against her side and revealed the chemise underneath, a filmy cover for her breasts. He kissed the skin of her breast that swelled above the silk.

'Get this dress off!' Mary almost screamed. 'Get it off! Get it off!'

His head was pounding and his erection had never been harder. Thought seemed to have left him as he spun her around and fought with the wretched fastenings, before pulling a knife from his boot and slashing the ties of the chemise. Both garments slid to the floor, leaving her in nothing but her drawers and stockings. She grabbed at his hair and pulling his head down, thrust her tongue into his mouth. He met her swirl for thrust, tasting her, devouring her. His jacket was gone and his breeches were down around his knees. Mary was fumbling for his rod and found his balls. She curled her palm under them and weighed them, then ran her hand up his length, gripping and pulling his foreskin up, then down. He tipped back his head and thought his eyes might burst out of their sockets.

'I need to be inside you,' and his voice was gravel.

In response Mary skipped up and slung her legs around his hips. He pushed her back into the wall hard and she guided him in. His tip found her entrance and it felt red hot, like a furnace that would cinder him whole. Without waiting, he thrust home and sank into a warmth he had missed all his life. Pulling back, he began to pound. Her back was banging against the wall and her mouth was demanding more and more from his. He drew back from the kiss, buried his head in her neck, and flexed his hips again and again. Lust roared and the scent of sex was intoxicating. He banged and banged and exploded.

He stood panting, taking her weight, sweat pouring down inside his shirt, his arse bare and his boots still on. And then she giggled. A girlish sound.

'You needed that,' she whispered in his ear.

'As did you,' he murmured back. Withdrawing from her body he let her slip to the ground and then gave a mocking laugh himself. 'I have yoked myself round the legs. If I try to walk I shall fall over.'

Together they pulled themselves into some semblance of order until he could walk, and then he lifted her and carried her to the bed. Dropping her onto the mattress he sat to remove his boots.

'Not dancing shoes. Do boots give you more support?'

'They do indeed. My left leg is still weak.' He looked straight at her, 'It may always be so.'

'Is that supposed to put me off?' Her eyebrows were arched high.

She watched as he moistened his lips and still panting slightly, yanked at the boot leather. Giving a soft laugh, she slipped off the bed and kneeling at his feet, caught hold of the heels and helped tug them off.

'I hate tight boots,' he muttered.

'Mm,' she murmured, 'I don't know, they may help keep you in one place.'

When he was stripped he rolled onto the bed and she climbed in alongside him. He lay back with his forearm over his eyes. He had never taken a woman in that way, with such desperation and ferocity. Sex with Elfie had been pleasant and comforting.

'You must be bruised?' he suspected. When he received no reply he moved his arm and looked for her. When they had entered the room there had been one candle left by her bedside, well away from all bed hangings and with a curl of metal arcing over to keep the flame in one place. Now Mary was drifting around the room lighting candles everywhere, three on the dresser, three across the room, two singles by the door. She was naked and seemed unconcerned. He watched her, enjoying the view. She was long limbed and taut with lithe muscle. Her breasts were not over-large, but were perfect, and her hair hung down her back in a wave of darkness that the candles seemed unable to illuminate.

She strode back towards him, her breasts bouncing slightly and revealing a thick thatch of dark hair at her groin. He felt his already partially stiffened rod harden further and his temperature was rising. She too was flushed, her cheeks a warm blush with a softer blush reaching down towards her nipples. He stretched out an arm for her and she joined him on the bed. Instead of lying beside him, she stayed on all fours watching him. He grew even harder and thought he might burst. She was as predatory as a wolf. She prowled up the bed to his hips and leaning forward, gnawed on his hip bone gently, then licked where her teeth had been. She crawled forward a little, stroking him with her tongue. He had a thick mat of golden-brown chest hair and she avoided that and licked up his side, edging away from where he really wanted her mouth.

He pushed up, knocked her down and covered her back, hauling her hips backwards. In this position he could stroke her breasts and let one hand slide over the satin of her skin until he found the moist area within the hair. He let just the tip on one finger slide along where moisture dampened his hand, then he slid it into her, rotating and thrusting a mere inch or two. She was writhing, trying to force his finger in deeper, but he held her firm and taunted her. She was panting and sobbing his name.

'Do you want me?' he growled.

'Yes, you bastard, yes!' she panted.

He thrust into her heat, deep, encased. She was tight; a perfect fit. He began to slide in and out, keeping it slow, but she was gasping 'Harder, harder!' so he obliged. The pace increased and he was losing control when she began to convulse and he could feel strong internal muscles sucking him deeper and deeper, pumping him as hard as he was pumping her. And then she screamed. A high shriek that should have had mountains to echo across. She suddenly went boneless and he had to tighten his arm muscles to hold her in place as he ground hard to his own completion.

They were both panting and soaked in sweat. They fell together into the sheets and blankets and bound together tight body to body. He didn't want to let her go and, it seemed, the feeling was mutual.

'I only went to that ball in the hopes of catching a glimpse of you,' he said softly.

'Disappointed?' she asked.

'What do you think?'

She gave a soft laugh and then sleep came swiftly.

James woke when light struck his eyelids. Sleepily her became aware of a warm presence beside him. Rolling, he gathered Mary up into his arms. She came awake quickly, as he had expected she would.

'Oh, that is better,' she said, 'light.' In a flurry of sheets she was up on her knees stroking him and examining him thoroughly.

'What are you doing?'

'I could only feel most of your wounds last night. Now I can see.'

James raised his eyebrows. He paid little attention to his body except the keep it clean. To his mind it was a tool that he could use, not much different to his sabre or his horse. And when it let him down, it annoyed all hell out of him.

Mary was sitting back on her haunches and cupping his balls. He watched her, now through narrowed eyes. He wasn't sure she might not bite them off.

'Goodness. You really are large all over.

'I thought you might have noticed that last night,' he commented dryly. 'Are you complaining?'

'Oh no. But you have ruined me for any other man.' She slid her hand up the length of him, squeezing and exploring.

James let his head fall back. He had thought he was hard, but she had just made him harder. She had rather long hands, with elegant fingers, that suited her height and slenderness, and now he discovered that whether or not she could play the pianoforte, she could certainly play him. 'Mary ...' It came out as a growl. To his disappointment, she moved to his left thigh.

'There is a large hollow where muscle should be,' she commented, letting her hand learn the contours of the scarring. 'And the hair hasn't grown back.'

His erection wilted slightly.

'But it seems to have healed well.' She moved on to roam around his lower legs before exploring his stronger right thigh. James stared up at the bed canopy and held his breath. Until last night he had been without a woman for a long time. If Mary didn't consent to another coupling after her exploration he thought his teeth might crack. And deep inside, hardly admitted, he was still anxious. At last she sat back to gaze at him.

'You are beautiful,' she said softly.

He heard himself laugh. 'Men aren't beautiful.'

'You are.' Her face was downcast and he frowned. 'What did you think of me when you met me?' Her voice was rather sad.

'I was fascinated by you. Once I woke up, that is.' He grinned. 'I was dozing by the fire and you sat opposite me with a book.'

'I was trying to teach myself Latin so that I could teach Jack.'

He smiled. 'You had a terrible fierce beauty that called to me. Have you ever heard of a Lammergier?' She shook her head. 'It is like a golden eagle, in many ways. I used to watch them in the Pyrenees. They fly high and then drop bones onto the rocks, then they swoop down to eat the marrow or meat from the pieces. Utterly wonderful creatures. Rare. Fierce. Amazing. You were all of that.'

'Birds don't eat bones.'

'Don't shift the subject. And yes, these do. I saw you and I saw yet another rare and gorgeous creature. Your eyebrows reminded me of the beard the bird has and your tooth was like its powerful sharp beak.'

'It has a beard,' her voice sounded cross, but she couldn't keep the smile away.

'Had I been able, I would have courted you then and there.' He paused, 'Not I imagine as fast as Hal courted Mags...' Her laughter made him pause. 'I wanted you then, Mary,' he reached to tickle her ribs, 'and I want you now.' In one swift motion she swung her leg over him and sat wide poised over his erection. She held his eyes and lowered herself slowly. He felt himself sink into female warmth. She was everything he had imagined she might be in bed, and more.

It was two nights later that they experienced their first disagreement. 'I will have the banns called as soon as we return home to Lincolnshire,' Mary breathed against his bare chest. They had barely been able to keep their hands off each other and it seemed prudent to remain for a while away from the keen eyes of two children for at least a few days. The amount of time they were spending in bed would be impossible under their watchful gaze.

'No, lass, don't,' was James' quiet reply. His tone suggested he knew he was in for an argument.

Mary pushed away from him sharply. 'Why not?' she demanded. He hated the hurt in her voice.

He reached and ran his fingers slowly through her hair, letting it sift gently so if fell against his bare skin. 'You aren't a woman to sleep beside an impotent man.'

'But you aren't!' There was pain in her eyes.

'But what if this doesn't last? What if my body lets me down again? Or what if I can't give you children? Once we marry, we will be tied together for life unless I swallow a bullet.'

'Swallow a ...' her voice tailed away.

'I considered it. I might have done it if I hadn't received your letter asking for help. The pain was increasing as the metal in my leg moved. I was barely conscious sometimes it was so great. I still don't know how Satan got me to Lincolnshire, or how I kept going once there.'

'But you are well!' Now she was annoyed. He was being ridiculous.

James drew in a deep breath. 'I am not confident this will last.'

Mary herself drew in a breath. She was sitting up now with the sheet clasped around her, 'I love you; I am in love for the first time in my life. I have never believed I might one day say that to a man. I love you utterly.' Her voice tailed away.

James reached for her and gripped her arms, 'You are every beat of my heart. But I will never tie you to half a man. And I am a soldier.'

'Don't I have a say in this?'

'It isn't just my health. Where are we going to live? You have huge responsibilities in Lincolnshire. You are one of the largest landowners in the country and I have inherited a small run-down estate in Wiltshire at the other end of the country and I am still in the army. I too have responsibilities. How do we marry the two?' His choice of words was deliberate.

Mary pulled away and sat up straighter. 'We discuss it. We resolve it. Tell me straight. Do you want me?'

He raised his eyebrows and had to smile. 'I do.' She was his Mary; strong, opinionated and so, so precious. The wanting wasn't in question. The keeping was.

'Right,' she said, sinking back against his chest, 'In that case, we need to have a discussion.'

'Later,' he murmured and kissed her.

What they did do later was send Mags home in the coach with most of Mary's clothes. She had no intention of attending any more balls or 'at homes'. The coach wasn't large enough for everyone and she was too parsimonious to hire a second coach for the baggage. James grinned and let her get on with it. Besides, Mary argued, Mags and Hal were newly wedded and had enjoyed very little time together. Again, James tried not to raise his eyebrows. It would take over a week for the coach to do the return trip and he had no complaint about spending a week in bed with Mary. What happened after that, well, he considered that that was not yet decided.

Mary didn't let the matter drop. They were in bed together. 'Are we going to marry?' she demanded.

'No marriage,' he replied.

Her eyes narrowed further. 'Isn't that supposed to be my decision? You ask and I answer.'

He closed his eyes and grinned. 'I haven't asked.'

'But you will.' Her tone suggested she would brook no argument. Then she frowned. He could sense it even with his eyes closed. 'Don't you love me?'

His answer was to slide a finger-tip along her shoulder, then to let it slide down navigating the rise and fall of her collar-bone until it found the swell of her breast. Tracing the slope, he circled her nipple then traced the curve as her breast fell and curved around towards her ribs. Heat had flooded her skin and she was beginning to forget her question. As her breath began to race, she asked again, but this time she couldn't keep the trace of grief out of her voice.

'Don't you love me?'

His voice was husky, 'Lass, you are why the sun rises for me in the morning, why the moon hangs in the sky at night and why a blanket of stars cover me while I sleep. Don't ask such a daft question.'

Mary swallowed, 'James, that was ... romantic.'

His eyes shot open, 'Me? Nay lass, I've always thought there was more than a hint of deceit about romance. I just tell the truth.' His eyes closed again and wandering fingers were once more tracing casual paths across her skin. Mary shivered.

'James, I am a puddle of passion. If you are going to make love to me, please, get on with it.'

'Puddle of passion, hey.' He was laughing quietly, 'Now I can't decide if that is romantic or not.'

She gave a shudder as pure lust rippled through her and so she flattened her body across his, breasts to chest. Her right hand roamed down across the sheet and gripped him. Finding him as hard as rock she moved so she could whip back the sheet and straddle him. She held herself above him, wide open and hot and welcoming. Well, that had opened his eyes fully. They were dark and intent and she could now see the same roaring need there that she herself felt. As she sank slowly down, taking him in, feeling him fill her she lifted back until she sat high above him. Leaning back further she began to rock. His eyes were slits now, his big rough hands grazing her skin as he explored the contours of her thighs and the curve of her backside.

'Why no marriage?' she hissed.

'Ask me later,' he gasped, and she gave a laughing sob of triumph.

Later came. Curled against him, sweat soaked and content, at least for a while, Mary explored the indentations and ridges of his various scars.

'How often has Hal nursed you back from the dead?'

'Hang on, love, it hasn't been as bad as all that!' He sounded indignant.

'Well?'

He took his time before saying, 'Three, I think. When he found me on the waterfront in India, then there was a bad sabre wound but Elfie did most of the nursing then, and lastly, after Waterloo when that bloody cannon blew apart. Rare event that.'

'And then when I cut holes in you.' Her hand ranged over the indentation in his left thigh. 'If you hadn't been so big and had so much muscle, you would have died you know?'

'That and a talented surgeon.'

'Who has retired.' Her voice took on a new urgency. 'James, I still have nightmares about that night. I dream of the blood, that you die, that you come back and attack me because I hurt you. You screamed, you know, just before you passed out. It was a ghastly sound.'

'I did? Odd that. I remember nothing.' He was filtering his hands through her hair, letting the strands slip and slide over his fingers. 'Your hair is finer than silk, softer, pure pleasure to explore.'

'Stop trying to distract me.'

'Is that what I am doing?' His grin was sleepy.

'So, why won't you marry me?'

He breathed in deep. 'I am no hero. I am not the man you think I am; I am a jobbing soldier, doing what he is told and going where he is put. You aren't the only one to have nightmares. There was a little lad who played the fife to keep the time when we marched. I was standing as close to him as I am to you when his head was blown apart. I often relive that moment, both awake and asleep. I have been a soldier for well over ten years and actively fighting for most of that time. When other soldiers were given periods of rest, Hal and I were out searching for the enemy, sometimes staying in hiding as they rode or sneaked by, then when we could, picking them off and getting away to safety. We sought out routes, watched the enemy, hunted men as prey. This year and a half of recovery has been the only real rest I have had since childhood. The army wants me back. Wellington has told them to keep me on half-pay for as long as I need. He wants me fighting the colonials.'

'What will you do?'

He sighed. 'How do I refuse Wellington?'

'By letting me speak to him! I will tell him that enough is enough. My turn now!'

He laughed. A genuine peal of laughter. He looked years younger and so gorgeous she could have eaten him up. 'Perhaps I should do that!'

There had been no more talk, just sleep, tied together in a knot Mary knew she never wanted to break. He was going to cross that Atlantic and go back to fighting over her dead body, she decided, besides, there was something else. They might have made a baby. She smiled as she sank fathoms deep.

Over breakfast the following morning she restarted her campaign. Perhaps when they weren't in bed they might manage to finish a conversation properly.

'Apart from being a soldier, what options do you have?'

'None, as far as I can see. Yes, I have inherited the Causton estate and the title, but the money that went with it is gone. At least for now.'

'So you have the land, but not the finance. Is it in a bad way?'

'From what little I saw, dreadful. I can't face taking it over, raising people's hopes, then not being able to improve anything. Besides which, I wouldn't know what to do. I didn't grow up thinking I would be a landowner. Chantel, my sister did. When both our parents died she was fourteen and said that she would take over the running of it. She could have too. She never got on with Lucian and he simply forbade her to set foot on the place. She complied. Not happily, but she was dependent upon him for support. Without that, she would have been on the street.'

'I'd know what to do. I have been running a huge estate since I was sixteen, only slightly older than when your sister wanted to. I suspect your brother made a huge mistake.'

'You could be right. She might not have married the Doughy Duke if she had been able to satisfy her ambition that way.'

'The what?'

James gave a massive and wicked grin. 'Her husband, The most honourable Duke of Daughton. Useless chap, as far as I can see.' She was now laughing so much she could barely breathe. 'But seriously,' he continued, 'you are tied to Lincolnshire and Causton is in Wiltshire. That couldn't work.'

Mary was now looking thoughtful. 'Couldn't it? One reason I can't employ managers, which I should like to do, is that they refuse to take a woman seriously. I had to chase one off with a pistol. There is currently a large hole in the study floor that I really ought to get a carpenter to.'

James' face had gone blank. 'You shot him?'

'Not him, just the floor, but as pistols come in pairs he decided to find other employment. The man he had replaced had thought I was ripe to be both embezzled and seduced. Now, if you were my husband, no one would try to commit fraud, or,' she hesitated, 'bother my person.' The look on James' face was now, to her mind, entirely satisfactory. Mary didn't think he had thought far enough ahead to consider what might be her fate if he followed Wellington's orders. She hoped his protective instincts, let alone his possessive, might now be completely engaged.

After a long pause he said quietly, 'Mm, I will have to make sure I leave you safe.'

Mary bit her bottom lip, hard, so that the smug smile that was rising from her gut was not allowed to blossom. Men! You had to lead them by the nose, sometimes. Leave her safe? Who with, she wondered?

She left James alone then, hoping, trusting, that he would begin to see the future the way she wanted him to. With them married. Partners. Patience seemed to be paying off when he said some hours later, 'There was a man staying with my sister. I think his name was Hawkhurst. An ex-army officer who she was training to be an estate manager. There might be a chance that you could employ him. If my sister has had a hand in him, he is likely to be good.'

'You think him to be trustworthy?'

'Probably yes. If he is worth his salt, how would you feel about employing him? As an ex-soldier and if my sister says he is trustworthy, then you would be safe with him.'

Mary narrowed her eyes. She wasn't sure his mind was travelling quite where she wanted it to. 'I could then live in Wiltshire, at Causton.'

'Possibly.'

Mary's face was split in two her smile was so wide.

'Is that finally a proposal?'

'No. I am still thinking.'

Mary forbear from screaming.

Chapter Ten

London to Lincoln was one hundred and fifty miles. Because all roads led to Lincoln they would have to go there before turning to head another seven miles back at a different angle towards Swann Manor. Which didn't sound much, but that road was atrocious. In the coach, this gave them at least three days on the road before stopping in Lincoln. Mary had James all to herself and she felt like the cat who had got the cream. They talked non-stop the first day. James told about his early life in the army, how he had thrived on every aspect and how he found it impossible to imagine life without it. Mary told him about her childhood accompanying her father all over his extensive estate, both learning about the crops and the denizens. She had a quiver full of anecdotes about the doings of Lincolnshire farming folk and their superstitions. At new year's eve it was common for them to put out a saucer of milk with a piece of bread, a piece of wood and a coin so the pixies would bless them with food, fuel and income for the following year. New shoes must never be put on a table; at which point James exclaimed, 'And old ones can?' And how when a cow calved, she must have a rhyme told into her ear to ensure that the calf thrived. In return James told her about the Hindu customs he had come across and about the gods he had come to feel fond of, like Ganesh, the elephant god. They both, however, kept their secrets. James about the girl who had died with his babe inside her and Mary about what Brewer had exactly put her through. The past was sometimes best left there.

It was on the second day as James dozed next to her that Mary had time to gaze at him and think. She drank in his face with its strong bones and regular features. She loved his dark blue eyes and the tawny hair, glinting with pale and old gold, along with every other part of him even, perhaps especially, the scars. He viewed the world with an air of quiet amusement, as if nothing could surprise him. Or perhaps more accurately, whatever it surprised him with he could cope with! Both men and women gravitated towards the aura of command that he wore like a cloak which, she suspected, came from his rock-solid confidence in himself.

He was army to the core and had known little else. So he had, in some ways, never had to think for himself. The army had fed him, housed him, and told him what it wanted him to do. His task had been to perform to the best of his ability and take care of his men. So was it surprising that when Wellington had told him, I want you in the colonies, he had simply got on with getting better so that he could fulfil his orders? It wasn't so much that he didn't want to marry her, she thought, it was more that his mind hadn't been flexible enough to think past the army command.

She moved across the seat to lean into his side and without opening his eyes his arm came around her, setting her against his body comfortably and holding her firm against the swaying of the carriage. She nestled into his warmth and breathed in the scent of warm man, horse and fresh air that was soaked into his skin and clothes. Unseen she pressed a kiss into the wool of his jacket. It was clear she would have to do the thinking for him for a while, until he became used to his new life and status. He seemed more embarrassed than proud of now being Major Lord Causton. He had an innate modesty that she adored. When she asked him how he had become a Major his answer was that all the good men had either been lost in the Peninsula or sent across the

Atlantic, so he had been the only one left. When quizzed about his title his attitude was much the same, he simply said that some better men than him had died. Which was true of all aristocratic titles! Yet she had never heard any other person be so self-deprecating about how they came into their inheritance.

Jack's own inheritance could be secured with a number of managers, especially with James to keep a keen eye on them, and James' own estate would prove a challenge to both of them. Besides, she knew she had the skills and he had the command; they would work well together. Slowly she had learned to have more sympathy for his response to the idea of marriage. For one, he hadn't thought that far, two, he hadn't trusted his body was healed and three, they hadn't really known each other. Well, she had settled all of that. Now she should plan her wedding. She closed her eyes and joined him in sleep. Neither of them, after all, was getting much at night.

At Swann Manor, Jack made it clear that he had expected James to return. He seemed satisfied with James' reply that he had, 'Been busy.' 'Mama is often busy,' Jack informed James seriously. Mary bit in her bottom lip and felt guilty. Elfie had finally stopped wetting the bed and crying out in the night and was growing tall. James wasn't lying when he expressed his amazement at how much they had both changed since he had last seen them. Both children had shot up in height and Jack especially was asking keenly perceptive questions. Elfie watched James from a distance for a few days sucking two fingers so much her chin went red with a rash before, having seen Jack climb all over him, she shyly edged up to his knee and leant gently against him. James hardly dared move, so he simply rested his hand lightly on her head for the moment. That evening she climbed into his lap, curled up like a kitten, and went to sleep. Mary watched James blink and wondered if his eyes were pricking. 'If that man doesn't believe he is marrying me,' she told herself, 'he has another think coming.' The cat, however, was displeased at having her favourite lap invaded and urinated on his boot.

The Army's Son

The row came two days later. Hal had been up to Mags' room, the one he had moved into as soon as he had met her and was passing Mary's room. James' voice was loud enough to wake the dead.

'Just who do you think it is you want to marry? I am a soldier. I have always been a soldier. I have no future except as a soldier! It is my trade and I am good at it.'

Hal nodded to himself in the gloom of the corridor. Too true he was. A bloody wonder with a sword. He could hear Mary's screamed response but couldn't make out the words.

'I am a man, Mary, just a man. I am not some sainted knight on a white horse, some hero in a story book. I kill men for a living and worse, I both teach other men to kill and then send them off to kill or more likely recently, die themselves.'

Hal headed out of the corridor towards the stairs in a hurry. He did not want to be caught eavesdropping if James came storming out, or if he was in a blind fury, be flattened by him.

Mags was downstairs and raised her face as he walked in. 'I didn't know James could lose his temper,' she commented. 'He always seems so utterly calm, as if nothing could disturb him.'

'Ah well, normally that is the truth. Could you hear them down here?'

'I can hear Mary shouting, but not what she is saying, but James was clear. I take it she has upset him.'

Hal chuckled, 'You could say that. It is probably for the best. They need to sort out their differences before the wedding bells chime. He can be too calm for his own good.'

'If I were her I'd be terrified. Does he get this cross often?'

'I've only ever seen it once before. A man who had been left in camp had been caught going through the men's things. He had taken all sorts, including a gold locket and a silver ring, all keepsakes from men's wives and sweethearts. He was hauled before James. James let rip. The man was being held between two corporals. James told him what a disgrace he was, how disappointed he was, how he had been proud of the man before this, how he had let his company down, he just didn't stop. Now this is a lad, like so many others, who had come from the Rookeries of London, whose mother was a drunken prostitute, never had a father and had been stealing anything not nailed down since he could walk. Yet, by the time James had finished, he was weeping and saying how sorry he was.'

Mags' eyes were wide open as she listened. Hal told a good story.

'James bellowed for the company to fall in and for the man to have ten lashes. Men were still scrambling into collars and coats and the lad was being tied to a wheel, when the Colonel arrived. Now he was as puce as a ripe damson. He hissed at James that the penalty was fifty lashes. James turned to him and said, "One, he had already received forty lashes of my tongue, two, a full fifty lashes in this heat is a death sentence and I want him to live, when he isn't thieving he is a bloody good soldier and three, if the little bastard does it again I will probably shoot him myself." By now the lad was twisted towards James blubbering, "I won't sir, I won't, I promise. And if I do I will shoot myself!".'

Mags found she was laughing. 'What happened?'

'The boy took his ten lashes and adored James for the rest of his life.'

When he sat beside her on the settle Mags curled into Hal's embrace. 'I am so glad we haven't been through all that.'

'Aye lass, but they are young. And young James can be as sour as an unripe apple when his peace is disturbed.'

'I thought that was the definition of a wife. Someone who disturbs a man's peace.'

'Never you, lass. You are my peace.' He kissed her soundly and gave thanks that he was no longer young.

Upstairs, now alone, Mary paced up and down in a furious rage. The stupid, stupid blockhead. Why couldn't he see what she was offering him! She would not cry. She never cried. She paced some more.

The argument between James and Mary, far from being resolved, erupted the following afternoon. They had slipped upstairs for a post luncheon 'nap'. Confident that wonderful sex would have softened him

Mary once again tried to discuss James leaving the army. His response was, if anything, even more violent than the last time. She was pacing to and fro pointing out how comfortable a life they could have together. His silence had given her hope until he erupted.

'Woman!' The word echoed from the walls. Mary stopped pacing. 'Just stop, will you?' James was sitting on the end of the bed, his elbows on his knees, his head dropped forward. Mary closed her jaw with an audible click of teeth. She had always thought the expression, his jaw dropped with shock, merely an expression before. Clearly not. She turned to face him. She hadn't thought he was capable of so much anger. She wasn't certain she was pleased to learn that he had such a temper and was willing to once more turn it on her.

'I am not certain I exist outside of the army. It has been my meat and drink, the air I breathe, for the whole of my life.'

Mary felt the blood leave her face. She swallowed. She had always recognised the army was her foe. Now, she thought, perhaps it really is bigger than I am? More powerful. He was looking up at her now, his face blank.

'I am not just a soldier. I am an officer. I don't just kill other men. I order men to kill, train them how, teach them where to aim their bullets and knife points. I send them into danger, again and again, to risk their bodies and lives.' His voice dropped, 'Perhaps their souls.' He looked up at her, his face hard. 'They belong to me, those men. They are my lads. Some are half my age, some twice, but they are all my lads. Mine. I take responsibility for them. I am the one who both sends them into danger and keeps them safe. I am the one who ensures that they are housed and fed to the best of my abilities. I know their strengths and weaknesses. I know the ones to trust and the ones to keep an eye on. They are mine. And I am theirs.' Mary took a breath and realised that she was shaking. 'I know no other life; am not convinced I know how else to live.' He made a wide gesture with one arm, 'I don't trust that I can change. Without the army, what am I? Just a useless lump of blood and muscle, with no skills and no future. What is it about that you do not understand?'

He stood and looked down at her. 'I am going for a walk.' When she heard the door close, it echoed her heart breaking.

Mary stood at the window and bit down on her knuckles. When she saw him storm out of the front door, hatless and coatless, she went to find her son and Elfie. She badly needed a cuddle.

When the letter from Chantel inviting James to The Court arrived it caused much discussion. Eventually, he wrote back to ask if he might bring Mary and her children for a visit. A reply was sent back soon enough for Mary to trust that the invitation might be genuine. She was burning with curiosity about James' sister, the one who had wanted to, but been forbidden, to run an estate, but who now ran a duchy. The day before they left, a letter arrived from James' Colonel.

'He wishes to know if I have, or if I think I will, recover from my injury.'

Mary glared at him. 'So the army really does want you back?'

James didn't dignify that with an answer, in fact, he barely raised an eyebrow. Their row had been left, but not resolved and simmered between them. 'He wants to know if I am fit for overseas service.' He raised his eyes to Mary, 'He says the King cannot afford to lose experienced soldiers like myself.'

'You really will go back.' Mary's tone was sharp. For the first time she wondered if she might lose.

'Mary, he mentions the King. If he persuades the King to personally request I remain in the army, I cannot refuse. To do so would be treason.'

'That is blackmail!'

To her intense annoyance, James simply ignored her and wandered out to go for a walk.

Hal was grinning. 'What is so amusing?' she snapped.

'He always does that. I thought at first he sulked, then I realised that when he is thinking he just shuts off. When he has thought, he tells you what he thinks.'

The Army's Son

Mary retired to her room. She hated that Hal knew more about James than she did. Hated it! Mags' frequent admonition that 'You catch more flies with honey than with vinegar' banged in her mind. Like James, she needed time to calm down. She felt no better when she did. If she forced James out of the army before he was ready, might it become a wedge between them later? She paced up and down and began to smile when realised she was doing exactly what James was, shutting herself off so she could think. The answer, when it came, was to write to Wellington.

Hal and Mags were to remain at Swann Manor and join James and Mary later, either at The Court or at Causton. James needed to chew over his possible futures and he wanted Hal with him. Mary didn't mind, she likewise wanted Mags for companionship. She might love James, but Mags was a part of her. In the coach as they headed for The Court, while the children dozed, Mary asked, 'What were your parents like?' What she really wanted was information about this sister who had managed to become a duchess.

James frowned, then admitted, 'I can't really remember. I must look like my father as both Luc and Tilly thought I was him back from the dead when they first saw me. I do have a sense that they were close and that they shared a lot of laughter, but apart from that, not much.'

'Does your sister take after your mother in looks?'

'Yes, in a way. Tilly is tiny and neat and much prettier than I remember, and she has cut her hair. As a girl I have a vision of her in breeches, riding her pony hell for leather, with her hair unmoving on the back of her head. Her hair was a mad tangle that sat like a bush and was almost impossible to comb. I know it took days to dry because I remember she was supposed to stay indoors while it was wet, but she was forever being scolded for escaping outside.' Then he gave a huff of a laugh. 'Now I think of it, she and a lad from the stables once climbed the huge chimney in the hall. They both came out black as soot, unsurprisingly. I seem to recall Mother scrubbing Tilly with a non-stop lecture in French. I learnt some new French curse words that day!' He grinned at her, clearly delighted with the memory.

'Did your mother speak French so that you would not understand?'

'Oh no, we all were brought up to speak, read and write French. It was my English writing that was poor when I joined the army.' Mary's face showed only confusion. 'Mother was French. Her family shipped her over to England when the French were cutting the heads of any aristocrat they could lay hands on. Father found her on a quay side. He sometimes called her his mermaid, or gift of the sea, or some such nonsense.'

Mary didn't think it was nonsense; she though it was charming and romantic, but annoyance and fear chewed together in Mary's chest. Why hadn't she known his mother was French? 'So was she a French aristocrat?'

James gave it some thought. 'No idea. I do think she had been sent home once from Versailles for upsetting the king, though.'

'A girl who gets close enough to upset the French king hardly sounds like a nobody, does she?'

'I really don't know. We will have to ask Tilly. Perhaps she might know something about her.'

With unspoken agreement, their argument was put to one side. Yelling abuse at each other was not the way respectable house guests behaved. Mary was relieved. Fighting with James was hateful and exhausting. That she might not win frightened her so much she could barely breathe. She wanted to relax and seduce him to her way of thinking and a stay at The Court might just be what she needed. No responsibilities except to be polite and slide off together whenever they could. Her spirits rose high.

Like James when he had first viewed The Court, Mary was underwhelmed. It appeared to be an Elizabethan brick building, but more to the point, it looked in terrible repair. There was a third floor, but Mary couldn't believe anyone had rooms up there, most of the windows were shattered and it was clear both ivy and birds had invaded. She was rather shocked and only later realised that her face must have shown her feelings as the coach door was opened and she stepped out at the front of the house. It was poor of her and she instantly regretted it.

Their greeting party consisted of a man of average height and plump girth, whom she suspected was the duke. He had receding hair, but appeared almost bald as his hair was rather fair. To his left was a tall dark man of severe good looks. He was standing very upright with his hands clasped behind his back and Mary wondered if he was the ex-soldier, Hawksworth. Either side of them were two large footmen, one tall and big boned who had shoulder length blonde hair and looked for all the world like a Viking, while the other man was as tall but dark and intense looking. Neither looked like the living statues she had become accustomed to in London that people decorated their halls with; both looked alert and vital. And then a woman arrived, rushing, with ink on her fingers. She was small and perfect. Perfect bust, tiny waist and perfect hips. A pocket Venus. Mary hated her on sight. Especially when she rushed to James and hugged him warmly.

Once settled, Chantel absorbed James' request for help and immediately sent for Hawksworth. The coach would be sent back to Swann Manor so that Hal and Mags might join them when they were ready, while Hawksworth would ride separately. Hal would introduce him to Ted Smith of Home Farm and leave Hawksworth to find his way around and prepare a report about how he might handle running the estate in Mary's absence and how many under-managers he might need. Hawksworth needed a job and Mary needed a manager. Why Chantel wasn't keeping him on herself puzzled Mary, but when she later met Lady Douglas McCloud and her daughters, she thought she might have the answer. Hawksworth looked at the woman the same way she found herself gazing at James and it made her blood run hot. Sensing his lust fuelled her own. And she revelled in it. In the way it fired her blood; in the way her eyes ached for James to fill her vision; and in the way she hungered for his body. This passion for him wouldn't last, of course. Nothing did. But while her body was obsessed with his, she felt more alive than she ever had and she wanted to glory in every moment. There would be time enough in the future for contentment and companionship; for now, she wanted to burn.

Mary hardly saw Chantel. She never appeared except at dinner and disappeared soon after. The woman seemed completely anti-social. Lady Douglas McCloud it transpired, was called Louisa and spent her day at her embroidery. She had two half-grown girls, coltish with long legs and manes of hair that were never pinned up securely, who often rode out together to visit other youngsters in the area. Mary had never stayed in such an uncomfortable and unfriendly house in her life before. The duke by contrast was ever amiable and rode out with both her and James each morning and played cards or billiards with them of an evening. She and James quickly decided to continue their precedent of always taking an afternoon nap. She thought it was a good thing the weather remained reasonably fine so they could air the scent of sex from the room afterwards. She wasn't a complete hussy.

Then Chantel surprised her. 'Lady Mary, might we find somewhere to enjoy tea?'

Mary schooled her features and nodded her agreement. She had, so far, spent little time with James' sister and was extremely suspicious of Chantel's motives. The last time someone had approached her like this he had been attempting to sell her a farm he did not own.

They settled in one of the dilapidated small sitting rooms. This one was furnished in carved oak so dark it was black and with burgundy curtains. Once the unwanted tea was served and the maid had left Chantel didn't waste any time.

'James is the image of our father. His is quite different in looks to his elder brother Samuel, Elena and Samantha's father, but they were both tall men.'

Mary kept her face still and considered. 'Hence Samantha, I suppose. It is an unusual name for a girl.'

'She was born the day after he died.'

'I see,' said Mary, although she wasn't sure she did.

Chantel lifted a cup and took a sip of tea that Mary was certain she did not want. Setting the cup with a rattle she said, 'Samuel, our eldest brother, died suddenly. I was only twelve at the time, but my only memories of him are of good humour and contentment. He was not a man unhappy with his life, he was healthy and strong. What I remember is the deep shock in the family. Clearly his death was a complete surprise and there had been no indication that he was unwell.' It was Chantel's next comment that froze Mary in place. 'Papa died in the same way. One minute healthy. Next gone. Mama had been fading for a long time. She was extremely unwell and there was only the faintest hope of a recovery. I remember it felt as if there was not enough air to breathe. The thought of life without Mama was unimaginable, she had been such a vibrant presence in our lives, never still, rarely quiet, always chattering or singing, but we all knew her time was close. But it was Papa who died. Mama went that night. I have always thought that she just gave up. She didn't have enough to live for any more. She was too sick to do anything for us and the man she had built her life on had gone.'

Mary sat stunned, trying to absorb the sense of what Chantel was saying. A part of her mind was shouting 'no'. Chantel had her face averted, staring out of the side window. Silence sat on them, as cold and heavy as water. Eventually she asked, 'Are you saying James might die soon?'

Chantel at last turned to face her. 'Disease runs in families. Some families have weak chests and are laid up every winter. Some are rarely ill and all make old bones, while others do well to last beyond their middle years.'

Mary had to agree. She had seen the same on her estate. Again, the silence filled the air between them until she found the wit to ask, 'How old was your brother and how old your father?'

Drawing in a deep breath, Chantel answered, 'Sam was in his early thirties, I think, and Papa in his fifties.'

'That is a twenty-year age gap, at least,' Mary said firmly. Chantel looked at her. Inside Mary thought, not while I have breath in my body. I will force him to live.

'Yes. But if you are to pin your future on James, I thought it only fair to warn you. He was such a little boy when all this happened, he may not have given it much thought.'

'But you have,' Mary said.

Chantel's 'Yes', carried a world of grief with such a small word. At that, she made her excuses leaving Mary alone. It was a long while before she left the room and the cold tea. She went to find James. To confirm he was as hale and hearty as she had left him. But mostly, she decided to ignore Chantel's words. People died for all kinds of reasons and at all ages. The only thing certain about life was that it would, one day, end in death. James could have died of wounds a dozen time, but hadn't. She had cut into his body and removed a piece of iron that had been heavy in her bloody hands and he had recovered. Any of them could drop dead tomorrow. Wasn't that the point of life? Surely, to live every moment as if it was the last and take out of it everything one could. Life had thrown her challenges that would have felled a lesser person and she was here to tell the tale. Now, she would take on Death in exactly the same manner. Just let the Reaper try to wrest James from her hands.

As Chantel had secreted herself away with Mary, James wandered the house until he found a sunny sheltered spot at one side of the house. He was weary. His leg pained him constantly and travelling around the country had aggravated it again. When he discovered Joshua dozing in a chair in the warmth of the morning sun, he joined him. All around them the gardens sat painfully still and green, only bees moving sluggishly around. In the distance dark trees offered black shadowed spaces but nothing moved. Where they were sitting might once have been a rose arbour, as some stunning blooms bobbed here and there over the mass of thistles and brambles. They both leaned back with their eyes closed, their arms crossed, and booted feet crossed at the ankles. Mirrored. A maid emerged from the house and crossed towards their left, probably on an errand. Or sneaking out to visit a lad. Neither were interested in her intentions, but both opened eyes to watch her until she disappeared again.

'That one is a plum,' Joshua said conversationally.

'A plum?' James queried.

'Mm. Dark hair and eyes, with red lips and cheeks. Luscious inside but deep in there is a stone as hard as anything. Therefore a plum. She will make some lucky man a wonderful bed partner, but she will rule him with a rod of iron.'

James had closed his eyes again but he asked, 'Do you always equate women with fruit?'

Josh's reply was sleepy. 'Always.'

'Give me some more examples,' James requested, rather amused.

'Strawberries are the ones to watch for. Lovely on the outside and often smell delicious, but when you bite into them they are insipid.'

James gave a soft laugh, 'Give me another.'

'Cherries; now they gleam in society calling attention to themselves with bright glances, but there is nothing inside but stone. The man that gets one of those is going to be severely disappointed.

Still in the same amused tone James asked, 'And what is my sister?' but Joshua's answer was instant.

'An unripe red apple.'

That did cause James' eyes to open. 'Oh yes?' He could see Josh was smiling smugly.

'A crisp outer skin, tart inside.' What he wanted to say but didn't, after all this was her brother, and he was huge, was that he preferred something sweeter.

James couldn't help himself, he laughed. A tart apple with a rosy skin. It summed up Chantel perfectly.

At that moment Mary appeared standing at one of the open windows. Clearly Chantel had finished with her. James watched as she took a step forward onto the sunny terrace. James rose to his feet. Without a word he headed straight for her. Seeing him she smiled and walked to greet him. When they were close enough she opened her mouth to speak, but he caught her wrist and tugged her towards him, his head searching left and right. Then he set off, towing her towards a summerhouse that sat, dilapidated, at the edge of the lawn.

'James?' she queried, but he didn't stop, so she gave a little shrug and let him pull her along. At quite a pace she noticed; he had her almost trotting and she gave a small breathless laugh.

At the summer house he gave a rapid glance around, moved her into position against the firmest looking wall, and with two hands swept up her skirts and holding her hips lifted her back hard against the support.

'James?' she murmured.

But now he was undoing his trouser flap and was edging close to her, finding his way. She opened her mouth but he closed it with a kiss, hard and hot. Then he was inside and she gasped into his mouth. Wrapping her legs around his waist she hung on. His hands were hot, and rough, and large, and held her firmly under her buttocks. Her spine banged a couple of times, but she didn't mind. He finished rapidly and she gripped him inside as hard as she could so he wouldn't withdraw. It had been fast and hot and she was throbbing with pleasure.

'What was that about?' she whispered. He was nibbling her neck now and she shivered. She was intensely sensitive there, which was lovely, but he was loosening her hair and it was all going to collapse if he kept that up. Not that she minded, she decided.

'Joshua sees women as fruit. Tilly is a tart apple.'

Mary blinked. That fit, sort of. She wasn't a woman easily known and how she attracted the easy-going and rather handsome Joshua was a mystery.

'So what am I?' she asked. He was around by her nape now and she shivered.

'A mango,' he stated.

'Oh? What on earth is a mango?'

'It has a highly coloured thick outer skin, but is luscious inside, exotic, erotic and is incomparable to all other fruit. Once tasted, no other fruit compares.'

'I rather like the sound of that,' she murmured, as he dropped her down to her feet and began to put her back together.

'Come on,' he said, taking her hand. 'You are wearing too many hairpins.'

She laughed softly. 'Yes, I know. My hair needs to be redone.'

'Not yet, I need to thoroughly undo it first. In bed. That was simply a taster.'

'James! We can't go back to bed, we have only just got up!'

'Clearly a serious mistake,' he muttered, as he began to tug on her hand again.

'I have created a monster!' she laughed, as she stumbled over re-attaching a slipper to one foot while still trotting along.

'Well, you did it. Now you pay.' His grin was feral. 'Besides, it may stop working again one day. We have to make as much use of it as possible now.'

The house was gloomy after the blank light outside and they were both blinded until their eyes adjusted. Mary was relieved that James had headed for one of the under-used back staircases. They were in their room and naked before she had time to even think about protesting. Thank goodness the door had a lock! But then he suddenly he slowed down and began to seduce her with painstaking slow thoroughness.

'A mango,' she whispered.

'Mm,' he murmured as his tongue ran under one of her breasts. She didn't really like her nipples being attended to and once he discovered that, he had left them alone, and that had touched her deeply even though she wasn't sure why.

'My mango,' he whispered, 'and mine alone.'

'And what would you do if I strayed,' she asked softly, teasing him.

'I would first rip all four limbs off the man and leave his torso to live to a ripe old age. Then I would tie you up and throw you aboard a ship heading for India.'

A sensual ripple shivered through Mary, though whether it was the violence or the idea of being tied up by James that had excited her she wasn't sure, but it wasn't a problem, they had a lifetime to find out; she was determined on that. 'Then what?' she whispered.

'When we arrived in India I would become a Maharaja and lock you up in my palace.'

'Ooo, what does that involve?' she wondered. He had reached her waist and was exploring nicely.

'I would drape you in brilliant silks that caressed your skin constantly and load you down with so many jewels you could hardly walk.'

'Would have to be a lot,' she murmured, 'I am very strong.'

He laughed softly into her navel.

'What does the palace look like? Just so I have the full picture.'

He lifted his head to grin at her, 'It is all white and pink marble, with arches and intensely decorated with lapis and gold. There are tall palms for shade and endless fountains softly singing with water.'

Mary swallowed and James continued to explore not India, but her. She gasped suddenly and totally forgot to breathe for a moment. Then their geography lesson was put to one side for a while. And Chantel thought this man was due a short life, Mary thought. It certainly didn't feel like it at the moment.

Hal and Mags arriving at last swelled the company to something more lively. They were all in the drawing room the afternoon after their arrival with Jack and Elfie, when the letter arrived. One of the footmen, the blonde one, came into the room and reaching James whispered in his ear. James rose and followed him out. He returned with a mud-splattered young Guards officer who gave a bashful smile as he was introduced to the company. Louisa took charge and escorted the man to a room where he could wash and rest as she gave him the promise that some refreshment would be sent to him. It seemed they were to have yet more company at dinner. The young man's starry-eyed absorption with Louisa's cool beauty caused Mary's eyes to narrow, meanwhile James was reading the letter.

When he looked up his gaze went straight to Mary. 'You wrote to Wellington?' It wasn't really a question.

'Yes. An officer should be allowed to sell out, you were being coerced.' There was no apology in Mary's tone.

'You went behind my back.' James' voice was low and hard.

'I met him a few times when I was in London. He was charming.'

'Did you not think that I too might have met him "a few times"? And if I had wanted to make a claim on our slight acquaintance I would have done so?'

'But you didn't! And you wouldn't! You are too proud!'

'You went behind my back!' James' voice was a roar. He stood and strode to the door. Elfie clambered up onto Hal's lap and stuck two fingers in her mouth. Mary rose with a shiver of skirts and headed out after him. The row could be heard continuing across the hall, echoing off the cold flagstones and on up the stairs. All thought of behaving as polite house guests had flown out of the window.

'Never known a girl who could swish a skirt like your Mary can,' Hal commented.

Mags bent and ruffled Jack's hair. 'You alright little man?'

Jack had looked up from where he was laying on the floor with a slate and chalk. 'Oh yes. She will be quiet soon.'

'Is she often like this?' Hal asked Jack.

Jack pursed his mouth and gave the question some thought. 'No,' he said eventually. 'The last time was when Farmer Simpson's Charolais bull died. Mama said he was careless and it was his fault. She shouted at him a lot then. At Christmas, I heard him say that he had never been the same since. But perhaps he won't kill any more bulls.' He then turned back to his picture, which seemed to be of a soldier on a horse wielding a sword.

Hal bent forward over Elfie to look closer. 'Good cutlass, lad. You have put an excellent curve on the blade.'

Jack grinned, 'Thank you Uncle Hal.'

Mags bit back a smile as Hal flushed with delight.

In their bedroom the row was still raging. 'Why go behind my back?' James demanded.

'I had to do something!'

'How will I ever feel I can trust you?'

'Of course you can trust me!' Mary took in a gasp of air. Had she miscalculated? Might James not forgive her? 'I am sorry!' she screamed at last, as her chest tightened with compressed emotion.

James strode towards her. With one arm he swooped her up and sent her flying through the air. She landed on the bed on her back with her skirts tangled. He landed on her with a thump, forcing his jacket buttons into her breast. 'You are heavy,' she gasped.

His mouth stopped all further protest. She kissed him back with desperation.

'I love you,' she sobbed.

'I know,' he muttered around a mouthful of her neck. She arched away so that he could reach more easily. He lifted up onto his arms and hung over her.

'If you had told me what you were doing I might have helped you write the damn letter.'

Mary's mouth made a round 'oh'. Then she asked, 'What did Wellington say?'

'That he had plenty of half-trained majors. I could serve my country just as well as a landlord or in Parliament and that he would ensure the king was not enrolled by my colonel, but it was my choice. Like all his written orders; brief and to the point. Just how interested in you was Old Hooky?'

Mary felt herself blush. She had danced with England's most famous hero only once, but afterwards he had escorted her to a quiet alcove. He had wanted to know why she was in London, so she had told him. His intent look had made her shiver.

'He is very attractive,' she admitted.

'He is a randy old ram. How interested in you was he?' he repeated.

'Not very,' but she could still remember his charisma. His sexual pull had been fierce.

'Not sure I believe you, but I am here and he isn't.' James' voice was muffled. His head was now under her skirt.

'He is married!' Mary blurted out.

'Unhappily,' James muttered.

Mary suddenly realised that the tape that held her chemise in place was undone and her dress was loose. 'You have unfastened me? How did you do that?' James was busily edging the fabric away from her shoulders and down her arms.

'Dexterity is essential for an infantryman.'

'So I see,' she whispered, as she undid the buttons on the fall of his trousers. If he could be busy, so could she.

Afterwards, when they were naked and curled together he said, 'I wish you had told me.'

Mary rose up and leaned over him. 'I truly am sorry. I have been making my own decisions for a long time. I just didn't think it through.'

'Nor did I really, when I hunted you down. I hadn't considered what having you and Jack and Elfie in my life would really mean.'

Mary edged down his body and took his rod in her mouth. He gave a gasp and arched off the mattress. Lifting her head to grin at him she said, 'But making up is nice.'

'Nice! Woman, am I ever going to tame you?'

She shook her head. Her mouth was too full to answer.

It was much later when she realised that James had hedged his responses. He had calmed her nicely. Manipulated even. He had said 'might' regarding writing the letter and had made no promises about resigning his commission. In fact, he hadn't said what he was thinking and Wellington had left the choice in his hands. Frowning, Mary sat in a nest of tangled bedsheets and wondered if she had been out-manoeuvred. Cross, she rang for her maid. He might believe he had the upper hand, but she was becoming wise to his stratagems.

Late that night, Mags lay curled up against Hal with her hand in the air, admiring the gold ring Hal had placed on her finger on their wedding day by the light of their single candle. 'Do you think James will put one of these on Mary's finger?' When Hal didn't reply at once, she turned to face him. 'Is he just playing with her?'

'James? Nay lass, never. Mary is the first woman I have seen him fall for and I doubt he will fall out of love with her easily. But he has his ways, as we all do. In battle, he is like quick-silver. Doesn't matter how the battle moves, his instincts are good. He told me once that when he is fighting, it is as if his heart beats more slowly. He can shift from rifle to sword to horse in an instant; turn and skewer a man who is behind him as if he has eyes in the back of his head; order his men to be just where they are needed. It is a rare skill. He has usually been more accurate at guessing what the enemy might do than any of Wellington's generals. But when he is not fighting it is as if he needs routine. We came back one evening from being out on the hills with spy glasses, watching French skirmishers. We had been moved from a falling down cow byre to a pleasant farm house. It was a generous act to move us into a far better billet, but James was unsettled for the next three days. He always follows the same pattern of washing and cleaning his weapons ready for the morrow before he can even think about eating, even if we have been out all day. He hungers for calm and routine in some parts of his life, so that when the world explodes around him, he is as calm as a summer's day.'

'So, how is he going to cope with a wife who has ruled her own roost for years and children who are never predictable?'

'He will manage, but I don't doubt it will take him time. He is army through and through, whereas I am a blacksmith who wandered into the army to keep an eye on my sons. Did you hear Jack call me Uncle?'

Mags had to laugh at the change in subject. 'Yes, and if James and Mary have children, you may yet be called granddad!'

'Now wouldn't that be something,' Hal said with deep satisfaction.

The arguments did not end. 'What if we did marry?' James asked. 'Are you sure you want to be an army wife.'

'I won't be.' Mary's tone was emphatic. 'You will leave the army.'

'What gave you that idea.' James' tone was equally firm.

'Of course you will leave the army!'

'There is no "of course" about it. I am a soldier. My whole life I have been a soldier. Why would I resign?'

'Because we would be married!'

'Yes, and you will be an officer's wife.'

'And how do I run the Swann estate that is Jack's and the Brewer estate that is mine?'

'We will have to find estate managers; we already have the possibility of Hawksworth.'

'Haven't you listened to me? I have tried hiring managers. All they do is try to cheat me.'

'Yes, but I will be there, behind you. That will make a difference.'

'When you are on the other side of the Atlantic! Fighting in the colonies? I have no intention of being a widow for the second time!'

'Being a widow is part of being a soldier's wife. The risk is always there. But I could cut my hand carving meat, get wound fever, and die tomorrow. The risk of death is around for everyone, every day. That is just a fact of life. And you could join me.'

'No. Think again.'

'Don't you want to marry?'

'Yes! But not like this.'

'I am sorry Mary. I adore you, and the children. But the bald fact is, I am a soldier.'

'Then stop being one!'

James shook his head sorrowfully. 'We have gone in a circle. There is no point in discussing this at present.' He made for the door.

Mary reached for a porcelain figure from the mantlepiece and hurled it at his head. Half way to the door he spun and caught the figure in his left hand, so Mary threw her hair brush. He caught that in his right. While she was seeking more missiles, he placed both items carefully down, and calmly stepped out of the room.

Mary stood biting the side of her thumbnail. The man was not just as large as an ox but as stubborn as one too. And she had a secret, far bigger than Jack's paternity. She had not found a Will for Brewer. She had simply continued as she was, running his estate alongside her own.

The world and his wife had seen her married, a sixteen-year-old girl in shock and an old man with a drip on the end of his nose, so everyone had assumed that as his legal wife she had inherited everything. She had no idea if the assumption was correct! But she was not giving up an inch of that estate; she had earned it. But equally, she could not hand over all of the estate documents to a manager, he might be bright enough to realise that the Will was missing, and if she shipped out to the colonies with James, who knew who might decide to investigate the true state of affairs? She took in a deep breath. She had already considered the problem and decided that forging a Will would not be too difficult; all she needed was her father's Will to model it on and to scrawl the signatures of a couple of dead old men who might reasonably have acted for Brewer. She had no conscience about it. Brewer had no known relatives and nor did she, so anyone making a claim would be off on a remote branch of a family tree, but she did not feel safe as yet, so she could not leave the country and follow James. She chewed her thumb some more and fretted about how to bring him around to becoming a land owner rather than an army Major.

Chapter Eleven

Chantel and Joseph gave James the loan of another coach for the trip to Causton. James fretted silently about the cost of the feed and keep of four more horses. At least the wages for the coachman and his apprentice were being paid for by Chantel, but every night in an inn was going to hit his purse hard and his pride hurt at the thought of asking for funds from Mary or Chantel. 'Bloody Lucian,' he thought not for the first time, before feeling guilty.

A courier had arrived at the Court with papers for Mary to see. She was edgy about leaving the estate yet again, but nothing too awful had occurred when she had left before. She bit the skin around her thumb and fretted looking out of the coach window. The fat wedge of papers sat on her lap.

'Read the papers, Mary, then you might relax.'

James' voice, so steady and calm settled her. She did as instructed. He, meanwhile, took Elfie up onto his lap and began to discuss military campaigns with Jack. Mary was amused to notice that he emphasised the boredom and incompetence of the Army, not its glory. Lifting her face from her missives, she shot him a grateful smile. His answering smile warmed her as nothing else could.

When the children fell to dozing in the sun shining in the coach windows, her papers being mostly dealt with, and after a large lunch, Mary asked, 'Did you question Chantel about your French mother?'

'Yes, but she knew little more than I did. Father did call her princess at times she says, but it seems he also called her mermaid and wren, so it probably means nothing.'

'It really was a love match, then.'

'Chantel seems convinced of it. But who she really was and where she came from, we never knew. Chantel looks very like her now she is older, I didn't think she did when she was a girl.'

'And what about money? Has she lost everything your brother gave her?'

'No, but it will take a while for her to collect the funds to begin to pay me back. It isn't really fair. If she were a man she wouldn't have to, it would be hers by rights. And they don't live as if they have much money. The house is falling down around their ears and they have few staff, so I don't believe she is making it up when she says that the duchy is struggling.'

'Will it pull around?'

'I should have persuaded her to let you see the books. I did ask, but she refused. She went bright red when she did so, so I think it was embarrassment. You are, after all, the successful landowner she wishes to be.'

Mary couldn't hide her pleasure at hearing James say that. 'I could have advised her,' she suggested.

James stared at her. 'And ice might survive in hell.'

Mary laughed. 'Well, yes, I wouldn't take kindly to someone looking over my books with a view of telling me how to improve!'

Talking of account books brought Mary's mind back to Brewer's Will.

'James, I am not sure I know what I have done with Brewer's Will. I searched for it a while back, but I seem to have misplaced it. Do you think it matters?' Misplaced was a euphemism. She had torn the house apart looking for it and spent many grimy and cobwebby days tearing Brewer's old house apart too.

James looked at her. She felt as if his clear blue eyes could scour her soul. 'I shouldn't think it matters,' he said.

'But what if I hand over to Hawksworth, or any other manager?'

'What of it? Your affairs are your business. You allow a manager to see only what you wish him to see. Before Hawksworth gets his feet fully under the table you will have to go back and ensure that he is properly competent. What does he have access to at present?'

'Only last year's accounts. Everything else is locked in my study.'

'Then he can do no harm, surely? And Ted Smith and Hal are around to keep an eye on affairs.'

She nodded feeling reassured. She had never had anyone to really discuss her worries with. Mags was wonderful, but she had never taken an interest in the actual business of the estate. She had been alone for so long. Looking back at James she wondered if he could see the relief she was feeling, just to have someone she trusted to discuss her problems with. The Will or lack of it had been giving her nightmares for years. And now she had met him, how could she live without him? How could he ever think of leaving her? The loneliness she would feel without him might slay her. His expression gave nothing away, but then he turned away to stare out of the window. She swallowed. Had he seen? Had he recognised how important he was to her? And damn it. She could be important to him. Just look how he cared for Elfie and Jack. He needed a family, roots, his own children, a proper home. Why couldn't he see that?

He turned back frowning returning to her question. Clearly he had been thinking about her worry. 'I am not sure I have any documentation proving that the Caustons own Causton. According to family legend we have been on that land since before time began. If asked to prove my ownership, I am not too sure I could. I suppose that there may be something lodged in a bank somewhere, but I doubt it. When Lucian left, I imagine that over time anything valuable was plundered from the house. With the state of decay in the place, parchments would have rotted years ago. Ownership for both of us probably comes under 'custom and practice'. We have been seen to own and steward the land for so long no one can challenge it. I shouldn't worry. I certainly do not intend to.'

'The old, 'ownership is nine tenths of the law' saying.'

'Exactly.' He smiled his wide, wonderful smile that shone too rarely. 'When do you think we can stop for dinner?'

Mary laughed, 'I am still full from lunch! How can you be hungry again?'

'An army marches on its stomach. Well, this part of the army does.' He turned to answer a question from a newly awakened Jack. At the mention of 'army', Mary felt as if she had been plunged into cold water. Wretched, stupid, stubborn, man.

They reached Causton on the third day and found an inn in the town to put up at. Leaving their baggage to be sorted, they continued on to Causton Manor. Late afternoon clouds had rolled in and it had begun to drizzle. They all stood in the darkening, dreary light and took in the wreck of what had once been a thriving and happy family home. There were great holes in the roof where the small red tiles had slipped away, ivy and moss grew all over the front wherever it could find a grip, the wide and low front door of solid oak was rotten all along the bottom where the wet had sat year in and year out and most of the diamond glass was missing from the windows. No one said anything until James found his voice. It looked even worse than he remembered from being here with Lucian during his last days.

'You all go back,' he said, 'I want to have a look around and then I will walk back to the inn.'

'Can I stay?' Jack asked. Mary wished she had spoken first. James ruffled his hair.

'No lad, I am probably just going to wander around the outside for a bit. We will come back tomorrow if the weather is better and we can explore properly then.'

Somehow they all sensed that James needed to be alone with his memories for a while, so collected themselves together and left him. But not before Mary had pressed a hard kiss to his mouth.

'Don't you dare go falling through any ceilings!' she instructed. He gave her a wan smile. It was, to his mind, all too likely.

He watched them all out of sight before he turned back to the house. A cold wind was now whipping around, shoving the tall grass that grew up to the house sideways. There had been a wide brick path running up to the front door; he thought that it might have had a herring-bone pattern, but that had vanished. He realised with a sense of something like shame that all the time he had been away in India or Portugal or Spain he had thought that his old home would still have been as he had left it. The fact that it hadn't been his responsibility didn't somehow lessen the feeling.

It had never been a huge house, but it had been large enough for his family and the servants, with undulating floors upstairs and beams that might concuss the unwary and a place for everything; the laundry; the pantries; the still room; the kitchens; the study; with cellars for cool storage of cheeses and wines. Everything a family might want or need. Slowly he began to move towards the front door, no longer sure that he really did want to go inside.

Because of the rot at the bottom of the door he was able to shove his way inside without too much effort. He stood for a moment on the threshold peering in. When he had last been here the air had been full of the haze of noise bees give a to a summer's day and a robin had been chittering that there was a cat nearby. He had been so caught up with discovering Luc here, a Luc who was clearly dying, he hadn't really looked at the house itself. That it was in poor condition had been evident, but the details hadn't caught at him. Then there had been the shock of discovering that Luc had followed his career closely; had wanted the outline he had in his mind filled in with the details that his younger brother had experienced. The state of his head then hadn't been such that he noticed much that was around him.

The flagstones in the hall were more uneven than he recalled. And suddenly he remembered running in, pelting as fast as his legs would carry him, smothered in pond weed and slime and trying to make the pump out in the back yard before any adult spotted him. The memory came back vividly in full colour. His arms had been cold and green with slime, his shirt and breeches both torn, or was it just his shirt? The sodden leather of his boots had rubbed harshly at his skin threatening bloody feet in the near future. James caught a breath at how intense the sensation was. Where had that memory been? He hadn't known he had it.

He walked slowly into the hall. One step, then two. The walls were bare of the ancient weapons that had fuelled his desire to be a soldier. He wondered where they had gone? The wooden handles would have rotted, probably, but the metal he supposed had been useful to someone. Perhaps the local blacksmith had melted them all down and made bill hooks and plough shares; useful things. The suits of armour too had disappeared, no doubt to a similar fate.

The stairs looked fairly sound, which surprised him. He stamped on the first couple of steps and the wood held. Looking up, he found he had no desire to climb them. All that there would be above would be rambling corridors and empty bedrooms. Was a room a bedroom without a bed in it? When he had come to find Luc, he had slept rolled in a musty blanket that had more holes than wool, trussed up having removed only his jacket and boots. He would have kept his jacket on but the buttons could be wretchedly uncomfortable. It had been a warm night and Simon, the lad caring for Luc, had been keeping a fire going all day so that Luc would never be cold. Not like now. Luc was very cold now. He wondered where Simon had gone and if it might be possible to find him. He had made a promise, after all.

He walked on, peering into the drawing room, unfashionably on the ground floor, the dining room, where it was as if he could still hear Tilly and Luc arguing, Tilly never giving an inch and Luc going first red then white with anger, before his father clipped them both round the ear and ordered them to behave. Tilly had been given, and expected, no leniency simply because she was female. His father had, he supposed now, always treated her as just another son. And that made him think about Mary. Her father had brought her up much the same, as if she, and not her husband, would run the estate. Perhaps marrying her off at sixteen to a septuagenarian made sense. All being well, the husband would die long before her, and she would be in charge. All at once, her father's will possibly made some sense. He wondered if she had thought about it in that way and a sudden longing to be back with her shot through him. He was no longer sure why he had stayed here, alone.

He walked on down the passageway that ran right through the house, from the front door to the back, leading out to the cobbled back yard, where there had been outhouses for laundry and aired larders, barns and stables. He carried on. The actual door was missing, the frame still attached to the soft scarlet bricks. He walked over slick cobbles and went to find the air larder. He had never seen another one in all his years of travel. Theirs had been on the north-east corner of the house. A small, square room, it had been built to have a lattice of wood on two walls that were at right angles to each other. Air had seemed to know what to do and had flowed between the two latticed openings making the room cool even on the hottest day. It was even smaller than he remembered, but the stone shelves were still there, waiting for buckets and jugs of milk, pats of butter wrapped in large green leaves and round cheeses maturing slowly for the winter to come. The floor had held much of the ale brewed in one of the outhouses. His mouth watered. He thought he remembered it as good ale.

Dark was looming. Returning to the kitchens, he intended to pass once more through the house and take himself back to the inn, Mary, and the children. He hoped Elfie was still awake so he could kiss her goodnight. Jack would still be up, that was for certain. Even if he had been forced into bed he wouldn't miss seeing James before he let himself go to sleep. He found he was smiling. He had a family. Possibly. But he didn't have a house. This one needed nothing more than knocking down; it was thoroughly rotten. Tomorrow he would find out who had the keys to the Queen Ann dower house and see if that was habitable.

Half-way up the passageway he realised he had reached his father's study. He paused. It was bound to be empty, every other room was. The door was jammed shut with damp and years of disuse. He put his shoulder to it and heaved. It didn't move. Thoughtfully, he stepped back, and forcing all of his weight through his painful left leg, slammed his right boot heel against it. He staggered as his damaged leg gave way then toppled into the wall with a curse.

The door hadn't opened by much, but it had shifted slightly. James took a breath, positioned himself, then kicked again. This time it moved further. On the third kick, it was open enough that he could slide around and inside. By now, although there was light outside as the day faded, inside the house it was full dark. Even so, he could make out that some furniture remained. He allowed his eyes to adjust for a while, breathing in the dust and odour of mildewed plaster and worm-eaten wood. Gradually, he could make out that his father's desk was still there with its back to the window. He reached out a hand and touched the edge with his fingers. He remembered then laughing as his father carried him on his shoulders. Or had it been Sam carrying him, his elder brother? He wasn't sure. And he wasn't sure he was enjoying these fleeting glimpses of a childhood he had wiped from his mind.

Finding his way mostly by touch, he edged around the desk, heading for the window. Once there, looking back towards the door, the room didn't seem so dark. He opened one of the top drawers and something rolled to the back. Reaching in it was a candle, which surprised him. It seemed the mice had missed this one. He reached into his pocket for his flintstone and lit it so that he could inspect the room better. Against his thigh was his father's chair. Made of oak, it had arms that curved around and a leather covered seat that when James eased into it, knowing his trousers would now be covered in dust, it fitted his backside perfectly and he grinned. He really had grown to match his father's size.

He sat there for a while, looking around at broken shelving and the ragged remains of velvet curtains. Mary would be missing him. She wouldn't worry, but she might set out alone to look for him. He grinned again. He couldn't imagine life without her now, so he supposed he really ought to marry her. He felt like laughing out loud. If he put that to her as a proposal she would spit in his face. He still wasn't sure about leaving the army completely. He had no money without his pay until Chantel could return some of the patrimony and that might take years. And he wasn't a man to live off his wife. Especially not if that wife was Mary. She wouldn't mean to, but she would fray his pride fragment by fragment. She was too strong and he would need every weapon he had to match her. The idea of having to ask her for money made him wince. Still not seeing any real way forward he sighed and because of his weakened left leg, pushed down slightly on the chair arms as he rose to stand.

Now he did laugh, as one corner of the chair fell through the floor completely. In the middle of fretting about managing his future he had fallen on his arse. He shook his head at how ridiculous life could be at times. Heaving himself up, he picked up the candle, intending to head for the door. For the rest of his life he never knew why he lowered the candle to gaze at where the chair had punched through the floorboards. As hot wax stung his hand there was a glimpse of something, then the candle wavered. Steadying it, he peered closer. He ripped at the floorboards with both hands, gaining splinters galore, until he held the hidden thing. It looked like a leather bag of some kind. Pulling it out, he turned it in his hands. It had weight and heft. He lay it down on the desk and thought for a moment. Then he blew out the candle and re-seated himself more securely with his hand resting on the bag.

The dark didn't worry him. He had, it seemed, spent half of his life in the dark, either checking sentries or silently allowing the night to wrap itself around him with its usual rustles and noises as he waited for an enemy, cheek resting on his beloved Baker rifle. Mary. Might she come to find him? Certainly there was a chance, but he had undressed her often enough to know about the knife she wore strapped to the side of her calf as naturally as she wore a shift or shoe, and he trusted her enough that if she headed out into the dark she would quite likely strap on his sabre, too. He shook his head. She filled his very soul. The thought now of life without her was unimaginable, yet, and yet. How could he leave the army?

He was still prevaricating, which was an educated way of saying the same thing Mary did, he was dithering. He remained rather put out about the letter she had written to Wellington. For goodness sake, what other woman would have written to him! England's hero! The most famous man in the country! That Wellington had paid attention didn't surprise him. Old Hooky loved strong, clever women, perhaps in contrast to his wife, Kitty, who was a little mouse of a thing. He had openly regretted his marriage, but James honoured him for it. When a young, untried, and frankly profligate, Wellesley had offered for her hand her father had sent him packing. He must have been deeply enamoured of Kitty at the time as he had rashly, it now seemed, asked her to wait for him. He had then headed off to forge a career and forgotten all about her, never contacting her to ask her to break that promise. Years later he had realised that she had waited and was sitting as a spinster, still in her father's home, for his return. He had married her then, sight unseen. It wasn't a happy marriage, but James doubted that Hooky's address to Mary had been anything other than proper. He wasn't a man to seduce a well-born unmarried woman; Harriette Wilson the professional courtesan was more to his taste.

He rubbed his hand over the package that lay under it. He was curious. But he was also feeling cautious. He had no idea what it contained, but he had an instinct that it might be important, buried right under his father's chair, the way it was. If the house hadn't been allowed to collapse so much and the wood had stayed in good condition, it would never have been found, which did not suggest that it was intended for him or his siblings, but perhaps for later generations. Which worried him rather and reinforced his sense that he needed to settle his future in his own mind without any influence from whatever it might hold. His main suspicion was that his parents had not been married, which could raise a question about his right to the Causton estate.

Did he really want it? He had been heading for an army life, he felt, from the moment he had breath in his body; he had never wanted anything else. It had become his family. He didn't enjoy killing, some of the things he had done and seen still came back to haunt him in daylight as well as in his dreams, but it was a trade he was good at, no different to a wheel-wright or ploughman. He took pride in that skill, but mostly in the competence of his men; the good and the bad, whom he had trained, whom he trusted, whom he relied upon. That comradeship had been his meat and drink for all of his independent life. He had never thought that he might inherit the estate; two elder brothers had put that idea well out of consideration. Second sons became clergy; third ones soldiers. He had been perfectly content with the way the world was ordered.

For the first time he gave serious thought to life after the army. He had never wavered in wanting Mary. It was the cost that had appalled him. It occurred to him that perhaps he was less courageous than his sister. She was hauling a dutchy out of penury; all he needed to do was modernise a relatively small collection of farms. Indeed, he had no money, but there would be some repayment from Chantel, she had promised that, and he could borrow from Mary. He could make it a proper contract with repayment terms. And then he gave a chuckle, she would probably insist on it! Was it the fear of entering into a new life that had been holding him back, or the knowledge that he needed to admit that his leg would never be the same again? Cold swirled in his stomach. He had recovered again and again. But the truth was he would never recover fully from this. He felt unstable except when on horseback and found he leant on his stick more than he was happy with. And the cold was the very bugger. It made the whole of his hip seize up and, although the pain wasn't intense, it was nagging and unpleasant. And there it was. The root of his stubbornness. For a man who had been the model of masculine strength and agility, he was handicapped. Brought down. Ashamed at his core.

He breathed in deeply. He should have admitted the fact months ago. He had been putting Mary through hell and the truth was staring him in his face. He was no longer fit for the army he loved. All he was fit for was the army that sat in Whitehall or Horse Guards behind a desk, and that was no life to his mind. He had to resign. He looked around the dark room, his eyes making out some of the shapes of the empty shelves as the moon played with the night-time clouds. Decision made, he grasped the leather bag. Whatever the future held, he would find a place in it, the pouch and its contents would not influence him. Though, if the pouch indicated that neither he nor Chantel should inherit Causton, his sister would be as mad as fire.

He rummaged for his flint and lit the candle again. Settling it to the side out of all draughts, he tipped the contents out. Inside were documents and a pile of heavy lumps; of what he couldn't make out in the dark. He picked up the first folded document. It seemed to be made of parchment, it was too thick and heavy to be simply paper. He unwrapped it and a sliver of paper fell out. Scanning that, he realised it was his parent's marriage paper; May 5 1790 in Plymouth. He breathed in and raised his eyebrows. Well, that answered one question, he was legitimate, so Causton was his, he supposed. He frowned at the signatures; Sir William Causton, his father, in his plain round hand. His mother had learned to write in France, and many English people would find it hard to decipher, but he knew it well. He peered at it now his eyebrows rising further. Without doubt it read, Marie-Claire de Bourbon. He frowned. What on earth did that mean?

He turned to the parchment and had just scanned it over, when he became aware that someone was walking along the corridor outside. Blowing out the candle he moved to stand against the wall, so that his silhouette was not set against the lighter night sky outside. A gleam of light slipped into the room and a figure peered in, then entered slowly.

'James?' It was Mary's voice.

'Come in lass. You have just what we need, some light.'

'I was sure I saw light. Did you have a candle?'

'It is almost burnt out, but your lantern will do.'

'I have two candles in my reticule as well.'

He breathed in deeply and audibly. 'Ah lass. You are the one for me.'

'Am I now? What are you doing?'

'Trying to read some documents, come and sit in this chair and we can look at them together. I have just found out I am legitimate.'

'Was there doubt?' Her voice had a frown in it.

'When I found hidden papers, I had begun to wonder.'

Mary settled herself and James perched on the desk. 'I haven't read it in detail, but it seems you are to marry royalty.'

'Up until now I had some doubts we would be married at all.'

'I know lass, I have been a fool. I need to sell out. Why haven't you banged me over the head with the truth?'

'Because you needed to decide that for yourself. It means giving up what has been your life and all of your ambitions. If I had tried to force you any harder, you might have hated me all our lives.'

He leant forward and dropped a kiss on her mouth. 'Pick a date and place and I will be there.' He felt her mouth curve into a smile beneath his lips.

'What do you mean "royalty"?' she queried.

'It seems, my mother was daughter to Louis-Stanislas, brother to the King of France, Louis XVI. This paper explains how she disgraced her father when a young girl and he effectively put her under house arrest at their chateaux and forgot about her. When the troubles arrived in Paris, she was sent with a female escort to England. The women all deserted her and my father found her and married her within days.'

'Goodness. What does all that mean? Are you even allowed to marry me, if you are a French aristocrat?'

'No one need know and I certainly am not going to give it thought. This is for you and me, and perhaps our children, to know, but no one else. Royalty bleeds the same as anyone else when cut; it is of no account.'

'James,' her voice was matter of fact, 'I suspect what you have just said is treasonous.'

'Hmm? Well, don't tell King George.'

In the shifting light of the lantern they grinned at each other. 'Was that all?'

'Oh no. I sat here and did a whole lot of thinking before I looked into the bag. I wanted to face what I wanted in my future before anything in the bag could influence me. I suspect this wasn't left for me, but for a generation in the future. When my father wrote this, he was still worried that my mother might be a target for assassination.'

'Goodness! I hadn't even considered that.'

He sat quiet for a while. 'She wasn't sent empty handed. He lifted the bag to reveal the items that had spilled out.

'James ...' Mary's voice was uncertain.

'It is what you think, lass. Mother was expected to marry an English aristocrat and spy for the French from inside the English court. She was sent with a rather large dowry. I suspect the idea was that if the family were exiled then she would be in safety and holding funds for the future. Only she married my father and promptly disappeared.'

'A dowry? Funds? Are they really what they look like: gemstones? And is that jewellery real?'

'Mmmm,' he hummed.

'How do you know they are not glass?'

'I don't. But I saw enough huge precious stones in India to suspect that these are indeed, real. I haven't worked out how to turn them into money yet, but I think I might say I brought them back from my stay there. A lieutenant I knew was sent to act as body guard to a Prince once and came back a month later with a ruby the size of a pigeon's egg as a thank you. I was pretty out of sorts I didn't land a similar task! We all were. Hal knows I came back with pretty much nothing but my skin, but I doubt anyone else does.'

'James, did you want to be a general?'

At this he laughed. 'No lass, I expected to spend my life as a lieutenant, many men do. I only made Major because so many better men were lost.'

'And you really want to sell out?'

'Yes, and I decided to do so before all this,' he waved a hand over the heap on the desk.

'And if you are rich, does this affect you and me?'

The Army's Son

He kissed her again, harder this time. 'Well, it means I can be your equal.'

He swallowed her reply in another kiss that suggested they needed to return to the inn. Soon. His future wasn't somewhere out there, it was here, with the warm, loving and loyal woman in his arms.

When he lifted his head, she whispered, 'Can we go to bed now?'

He was grinning widely as he scooped everything back into the leather bag and blew out the candles. Taking the lantern, he said, 'Let's go home.'

Author note

James joins the army at age eleven. All rules and regulations were much looser at the beginning of the 1800s than later. People from 1830 onwards looked back on the early days of the century as far more regulation-free than their own times. By sixteen he is actually fighting.

James unwittingly, but instinctively, trains himself very much as medieval warriors trained. At the age of 7 they would begin learning sword-play with wooden swords. By sixteen they would be skilled with metal ones. Few modern men could stand up in the armour of those days, let alone get up and down from a horse in it or actually move to fight once inside it. On 26 August 1340 King Henry V at the battle of Crecy II divided his army into three. He placed the sixteen-year-old Edward, the Prince of Wales, later known as the Black Prince to, control and lead the most vulnerable spot of the centre defensive line of the army. Edward indeed led the troops and all contemporaneous sources state that he 'won his spurs', in other words performed perfectly adequately.

In 1812, Britain was fighting American forces at the battle of Snake Hill. The fallen at that battle have relatively recently been exhumed. Nine of the bodies examined were under twenty.

In armies of all ages it appears that if a soldier performed well, age was, perhaps is, not a factor. James joining an army at such a young age is unusual but by no means impossible.

. . .

Mary has successfully delivered 20 babies. The woman who teaches her is insistent upon cleanliness during childbirth. The four killers of women in childbirth are illegal abortions, haemorrhage, convulsions and puerperal pyrexia. All four of these still kill women today around the world. The first Mary has never been involved in. The two following are down possibly to luck in her day, but the fourth she mitigates. The woman who taught her has spotted that puerperal pyrexia, an infection that can be passed on, exists. The first doctors who said this openly were hounded out of the profession because they identified that the people doing the delivery were carrying this deadly infection and spreading it, killing the mothers. The profession refused to recognise this and women continued to die. Because Mary is not constantly delivering, and because she has been taught to be as clean as possible, she is so far successful with all of her deliveries. In undeveloped parts of the world today, infant and maternal mortality has been dramatically improved in some areas after the nurses and midwives were taught to wash their hands before undertaking a delivery. Life can so often hang on a bar of soap.

Acknowledgements

As always thanks to wonderful Janet who reads everything first and also Becky who is so great at cheering me on. To Jaycee, whose professionalism has made this book a reality. And to all of my friends who support me, Janet R, Cassie, Sam, Linda, Jayne, Leslie and Shirley. Thanks guys.

Book Group Questions

1. Should James, at 11, have tried harder to keep in touch with the remnants of his family?
2. Do you think that the army did a reasonable job of looking after him while he was young?
3. James and Hal become as family. What do you think is the basis of such a strong relationship?
4. Did Sylvester make a mistake in not courting Mary? Who lost out the most?
5. Mary admits to having nightmares about the time she operates on James and James admits, at least to himself, that his experiences have left him with nightmares. Do you think people were better able to cope with PTSD in the past?
6. Did you understand James' point of view when Mary was asking him to leave the army? Did you understand hers?
7. Are James and Mary suited?

THE CAUSTON SERIES

The Army's Daughter

At seventeen, Louisa is married off to brutal Rupert. A determined survivor she lives her new life with an iron spine and lifted chin. When the chance of a respite appears, she takes it. But freedom tastes sweet and, never lacking courage, she builds a new life. When that too is ripped away, now with two little daughters to protect, her determination to survive is again tested. When Xavier Hawksworth offers a chance of a late love, should she trust life yet again and grasp it?

The Army's Son

Eleven-year-old James has always known that the Army is his destiny. Big boned and well nourished, the Army takes his shilling. Years later Hal finds him left to die on a quayside and nurses him back to health and a return to service. After the battle of Waterloo James is seriously injured again. When he meets Mary, he believes that his only possible future is to die in uniform, still serving his country. As china ornaments whizz past his ears, might he take a chance on a very different life? One of love and children?

Chantel

A mathematics prodigy, Chantel solves her first coded message at eight-years-old. Ten years later she enters society and the marriage mart. After four years she is bored until Joshua, Duke of Daughton, offers her marriage and a challenge to last her a lifetime. Marriage is literally, 'Until death do us part'. When Joshua tires of her and her childhood friend Daniel reappears, how far can social rules be pushed aside to allow her and Daniel to be together.

Elena

Louisa's daughter, Elena, is born while her mother is still legally married to the brutal Rupert, making her the legitimate heir to his title and fortune. Unprepared, she is thrown into society, which does not go well. Wounded, she wraps her independence around herself and strikes out into the world by going into business with Harrison Weeks, an iron foundry owner. A female earl and a working man, surely a romantic relationship is impossible? Except no one told their hearts.

Samantha

Samantha writes and solves codes like her Aunt Chantel for the spies in Whitehall. But she is too lively to want to help her country by only sitting at her desk. When life goes horribly wrong she offers herself in marriage to the one man she can think of. In his wildest dreams, Toby never imagined he might ever be considered eligible to marry Samantha, but all he has ever wanted to do is protect and love her. Now he has his chance, except Samantha, knowing she forced his hand, wants to set him free.

Printed in Great Britain
by Amazon